I0596621

THE REVENGE OF FANTÔMAS

A FANTÔMAS DETECTIVE NOVEL

BY MARCEL ALLAIN

Translated by A. R. Allinson

Bibliographical Note

This Antipodes edition, first published in 2017, is a republication of the work first published by Stanley Paul & Co, London, in 1927. The original translation has been altered to reflect modern spelling and usage.

ISBN 978-0-9966599-6-3

Contents

THE REVENGE OF FANTÔMAS

1. One Thing Certain

"Quicker, man! Get a move on, do!"

"But how about fines, sir?"

"Don't care a hang!"

"Perhaps not *you,* sir, but what about *me?*"

"Same for you! Only drive ahead. I'll be answerable. They'll never punish you… I am Juve!"

"Juve?"

"Yes, Juve, by God! Get on, my lad, get on! I've just arrested Fantômas.…"

Hanging halfway out of the window of the taxi he had hailed at the Paris barrier, the renowned police officer was yelling to his driver. Nor was it any exaggeration to say his guarantee would clear the poor Jehu of all pains and penalties for excessive speed and breach of bylaws.

Fantômas arrested, Fantômas a prisoner—a noxious beast in chains and harmless henceforth—here was the end of a hideous nightmare that had brooded over the world for long years. All Paris, all France, the whole earth would be holding high holiday in a few hours' time, soon as ever the news should be known—scattered broadcast by the Press, by telephone, by wireless, to the uttermost confines of the universe.

"Drive on! drive on!" Juve reiterated—and a sharp jolt of the cab told him the driver had realized the news.

"Fantômas! Fantômas a prisoner!" stammered the fellow, his face white with excitement, "and you are Juve!"

The Paris cabby and taxi-man is well used to being mixed up in the most sensational affairs, but the knowledge that he was driving the great Juve, the police officer of genius and gallantry, and that his fare had just arrested Fantômas, put the man in a perfect fever.

"Drive on! drive on!" screamed Juve once more—and the

man started off his taxi at racing speed. Its passage was marked by whistling, shaking of fists, even a motorcycle from the Préfecture of Police in hot pursuit; but Juve was undismayed and continued to urge on his *Automedon:*

"Get on! get on! I take all responsibility!"

To the terror of the public, the rage of brother cabbies, the impotent fury of the police, the vehicle shot across Paris, swung onto the quays, pulled up at last before the vast building facing the Palais de Justice that houses the police administration of the city.

With one bound Juve was on the sidewalk. Fatigue, exhaustion were gone, banished by the joy of victory; vigorous as ever, he felt all the spirit and elasticity of youth. Two steps and he was at the porter's lodge.

"The Préfet? Out? In?"

"But—" stammered the official.

"Answer my question! In his room?"

"That's to say... I—I think—"

"Good day!"—and swinging round on his heels, with a boyish glee worthy of Fandor, half mad with triumph, the weight lifted that had for so long oppressed his spirit, Juve dashed four steps at a time up the grand staircase leading to the private room of the Police Préfet, supreme head of the department entrusted with the detection and punishment of evildoers.

An usher sat half asleep in the sumptuously furnished anteroom, sorting papers that clerks came from time to time to collect and dispatch to the individuals concerned. Juve sprang at the man and shook him.

"The Chief?" he demanded.

"Monsieur le Préfet?"

"Yes! Within?"

"Busy, M'sieur Juve! The mail..."

"Oh, that all?... Take my name in."

"Impossible! I have orders—"

"Idiot!"—and losing all patience, knowing indeed that all orders counted for nothing before the importance of the news he brought, Juve darted to the door of the great man's room.

Turning the handle, he tried to open, but the door refused to yield.

"Locked!" grinned the usher.

"Well, unlock it!"

"Can't be, M'sieur Juve!"

"When I tell you—"

"Maybe! But my orders!"

A trivial obstacle, the silly obstinacy of a humble menial who cannot realize there are orders, even important ones, which must be disobeyed, when an unlooked for emergency comes—Juve ground his teeth.

"I take all responsibility!" he declared.

"M'sieur Juve, I'm ever so sorry, but I can't risk the sack to oblige you."

"But, in God's name, listen here! I've just arrested Fantômas!"

"Fantômas?… Fantômas?"

"Yes!"

"Oh, in that case I can't say now what I ought to do—I can't!"

The poor fellow's hesitation indeed was so manifest that Juve suddenly clenched his fists in a spasm of rage. He knew, of course, quite well that the Préfet's sanctum is barred against importunate callers—it must be so. He was perfectly well aware of the existence of a special lock securing the door, of which only the usher on duty and the Préfet have keys. He had often and often been in the room and had seen how four heavily padded doors separated it from the anteroom, so that his loudest appeal could never reach the Préfet's ears.

Yet it was imperative the Chief should be informed, and every second was of priceless value. To capture Fantômas was well; to keep him better still; and, to make sure this ever-elusive Prince of Daring should not again escape, instant measures must be taken, measures which none but the Préfet of Police could organize. What was to be done then?

"One… two… three—have you made up your mind?" demanded the police officer. "The Préfet's got to see me now, this instant."

"My orders—"

"So be it then!"—and he prepared for action. No! Juve was never at a loss for a plan. Juve was not the man to be balked by so childishly simple a difficulty. True, visitors might shout and bang their fists on the outer door, and never be heard inside the guarded room. Granted. But the explosion of a firearm?

Juve hauled out his revolver—Monsieur Havard had provided him with one—pointed the weapon at the ceiling, and emptied the six chambers one after the other.

"You're going mad!" screamed the usher.

But at that same moment the doors opened and the Préfet appeared.

"Juve!" he cried.

"Myself!" the police officer assured him. "I knocked—"

"Knocked?"

"And fired. I was bound to see you instantly."

"Very good! very good! But I was afraid—"

"I apologize, but—"

"No need to apologize, Juve—come along in!"

The Préfet was a man of energy and prompt decision. Needless to say he knew Juve and felt the same admiration for his talents as everyone else. Could he fail then to guess that the police officer had not behaved as he had just done without weighty and serious reasons?

"Come in," he repeated. "Quick's the word"—and the instant the door was relocked and the heavy curtains dropped, he demanded:

"What's to do?"

Juve never hesitated a second. Another man perhaps would have boasted—couched the tremendous news he had to tell in some grandiloquent phrase; *he* out with it in two words:

"What's to do, sir? A very interesting to-do, Monsieur le Préfet. Fandor and I have just arrested Fantômas."

"Arrested Fantômas?"

"A couple of hours ago."

"Arrested Fantômas!" exclaimed the Préfet again.

"Right and tight!" asseverated Juve.

"Mercy on us!" groaned the *puissant* Chief, and there and

then, as though a spasm of sheer terror had mastered him for the moment, he staggered, his legs all but gave away under him, and he had to grasp the back of a chair not to fall. Was it mere joy, triumphant joy at a capture that must make his period of office forever famous? So ghastly was the man's face that Juve was filled with a nameless terror. Men of his type, accustomed to see the most unlikely, the most unlooked for occurrences come to pass, have strange presentiments. There is nothing to account for them, yet are they real enough. Juve demanded breathlessly:

"'Mercy on us?'… Why?"

The words were incoherent, but the meaning plain. "Why do you say 'Mercy on us?'" reiterated the police officer. "Why so upset at a moment like this?"

No answer for a space; then, trembling still, the Préfet continued:

"You have left Fantômas to his guards?"

"Yes, ten minutes after his arrest."

"What madness!"

"No, no! rather say prudence. Fandor and Havard are bringing him in a car—"

"Where to?"

"To the Depot. I came away at once to inform you. A system of surveillance must be organized, precautions must be taken—"

"Besides Fandor and Havard, who guards the scoundrel on his road here?"

"Fifteen or twenty constables, Monsieur le Préfet. Oh, make your mind easy, sir."

"My mind easy?"

"He can't escape."

"Are you sure?"

"Sure—and more than sure! Just listen to the arrangements made. An open car heads the march, seven or eight inspectors of the Department in it, revolver in fist, never losing sight of the car behind. In the second car rides Fandor and the prisoner. He and Fantômas are alone in the vehicle, no complicity possible therefore."

"Good! But—"

"Hear the rest. Behind this car comes a third, in which Monsieur Havard sits, surrounded on every side by constables, all armed to the teeth. All eyes are riveted on the car containing Fandor and Fantômas. With all this, Monsieur le Préfet, you must agree Fantômas could *not* escape, if he were the devil himself. Impossible to stir a limb without Fandor seeing; impossible to spring from the car without a score of shots greeting his appearance. Into the bargain, he is wounded, half dead, and tied hand and foot."

Juve said no more. After detailing the conditions under which the prisoner was being conveyed, he had recovered all his calm equanimity. If the Préfet had manifested such keen anxiety on hearing of the momentous arrest, this was evidently because he was filled with alarm at the mere possibility of an escape. But an escape was *impossible*—a sheer impossibility! Juve was no daydreamer—far from it. His was one of the most practical and well-balanced minds in all the world. He never paltered with facts actually verified, but on the other hand, he was not one to be scared off by the improbability of apparently nonsensical suppositions.

All smiles, he turned to the Préfet. But, paler than ever, the great man was staring at the police officer, his eyes wide with bewilderment.

"We are being tricked!" he announced suddenly.

"Tricked?" Juve repeated the words.

"Yes! Made a mock of. Hideously deceived! Oh, Juve, my poor Juve, what a disgrace!"

"Disgrace? Who's disgraced?"

"Why, you—and me. I—"

"I must be going crazy!" thundered the detective. "What the devil are you telling me?"

"There, read for yourself, then you'll know"—and with dragging steps the Préfet crossed to his desk. With a shaking hand he opened a drawer, drew out a crumpled sheet of paper, and held it out to Juve.

"Read that," he bade him—adding in a faltering voice: "I may as well tell you straight away how I came by it.… Three quarters of an hour ago I was working here quietly. Suddenly a crash of broken glass, and a stone drops on my desk."

"So an attempt on your life, eh?"

"I thought so, at first. But no! The stone they'd pitched through my window was ballast for a piece of paper—a letter—the letter there. Take it—read it! *I*—when I'd read it—I locked myself in my room. I felt half mad. Yet I still thought it only some grim jest. But now, now I've heard your story…" and a wild gesture said more than words could express.

Juve, meantime, hearing his Chief's account of the way the paper had reached him, frowned darkly. He could not fathom—that was impossible—the precise cause of the Préfet's extreme agitation, but he suspected something sinister, something monstrous—and his presentiment grew graver every moment. Mastering his feelings, however, fighting down the fears that beset him, he merely said, after glancing at the letter:

"Hmm! it's typewritten, I see. No handwriting to recognize, consequently nothing for the experts to make out"—and with these two remarks, that showed how his sagacity as a detective was ever on the alert, he proceeded to read the missive the Chief of Police had received under such odd circumstances. It ran as follows:

Dear Sir,—Juve and Fandor, whose recklessness defies all peril surely, have just arrested me. Havard, a bigger fool than they, gave them a free hand. They have just arranged for my return to Paris, by motorcar, with an elaboration of safeguards that robs me of all chance of escape. You will realize that this is disturbing for me—disturbing in the highest degree. Well, my dear sir, in face of these facts, I do not hesitate to address this note to you—which I have decided, for greater safety, to deliver to you personally.… Here is what I have to say: I have but a few orders to give you, but these are of the highest importance. I recommend you therefore to treat me with all the consideration that is my due. To begin with, you will free me of my handcuffs and fetters. Then you will summon to my bedside, to attend me, a Professor of the Faculty of Medicine of Paris; I have a horror of your general practitioner. Lastly, if I have not a temperature, you will have a good meal ready for me about nine o'clock, and send to the Place de l'Opera to fetch a good motor-brougham from a first-class garage. Needless to add that all the necessary formalities of my discharge from custody will be carried out while I am at breakfast. Thus you will be setting me at liberty say at ten o'clock at latest.

By the way, supposing you are disposed to act contrary to these formal instructions, I am then bound to consider this eventuality of your not agreeing to what I wish…. Accordingly, please understand this: If you fail to obey me to the letter, you will die in the course of the day and with you some hundred or hundred and fifty thousand Parisians. I cannot, of course, say for certain; but I am persuaded you will realize where your true interest lies, and that is why, relying on your docility, I permit myself to assure you of my very best wishes for your welfare.

FANTOMAS.

"The deuce!" growled the police officer.

"You understand now?" questioned the Préfet.

"Not the very least!" declared Juve.

"Yet it's perfectly plain, alas!"

"Perfectly plain, eh?"

"Why yes! Fantômas is poking fun at us. And if he pokes fun at us, that means he's free; it means, he has escaped; it means he has taken to his heels the moment your back was turned."

But Juve shook his head positively. "That," he protested, "is impossible!" And Juve closed his eyes a moment. Anyone seeing him thus would have deemed him entirely calm, almost indifferent in fact. Yet the veins on his forehead were swollen and the whole face seemed frozen in an expression of rage and savage determination. The truth is the police officer was thinking intensely. Fantômas escaped? No! he could not bring himself to fear that. He was positive—absolutely positive—that an escape was physically impossible. Yet the wording of the first part of the letter clearly implied that he was free; there was one sentence read word for word: "I address this note to you—which I have decided to deliver to you personally!"

"True," Juve continued his soliloquy, "but, then, the end of the letter contradicts the beginning. If Fantômas is a free man, what can this order mean about having to set him free tomorrow morning?"—and the detective gave a sudden shrug. Yet certainly this strange letter that had so mysteriously reached the Préfet's hands was like the brigand's work, but for all that, for once, the thing was impossible. The villain could *not* have written it! And lifting his head and reopening his eyes, Juve announced:

"I understand now, Monsieur le Préfet."

"You understand? Understand what?"

"That we are indeed tricked."

"Oh!"

"But not by Fantômas?"

"Not by Fantômas?"

"No, but by an impostor. The letter is the letter of a practical joker. It's just a silly jest. It can't be anything else. And besides, everything goes to show this."

"Nonsense!"

"No, sir, it's sense. Just consider the threat it contains: 'If you fail to obey, you will die, and with you some hundred or hundred and fifty thousand Parisians; I cannot of course say for certain.' It's too silly. Do *you* know any sure way of killing a hundred or hundred and fifty thousand men at one blow?"—and again Juve shrugged his shoulders.

"Grotesque!" he reiterated, tossing down the letter contemptuously on the desk.

At that moment a crash was heard and a wild scream for help.

"What!" exclaimed the Préfet, while Juve made a headlong dash for the padded doors—from the inside of the room they open easily enough—and flung them wide in frantic haste.

Then an oath broke from the police officer's lips. In the anteroom he had caught sight of two men still struggling together savagely as they lay sprawling on the floor. One held the other at his mercy, his fingers gripping his adversary's throat, ready to strangle him.

The victor looked round, and Juve gave another cry—a cry

of utter bewilderment:

"Fandor! Why, it's Fandor!"

Yes, it was no other than Fandor who had just borne down the unfortunate usher and seemed on the point of choking him to death!

*   *   *   *   *

So little was Juve at that moment expecting to see Fandor—Fandor, who was not to quit Fantômas' side under any pretext whatever—in the Préfet's anteroom, above all so little did he expect to find him busy throttling the usher on duty, that for an instant the sight he beheld left him speechless. "Never," so Fandor used to say in his picturesque diction, "never did old Juve lose his nut." Yet on this occasion there was no doubt he *was* dumbfounded as he stood there staring about him in all directions with haggard eyes.

"Midsummer madness!" the Préfet was declaiming, while Fandor got up quietly and deliberately from the floor, like a man who has completed a complicated job and is not sorry to have got done so easily with an unpleasant duty.

"Yes, perfect madness," he chimed in calmly. "The obstinacy of that fellow!"—and pointing to the usher he concluded: "And, to top all, he has buttons to his trousers' pockets, so I couldn't manage to search him."

"Search him?" put in Juve.

"Why, of course!" Fandor assured his friend. "I was choking him because I wanted to go through his pockets. Anyway, it was only a 'very little' choking—a mere strangling for form's sake."

"I'm dreaming!" stammered Juve, but the journalist strode up to his friend and administered a friendly slap on the back.

"Not you, not a bit of it," he cried. "Only, my good old Juve, you don't grasp the thread of my discourse. This is it—I wanted to join Monsieur le Préfet and you as quickly as possible, and the usher refused to take in my name, under some preposterous pretext or other."

"So you threw yourself on the man?"

"Anything else you would have had me do, eh?"

"Why, certainly," grinned Juve. "You might have called out, shouted, fired off a revolver, so there!" And, signing to the Préfet not to say a word, the detective drew to one side and invited the young man to enter.

"Yes, in a moment," Fandor agreed. "But first…" And with the word he marched straight for the usher, who had now got to his feet, though still looking bewildered.

"No ill feeling, eh? I warned you, old chap! I just *had* to get by!"

He wrung the fellow's hand, and without more ado joined Juve and the Chief of Police in the room so jealously guarded.

But then, as Fandor made his way into the Préfet's office, all his natural lightheartedness seemed instantly to desert him. In fact, the young man was hardly inside and the door shut, assuring the privacy of the communications to follow, when Juve, springing to his friend's side, adjured him to speak.

"Speak? Speak about what?" asked the other teasingly.

"Oh! a truce to chaff, I beg and beseech you, Fandor."

"Very good, Juve!"

"What have you come here to tell us?"

"To tell you? Hmm! I was hoping not to have anything to say to Monsieur le Préfet."

"So it was to me—"

"Faith, yes, Juve, it was to you I wanted to talk."

"To me alone?"

"I should so much have liked—"

"But, anyway—Fantômas…"

"Oh! Beg pardon, Juve," interrupted the journalist, "but don't let's go putting the cart before the horse. That's no way to get on. First let me say what I have to say."

"Well, go ahead! Go ahead, pray!"

"Sit down, friend Juve. There, facing me. Monsieur le Préfet, tell him to sit down."

But the latter was at that moment passing his hand over his brow with the look of a man awaking from a terrifying and incomprehensible dream. These remarks exchanged by the two friends left him more dumbfounded than ever, manifesting as they did a state of breathless suspense and nervous tension in Juve, and imbued with a quality of rather grim and somewhat forced humor on Fandor's part.

"Sit down, Juve!" he ordered nevertheless.

"Now speak, Monsieur Fandor… Fantômas?"

"Fantômas? No! Juve, it's Juve is in question."

"What, I?" cried the police officer.

"Why, certainly!" declared the journalist. "You are past your prime, old man."

"Past my prime?"

"Yes! And that, Monsieur le Préfet, explains the hallucinations, the blunder… In one word, you mustn't blame him for it."

"Mustn't blame me if—if what?" cried Juve. "Have done! You're killing me!"

"There, there! Calm yourself, my dear fellow. No, we mustn't be angry with him, this poor effete Juve, if now and again he commits gross blunders."

"Gross blunders? I have committed—?"

"Why, yes! But I'm not talking to you, my dear man. As I find you in company with Monsieur le Préfet, it's to him I address myself. Anyway, let's get done with it."

But as he said the words, Fandor seemed to hesitate—and fell silent.

"By all means let's get done with it!" stammered the Préfet. "So, then…?"

"So, then, it's all quite simple—or it ought to be quite simple. Hmm! All the same, I hardly know how to put it."

"Put what, Fandor?"

"Hush, Juve! See here, Monsieur le Préfet, what has Juve been telling you since he has been with you?"

The Préfet of Police turned white as paper, and it was in a barely audible voice he brought out:

"Juve told me—reported to me, in fact—that he and you, the two of you, had arrested Fantômas."

"Really?"

"And that you were bringing him here with Monsieur

Havard."

"And police constables?"

"Yes, and police constables."

"Well, Monsieur le Préfet, that's just what I was fearing."

"What say?"

"I say 'that's just what I was fearing!' If only I'd got here quicker, I'd have stopped Juve telling you these cock-and-bull stories."

"These cock-and-bull stories!" shouted Juve, who had sprung from his seat. Now, running up to the journalist, seizing his arm, shaking him soundly, he yelled:

"You call this a cock-and-bull story?"

"Faith, yes, I do!"

"But you're mad."

"Oh, no, Juve! Not a bit of it!"

"To have Fantômas in custody—a mere nothing!"

"Why, yes, Juve, because—"

"Because what? Speak out, for God's sake!"

"Because Fantômas is *not* in custody, you poor old chap."

"Not in custody?"

"Why, no! No more in custody than I am!"

"He escaped, then?"

"Escaped? Not he! He couldn't have escaped."

"Then?"

"Then, Juve, the rest is plain enough, seems to me."

"But it just isn't plain to me! It's enough to drive a man mad! You say he hasn't escaped—you say he's not in custody. That's to say he's free."

"Free? Yes, that's so!"

"Free! Free! Free, when I put him in your charge—yours, Fandor, and Havard's."

"No, Juve, Monsieur Havard has nothing to do with it. *I* did it all."

"But did what, man?"

"Yes, what? I tell you Fantômas is not in custody. I tell you also he could not escape. Draw your conclusion!"

Juve turned a more ghastly color still. He was glaring at

Fandor with eyes like gimlets that seemed bent on piercing the young man's skull in their effort to discover beneath the reticence of his words the actual thought that he would not out with. Then suddenly:

"Oh, ho! Fandor, you haven't…?"

"Yes, I have!"

"You've let him go?"

"Yes, Juve, I've let him go—or as good as…"

"Or as good as?"

"Oh, it's all one! Let's say I've let him go."

"But you have a motive, a reason?"

"Yes, that seems likely."

"Well, then, tell us."

"No! I shall tell you nothing."

"You refuse?"

"Yes, I refuse to tell, Juve. Listen, here—here's all I can—for the moment, you understand, for the moment—let you know. Fantômas was sitting beside me. We had a talk. As we talked we came to think alike in several important points. In one word, I put myself in his hands."

"You! You, Fandor!"

"Myself. Then, next instant, I started the engine off full blast. I had a first-rate car, quick and sensitive. Full blast. You take me?"

"I'm dreaming!"

"The obstinacy of the man! I tell you you're *not* dreaming! I clapped on the gas—a quick turn, to the right—another like lightning to the left—and then straight ahead. The first car, with the constables, dropped out instantly—bad driving! Havard's stuck to it longer. His shots pierced the woodwork. It's a mercy I was not killed. But I left him behind on a downgrade. He did not dare to make as sharp a turn as I did."

"And Fantômas?"

"Very plucky. Kept telling me: 'Go ahead! Go ahead!' What would you have, Juve? I went ahead."

"But in the end—"

"Let me speak, Juve," broke in the Préfet. "Now, Monsieur

Fandor, do you realize the gravity of your statements?"

"Certainly, sir, I do!"

"And that they can't be accepted?"

"Still, they'll have to be accepted, Monsieur le Préfet!"

"Hmm! We shall see. In any case, I know you—I know you are a hero—I know you've risked your life a hundred times, a thousand times over, to arrest Fantômas."

"Precisely so! And today I've risked my poor little life to save him."

"Just what I was going to say!" declared the Préfet. "After that, to guess that an overmastering, a supreme motive, actuated you is a short step."

"Monsieur le Préfet, you are more perspicacious than Juve!"

"But you had no right to—"

"Hush, Juve! Say no more. Leave me to talk things out with your friend Fandor. Very good then. An overmastering motive urged you to set Fantômas at liberty."

"Hmm! That's true enough, if you put it so! But go on, sir."

"Well now, read this letter I've had—note the threats it contains. And, that done, speak! Tell us what you're bound to tell us."

Fandor bowed. Ever since his entry into the Préfet's room he had avoided looking Juve in the face, seeming to fight shy of his impetuous friend. Was he aware, then, of the monstrous strangeness, the incomprehensibility of his behavior? But, if so, why had he come to visit the high Chief of all police officials? Fandor had helped Fantômas to escape—a thing that staggered the imagination. He had betrayed Juve, joining hands with the murderer, the villain, the grim Lord of Terror—surely the maddest of all the mad turns of fortune that so often marked the career of Fantômas!

The young journalist, now looking rather white, held out his hand for the paper the Préfet handed him and read it slowly through, weighing the contents.

"Well?" broke in Juve, boiling with impatience.

"Well, it's very evident—"

"What? What's very evident, pray?"

"That I did well to act as I did."

"Explain, then!"

"At this moment? No!"

"But, come, you take into account—"

"Everything, Juve, you want me to. And of something else *you* seem to forget."

"And that is?"

Fandor rose from his seat and stepped up to Juve. With simple directness, paying no heed whatever to the presence of the Préfet of Police, he held out his two hands to the police officer.

"It is this, Juve," he cried. "You love me like a son, and I love you like a father. We two have always shared the same dangers. We two have always fought side by side. You would give your life for me, and I would kill myself ten times over to save yours. Then you cannot, you must not, you have not the right to suspect me!"

This time the young man spoke slowly, in his voice a tone of infinite earnestness and acute distress. Till that moment, it may be, Jerome Fandor had tried to smile, to defy the storm, to pretend an indifference he was far from feeling. But suddenly he had thrown off the mask. Pale and trembling, his brow wrinkled in anxious thought, he was speaking gravely, sorrowfully. It was the heartrending call of a lifelong friendship to a friendship no less enduring.

"God forgive me!" groaned the detective. For one second, one fraction of a second, he held back. Now he understood! If Fandor had acted as he had, it was because it was right for him to have acted so. It was because honor and duty commanded him to do what he had done. If he still refused to speak, it was the same honor, the same scruple of duty, that sealed his lips. And Juve gripped the two hands Fandor held out to him. He drew Fandor to his breast and pressed him to his heart.

"Fandor, my little lad!"

"Juve, my dear old Juve!"

But the embrace was brief, fugitive, over in a moment, and Juve went on:

"Listen here, Fandor, let's see how we stand. Yes or no, can you let us know the secret of your behavior?"

"No, Juve, I cannot."

"Yet you admit you released the prisoner?"

"I admit having carried him off in a car."

"Then you understand where my duty lies?"

"Your duty, Juve?"

"Yes, Fandor. So long as you have not spoken out, justified your conduct."

"You are bound to arrest me, Juve?"

"I am bound to arrest you, Fandor."

"But I won't let you do it!"

"Too late!" The cry burst from the Préfet of Police. "Hands up, Fandor!"—and he leveled the service revolver he always kept within reach of his hand.

The Chief of Police hesitated no longer. For some moments, as he marked the cordiality of the embrace that had thrown Fandor and Juve into one another's arms, the Préfet had experienced an uncomfortable feeling of suspicion. Who in his place could have done otherwise? So dark and tortuous were the machinations in which the sinister name of Fantômas never failed to recur, like a refrain, no man could boast of having ever fathomed the exact truth.

The Préfet thundered: "One step, and I fire!"

But in a bound Jerome Fandor was on his feet.

"It is I you threaten?" he demanded.

"In the name of the law I arrest you!"

"Well, in the name of my duty I defy you"—and, quicker than lightning, Jerome Fandor sprang for the door.

His hand was on the knob; in another second he would have escaped, when a sharp click reached his ear, a sound only too easy to recognize; the Préfet had snapped off the safety catch of his weapon.

"Hands up!" he ordered, "or I fire!"

"Oh, but you'll never fire on Fandor!" protested Juve—and in an instant, mechanically, without a thought of the risk he ran, Juve threw himself between the great official and the simple journalist!

"It is I you will kill!" he declared calmly.

"Thank you, Juve!" cried his friend, and he was already outside the door by the time the detective had rushed at his Chief, barring his way, seizing him by the shoulders, crying in a voice of frantic distress:

"No, no! You cannot suspect Fandor! I stand sponsor for him! If he has let Fantômas go, it is because it was his duty to release him."

"It only means you are his accomplice!" stormed the Préfet.

"I? Then why should I have come to see you?" Breathlessly the two men stood staring at each other. True, the Préfet was not, could not, like Juve, be convinced of Fandor's innocence; still, he felt somehow that Juve must yet be right. No arguments surely, however cogent, no suspicions, however well founded, ought to prevail against the plain fact: Jerome Fandor was an honorable man; nay, more—a hero.

"There is one thing certain—" began the Préfet, but at that moment the door of the room, left unlatched by Fandor in his hasty flight, opened again to admit a fresh arrival.

This was Monsieur Havard. The famous Head of the Criminal Bureau was smothered in dust. His face was livid. He caught and echoed the Préfet's last words. "You are right," he approved. "There *is* one thing certain—at this present moment either Jerome Fandor is dead, or—"

"Or?" queried Juve.

"Or he is the most abandoned villain still unhanged!" And the Head of the Criminal Bureau sank into an armchair like a man utterly exhausted, incapable of further battling either with fatigue or agitation.

2. Diamond Cut Diamond

An hour later Juve was leaving the Préfecture of Police. He was not much better posted than before, but if he *had* made some small advance in his efforts to get at the truth, this was merely from force of circumstances, and with no spark of enthusiasm in the search. The fact is, he had just pocketed a document the contents of which simply horrified him. It was a warrant of arrest—a warrant to arrest Fandor!

It was veritably under compulsion and against the grain that Juve had taken on the task of apprehending his young friend. The mere notion of suspecting Fandor revolted him. This comrade in so many grim battles, this gallant lad who had risked his life, poured out his blood, affronted the direst tortures, to hasten the arrest of the atrocious brigand, he knew beyond possibility of doubt could have done nothing blameworthy.

Yet how prove him innocent in the eyes of the Préfet of Police, in the eyes of Monsieur Havard, without compromising himself? The latter, indeed—Monsieur Havard—had been very fair, very just, very impartial. If at times, in regard to Juve, he *had* shown a certain jealousy, the feeling had, at any rate tonight, led him to utter no ill-natured word. No, he had simply and plainly reported to his Chief the facts he had personally witnessed, and these facts had strictly confirmed the two depositions made by Juve and by Fandor. In fact, after analyzing the incidents that had marked Fantômas' arrest—an arrest carried out under his own eyes—Monsieur Havard had, point by point, corroborated the statements made by the young man.

"Fantômas was with this confounded journalist in the cab," he explained. "Suddenly I saw him speed up. After that I saw nothing more, except that the car in which, as I said, Fandor and Fantômas sat was taking to flight. My men fired. My driver gave chase—in vain!"—and he summed up:

"Two alternatives, therefore: either Fantômas had killed Fandor and then bolted, alone, after he had pretended to be wounded, or—and this is what I believe—Fandor was the scoundrel's accomplice, and helped him to escape."

Two minutes later Monsieur Havard, informed of Fandor's coming and taking to his heels, had felt no hesitation as to which solution to adopt.

"In that case," he exclaimed, "no doubt remains. He is an accomplice, a vile accomplice of the Lord of Terror"—and there and then, without a moment's delay, in fierce indignation, Monsieur Havard had made out the warrant of arrest the unfortunate detective was now carrying away with him, muttering under his breath a heartfelt wish he might never have to execute the duty he had been forced to accept.

"I could not well refuse," he kept telling himself. "Havard and the Préfet would have thought I, too, was in league with Fantômas. But, anyway, how the devil came Fandor to behave in this fashion? And why does he refuse to give explanations?" The thought haunted Juve's mind and could *not* be banished. In Fandor's guilt he could not believe. Fandor outwitted by Fantômas—this hypothesis was equally untenable. It followed Fandor had just simply entered into some bargain with the ruffian.

"And yet," he groaned, "I know perfectly well that cannot be the case either."

The debate might have gone on forever in this way without any plausible explanation resulting. So fully, in fact, did he realize this that he abandoned all further attempt to explain the inexplicable, and presently asked himself the question:

"All this being so, what am I going to do?"

But an answer was just as difficult as before. Quite recently restored to the ranks of the police—he had been cashiered as the result of a political intrigue—Juve felt convinced the time was not one for taking independent action.

On the other hand, to track down Fandor, to give chase after his friend as if he were a common criminal, this was utterly repugnant to him.

"So, then?" he asked himself. "So, then, I can only give in my resignation?"—and, as he alighted from the Montmartre motorbus two doors from his home—he still lived at No. 1 Rue Tardieu—Juve thought so seriously of doing this that he was on the point of retracing his steps to the Quai des Orfèvres.

"But no," he told himself, on second thought, "that would be silly. Fandor has acted with a purpose—one I cannot fathom, but one that is bound to be weighty. I may, therefore, assume for sure he's not going to be so foolish as to let himself be arrested. Wherefore—" But, ponder the whys and wherefores as he might, Juve's dilemma remained as cruel as ever.

"If only," he exclaimed suddenly, "if only I was sure he's not risking some dreadful danger."

So much for Juve's anger with his friend. The first moment of stupefaction over, the police officer was ready to give the young man the benefit of the doubt to the fullest extent, completely ignoring the fact that by letting Fantômas escape—for that was actually what Fandor had done—the journalist had robbed him, Juve, of an unparalleled triumph. His only thought was of something infinitely more important in his eyes—to wit, that the gallant fellow was in all likelihood embarked on some new and terrible adventure.

Stepping lightly, as his way was, and making no more noise than a Sioux brave on the warpath, he entered the outer hall of the block of flats, and passed the concierge's lodge without anyone seeing him. He mounted the stairs, equally unobserved, to his own chambers on the fifth floor, and rang the bell. Jean, his old servant, opened the door, as unconcerned as ever.

"Ah! Here you are, sir," he remarked. "I was just saying monsieur won't be long now."

"Who were you saying that to, Jean?"

"To Monsieur Fandor."

"To Fandor? So he's here?"

"Been waiting over half an hour for monsieur."

"Great God! The idiot!"—and Juve all but turned tail. Fandor was here, come to see him, waiting for him—and in his coat pocket he had his order to arrest the young man. Why, it was lunacy! Fandor was truly an "idiot" to have come like this to get himself arrested.

"If I take to my heels," thought the detective, "that's a breach of duty."

In fact, his very first thought had been to run away. However, he was not given long to fight down the impulse. The door of his working room opened, and Fandor appeared on the threshold.

"So, Juve, here you are!" the young man greeted him.

"Here I am—yes."

"No offense, but you were in no hurry. I saw you from the balcony coming up the street."

"You saw me?"

"Don't I tell you so?"

"And you couldn't—"

"Couldn't what, Juve?"

"Why, cut your stick, man!"

"Cut my stick? Because I saw you? Why, I was in your rooms, Juve, I was waiting for you."

"A pretty notion!"

"An obvious notion, if I may say so; we've got to have a chat."

"You think so?"

"Well, the idea did enter my head. A cigarette?"

"No. And here's another thing to put in your head: as I've just told you, you ought to have made off when you saw me coming."

"Why?"

"Because if you hadn't been an imbecile you'd have guessed—"

"Juve! Juve! I'm not a conceited man, but really, you hurt my vanity. I did guess, so there!"

"You guessed what?"

"Breast pocket of your coat, left side, Juve! You want me to tell you what you've got there, eh? A document that concerns me."

"Well, if you know, Fandor—"

"I do know, old man. But I know another thing, and that is I want to have a talk with you. Now, do you refuse to hear me?"

Juve gave a cough, in manifest embarrassment. Presently he began again.

"Listen here, Fandor; *I* don't doubt you."

"That's a good thing."

"But I know, and you know yourself, duty must not be shirked. Well, my duty is to arrest you. Therefore, say what you may to me, I *shall* arrest you."

"But that's understood, man! Settled up! Agreed upon! Only, do you make a point of arresting me right away? Or do you wish for the explanation of my conduct?"

"The explanation? You are going to explain?"

"I'm here for that, and nothing else!"

"But you refused—"

"Refused to speak? Why, what a question! What I said was, 'For the moment I can't say anything.' 'For the moment' was a polite way of giving you to understand that the worthy Préfet of Police was *de trop*. You failed to understand?"

"I understood nothing," sighed Juve, "neither this nor anything else."

"Well, come, question me!"

Fandor now spoke in a voice betraying agitation. True, there was, as always, a touch of boyish roguery in his accents, but it was easy to divine an undercurrent of sadness and profound feeling.

"Listen to me," said Juve. "To begin with, tell me the truth. Did you really help Fantômas escape?"

"Juve," protested Fandor, "your question is offensive. How can you ask me such a thing? Most certainly not! No, I did not help Fantômas to escape."

No single thing Fandor could have said would have more surprised the police officer. Not Monsieur Havard only, but Fandor himself—had not both of them established the actual facts categorically?

Giving a start of sheer amazement: "But you said just the opposite," cried Juve. "*Everything* proves you let Fantômas escape."

"Well?"

"Well, now you will have it."

"Come, Juve," was the journalist's calm retort. "You're not your old self today. What the devil's come of your powers of observation? I did not let Fantômas escape—but I did help the prisoner to get away. Now, is it impossible for these two facts to be both true together?"

"God pity me!" cried Juve, while his friend went off in a peal of laughter.

"At last!" grinned the young man, "at last the great, the renowned detective has grasped the truth! Why, of course, I let the prisoner escape and I did not let Fantômas escape—because the prisoner was not Fantômas! There's the whole mystery!"

The last sentence was uttered in a tone of triumph, while Juve gave another violent start.

"Not Fantômas!" he stammered. "It was not Fantômas. But if he cried out—"

"A falsehood."

"Well, then, who *was* it?"

It was Fandor's turn to hesitate.

"Who was this prisoner? That, Juve, is the one thing I cannot tell you."

"Because?"

"Because I do not know, Juve, who this prisoner was."

"You swear you don't?"

"I have a suspicion, Juve. Yes, I have a suspicion, but nothing more. And I have no right to tell you my suspicion."

Fandor's voice had trembled as he spoke the words. Juve looked hard into the young man's face before he answered:

"So be it! If you talk of 'right,' I cannot insist. But can you tell me other things?"

"Yes, everything else."

"Speak on!"

"You condemn me. Oh! yes, I can see you do! Oh, Juve! my good old Juve! this is a frightful business. I tell you, whatever happens, I have nothing to reproach myself with."

"Do *I* reproach you with anything?"

"No. But first hear the facts. You had just gone. You were hurrying to see the Préfet."

"In triumph, Fandor."

"Certainly, in triumph. And I too at that moment was triumphant. Fantômas was captured; I believed it as surely as you did. They had carried him to a conveyance called up for the occasion. They put him in my charge. *I* was to have the honor of personally guarding him. He was bound, fettered, the handcuffs on his wrists. Oh, how proudly my heart beat, Juve, as I thought how here was the end of all this horrid nightmare, that Fantômas was taken, that his victims were avenged, that he would never commit another of those atrocities that have set all the world shuddering."

"Then? Then?"

"Then, Juve, the car, crammed full of police constables, started off ahead. Behind, the other car, in which Monsieur Havard had taken his seat and in which more police officers rode, was on the point of following me. I threw in the clutch—"

"After that? Go on!"

"I was just saying to myself: 'Here's the first turn of the wheels taking Fantômas to the scaffold—'"

"You were in the right, Fandor!"

"No, I was not, Juve. I was in the wrong! And I found that out pretty quick."

"When precisely?"

"Five hundred yards farther on. See here; lying on the floor of the car I could hear Fantômas panting, suffocating it seemed. I was afraid he was going to die on my hands. I leaned half over him. He was groaning: 'Oh, this mask! This mask!' Then—"

"Then, Fandor? Out with it, do!"

"Then, in spite of everything, I pitied the man, lying in such pain. I said to him: 'Take off your hood, Fantômas. What good keeping it on? They'll have it off at the Depot, anyway.' And, Juve, the prisoner answered: 'No, I won't take off the mask. And I'm not going to the Depot. And you're going to save me!'"

"Save him! You didn't answer him, I suppose?"

"Juve, I stooped lower. I meant to drag off the hood by main force. Why? I don't know. A presentiment. Then the prisoner half sat up—pushed me away—put out a hand. And, when I saw those hands, quite little hands—well, I understood."

"Understood what?"

"That it was—that it was a woman, Juve, we had just arrested!"

"A woman?"

"A girl, Juve!"

"A girl! A young girl! Ah! Fandor—" But Juve left the words unfinished. He had not the courage at first to end his sentence. *Who* was this girl they had captured wearing the ill-omened uniform of Fantômas? Who and what could she be? Nay! was not her identity of necessity known to the detective, who fixed his gaze on the other's face in grave scrutiny? The journalist's sensitive features betrayed profound agitation. His eyes were riveted on the ground, as if he were afraid his thoughts might be read in his face.

"Fandor," Juve besought him, "was it? Was it Helene?"

"Juve! I assure you on my oath I do not know!" came the reply in hoarse, broken tones.

Helene! Fantômas' daughter! Helene, the sweet, innocent child who yet was born of the blood of that execrable monster! Helene! Ah, yes, if it was Helene who had been found in the hands of the police, arrested by a hideous error in place of her father, was not Fandor's whole behavior explainable? He had loved her, he had destined her to be his bride. Fandor, and Juve no less, knew her to be innocent, absolutely, entirely innocent, of her father's crimes. Juve's thoughts flew fast.

"If she was there where we seized her, poor child, if we caught her clad in the traditional garb of the Lord of Terror, the hood of darkness and close-fitting suit of black, it meant that she was vowed to some work of rescue, that she was employed, no doubt, in paralyzing one or other of the scoundrel's sinister designs."

Juve shook his head disconsolately.

"If the prisoner was Helene," he said slowly, "you did well to save her, Fandor."

"I tell you, Juve, I do not know who the woman was I let escape. I only know this much—that she proposed a bargain to me, that she put herself at my disposition to enable me to frustrate an atrocious, an abominable scheme of Fantômas."

"And this scheme was, Fandor—?"

"I have sworn not to tell you, Juve. I have sworn even, now the pursuit is renewed, not to attempt Fantômas' arrest. I have promised only to intervene to save human lives."

"You have done well, Fandor. And it was Helene. But are you sure you are not the victim of a ruse?"

"No, Juve, I am not certain of that. I am playing a terrible game. But I held it to be my duty."

"Your duty—yes, your duty. But mine, alas—"

"I know, Juve. Your duty is to arrest me. So be it. But I have the right, surely, to try to escape you?"

"The right—why, yes!"

"A cigarette, Juve?"

Fandor had opened his cigarette case, but the other did not take one. His face expressed a painful embarrassment.

"Ah, Fandor," he sighed, "but it is horrible to have to be always fighting against one's sense of right, against one's affection. If you were to escape me, you swear you would be prudent?"

"So far as possible."

"That, your task once done, these innocent folk in danger once saved, you will resume the struggle against Fantômas?"

"Yes, I swear it, Juve."

"Give me that cigarette, Fandor,"—and he took one from the case the young man handed him. His hand never trembled as he applied the match, but his face was very grave.

He inhaled a mouthful, then another. Then, suddenly, he fell, with arms spread wide, as if struck by lightning.

"Ah! poor old Juve!" groaned Fandor, and, dashing forward, he took the police officer in his arms and carried him to a couch.

"A marvelous narcotic!" thought Fandor. "I was sure of escaping him, if only he agreed to smoke"—and he went on: "And

Juve himself had guessed what I was at, suspected the trap laid for him. What a friend! He trusted me! He let himself be put to sleep so as not to have to arrest me!"

For a brief while the journalist stood pensive. The narcotic he had administered to Juve he knew to be harmless. In an hour the police officer would wake up, fit and well.

"Come!" he exclaimed presently, "to get to work! Ah, Helene, is it you? Is it you I have saved?"—and he left the room on tiptoe.

Without a suspicion of what had occurred—impossible, of course, to mistrust Fandor—old Jean, Juve's manservant, opened the outer door for him.

"Monsieur Fandor is going?" he asked. "Monsieur isn't staying to dinner?"

"No, I have to go," replied the young man. "But I shall be back again—"

It cost him an effort to disguise the trembling of his lips as he said the words. He would be back again? Yes, but when?

*   *   *   *   *

When Juve awoke from the heavy sleep induced by Jerome Fandor's narcotic he did not do what another man would have done. He did not open his eyes.

"Now's the time to think things out," he reflected, and, preserving the most absolute immobility of body, but his brain hard at work, he proceeded to review the situation. His thoughts could hardly be other than gloomy, and truly the circumstances were embarrassing.

"Devil take me if I know what I'm to do," he muttered. A few hours earlier in the day, when the Préfet of Police had instructed him to arrest Fandor, whom he accused of being an accomplice of Fantômas, Juve had readily enough guessed that the high functionary in question was not very far from including him also in his suspicions. In truth, the police officer's adventures had often been so amazing that it was hardly surprising if the question came at times to be asked whether he too was not in Fantômas' pay.

"The Préfet dare not arrest *me*," reflected Juve. "So far, so well; but it won't do to drive the man to extremities. So what am I going to tell him? If I let him know that I have let Fandor slip between my fingers, one of two things will happen—either he will set me down as an idiot and a clumsy fool, or he will again accuse me of complicity. If, on the other hand, I hold my tongue about the adventure, what is there to show I shall not be confronting a worse danger? He is quite capable of having had me shadowed and so discovering all about Fandor's coming and going. Damn the boy!"

Still lying perfectly still, Juve continued his reflections:

"Then, into the bargain, the confounded fellow is dead certain to go running himself into some terrible adventure. Therefore—"

But the worthy man never finished his sentence. At that moment, close beside him, a faint sound had caught his ears— the sound of a deep-drawn breath, a half-stifled sigh. And, for the second time, Juve had the presence of mind to refrain from doing what anyone else in his place would have done. Police agent to the core, in fact, trained to master his emotions, to dominate his nerves, Juve could school himself never to act without having first taken time for reflection.

"Ho, ho!" he merely told himself, "one would think there's somebody standing beside me. Who can it be?"

He had only to open his eyes to find out, but to do this might have been perilous—to reveal to his visitor that he was in full possession of his senses. Better make a try first to guess the newcomer's identity. He thought:

"Jean? It might be my manservant Jean. But no! Jean would never be able to keep still without doing anything. I feel perfect- ly certain Jean, while waiting for me to awake, would be polish- ing up something or other. Who, then? Fandor? But Fandor is certainly gone. If he made me take a narcotic, his object was to avoid my arresting him. True, he might have come back again. But Fandor would be doing something better than sighing like that. He, again, is too energetic for that. He would be shaking me to rouse me. Then is it a police officer from the Préfecture?

An emissary from Monsieur Havard? Never in this world! I know my colleagues; they are all chatterers. If it was one of them, he'd be talking to Jean—" And he concluded:

"Faith, no! I cannot tell. Ah! A doctor, perhaps? Yes, possibly Jean may have been to fetch one. But a doctor would be bleeding me, and not sighing. Well, well, I'll risk one eye, as I can't divine who is there"—and he cautiously lifted an eyelid.

But what he saw was so utterly unexpected, he could not help looking closer. Still not moving, but opening both eyes, and opening them wide, Juve was on the point of exclaiming:

"A woman! It is a woman!"

It was in truth a woman there in his room, waiting for him to awake. Holding his breath, the police officer scrutinized his unlooked-for visitor.

It was a very beautiful creature he saw. Dressed entirely in black, her face half hidden under a flowing veil of black crepe, which she had thrown back a little over one shoulder, she stood near the window, pressing her forehead to the glass, gazing, doubtless without seeing them, at the workshops and masons' yards that have for so many years disfigured the ancient Square Saint-Pierre. Tall, slender, elegant with a simple and unassuming elegance, the unknown displayed in all her attitude a grace and charm truly entitling her to the epithet of queenly. He could not discern the features, but, to make up, he could perfectly distinguish beneath the rim of her hat the brilliant, tawny gold of her magnificent hair.

And in a moment he knew. It was—yes, it was none other—it was She! Juve spoke no name to himself; but it was that of Fantômas that flashed across his brain as he looked. Was not the unknown *his* wife? Was not this visitor, by some incomprehensible aberration, aiding and abetting her terrible mate, while at the very same time abominating his crimes?

Lady Beltham! Helene! The wife and the daughter of Fantômas. For Juve, in the confusion of his whirling brain, united the two in his thoughts. Both loved the Torturer. Both, enslaved by their love, would have attempted the impossible to save him from falling into the hands of justice, being dragged to the steps of the scaffold. Nay, many a time already had they striven to paralyze his plans, struggled to frustrate his designs, risking their lives, defying his fury, working to nullify his success in the grim and dreadful exploits he accumulated in reckless triumph one on top of another.

"Extraordinary!" thought Juve. "Fandor would seem to have encountered Helene, and I—*I* shall meet Lady Beltham. This should verily mean that the hour is grave. Good! We must be prepared."

Another than Juve might well have been afraid. Lady Beltham's presence proved beyond a doubt that Fantômas could not be far off. But the police officer was impervious to terror. He was one of the men ready to confront the worst dangers with a smile, who hold it only natural to risk their lives on all occasions.

"Well, one must be prepared!" he repeated, and at last made a movement—rather, tried to make a movement, and failed utterly. On attempting to sit up on his couch, he undeniably discovered this was simply impossible. Arms, feet, were bound, firmly tied to the legs of the sofa on which he lay. Advantage had evidently been taken of his state of lethargy to manacle him in this fashion.

Still, on making this discovery, Juve seemed in no wise astonished.

"A pretty thing, truly, to awake like this!" he growled to himself. "However, there's nothing to be gained by making a fuss." And he took another second or two for further reflection. Then suddenly he spoke in a tone of irony:

"Lady Beltham, may I offer you my respects—"

Instantly the visitor wheeled round and faced the speaker.

"—and ask if you are responsible for tying me up in this highly workmanlike fashion?"

But he stopped abruptly. So deadly pale was the woman's face, such livid horror was depicted in her eyes, he almost feared to see the poor creature lose consciousness and fall to the floor. At first her lips seemed to move, but no sound left them.

"You do not answer, madame?" insisted Juve.

"Oh, yes, I will answer you," came a hoarse whisper from the quivering lips. "It was I who bound you."

"Really? If I am not indiscreet, may I ask you why?"

"Oh! Juve, Juve! A truce to raillery. You know very well—"

"I know nothing, madame, believe me!"

"Oh, but you do. You know how I suffer, that my life is a hell, and that I am here—"

"To tie me down to a sofa?"

"Juve, you have no pity. If I am here, it is because I must be. If you are bound, it is—"

"It is because I must be, eh? No offense, madame, but you speak without saying anything!"

"Juve, listen to me! Now, candidly, if I had not bound you, would you not have tried to arrest me?"

"I do not deny it, madame."

"Then was I not right in taking this precaution?"

"Admirable," sneered Juve cuttingly, "an admirable precaution! May I offer my congratulations?"

"Juve, I am here to talk seriously, to beg a favor, to beg it on my knees."

"You amaze me, madame!" And now the kindhearted detective was really serious. In secret, at the bottom of his heart, though he would have been ashamed to own as much, he felt a certain pity, not unmixed with respect, for the unhappy lady he saw there trembling before him. And was he not convinced she could not be there without grave, even terrible, reasons?

"Madame," he resumed, "I ask no better than to hear you speak—the more as I know no way of stopping you! But I would wish, to begin with, to clear up one detail. How did you get in here?"

"Quite simply," declared Lady Beltham, "with a key! I saw Fandor come out. A little later I saw your manservant leave the house, and I walked upstairs."

"So you were watching my house?"

"Yes!"

"And you had a key of my rooms?"

"He had one."

"He? Fantômas?"

"Do not force me, Juve, to utter a name that fills me with horror!"

"Better and better! And if I had not been put to sleep by Fandor? If you had found me awake?"

"I was convinced of the contrary—after seeing Fandor leave you again a free man."

"Then you were aware of the duty I was charged with?"

Lady Beltham's voice dropped to a whisper as she explained.

"Need I tell you, Juve, there are means of intelligence at the Préfecture of Police itself?"—and to this the detective offered no reply.

In this amazing interview with the wife of the most formidable brigand the world has ever known, everything was strange, abnormal, terrifying. But he, the police officer of genius, was he the man to be dumbfounded by anything Lady Beltham told him? That Fantômas possessed a key of his own private rooms, *that* he had never doubted. That Fantômas again had made such arrangements and suborned such accomplices as enabled him to know whatever was spoken at the most secret colloquies in the Préfecture of Police—no! *that* could not, was not likely to, surprise him.

"To proceed," he said quietly. "So you got into my rooms, it seems, and made it your business to tie me down to avoid the risk of arrest. Go on, madame. You came here with an object, I presume, madame?"

"I told you what it was—to beg, to beseech a favor."

"My favor—for whom?"

"For Him."

"Impossible!" For once Juve was dumbfounded indeed. That Lady Beltham could have dreamed of actually begging his favor for Fantômas left his brain reeling. Could she fail to realize that no prayer could move him where this monster, this murderer, was concerned?

Suddenly a wild idea flashed across his mind:

"Why, yes! Does Lady Beltham know that the prisoner was

not Fantômas? Does she know that this prisoner was a woman? Does she know how this same prisoner was released, thanks to Fandor?"

He asked her eagerly: "What is it you want to ask me?"

"Oh, Juve," groaned Lady Beltham, "I have come to ask you—his liberty—"

"His?"

"The prisoner's."

"Hm! So you know that the prisoner—"

"No, no! Not a word! Do not tell me. I do not wish to know. I cannot know! But, Juve, I must tell you—it is serious, desperately serious! It is horrible, hideous. Never—you understand me?—never must the prisoner—be retaken—"

"Oh!" groaned Juve. To tell the simple truth, he was again entirely in the dark.

"So," he kept telling himself, "Lady Beltham knows I have to arrest Fandor. It follows Lady Beltham knows that Fandor has released the prisoner—the woman who was a prisoner. On the other hand, it is plain she does *not* know this woman is—Helene."

But at that moment Lady Beltham was interposing:

"His vengeance would be terrible."

"Fantômas' vengeance, you mean?"

"His vengeance."

"You will not say his name?"

"No! I do not wish to understand. Think what a horror I feel for his crimes!"

"Well, madame, how the devil do you expect me to recapture the prisoner, or anyone else to do so?"

But, gazing at the police officer, the poor lady seemed more and more embarrassed.

"Am I cursed then of God?" she groaned. "At one and the same time I must speak and I must not. Oh, Juve, the torment my life is! Listen now. Fandor loves you. He must be warned. He is running appalling risks. Yes, and all unwittingly he may stir up catastrophes. Look you, I know—you hear what I say, Juve—I know that Fandor will meet with a fearful disappointment. And I am afraid that, heartbroken, he may commit a dreadful imprudence—that he may try—what must never be attempted."

"Madame, I do not understand a word you say," Juve admitted. "But I am going to call people by their names, I am!"

"No, no!"

"But I say yes! Fandor should be with Helene—"

"He will not see Helene."

"Whom will he see, then?"

"I cannot tell. But he must not arrest him."

"By God," burst out Juve suddenly, "it's enough to drive one mad! See here, I trust you—more or less. You prophesy catastrophes; I would fain avert them. But I must know how to set about it. What am I to do, according to you?"

Juve was forced to lower his eyes before the fiery look in Lady Beltham's.

"You must," she began, "you must—cost what it will—arrest Fandor."

"Arrest Fandor?"

"That is the only way to stop his acting."

"But where to find him?"

"Ah, Juve, I tell you—Fandor will come back to you."

"Hmm! Is that so?"

"I came here to tell you this, Juve—and no other thing. Oh, and it is so grave, so serious! Think, and you will understand. It is simple too—why, yes, quite, quite simple. Arrest Fandor! Arrest him, to hinder him from arresting anyone!"

Lady Beltham had spoken in a voice barely audible. Now she fell silent, and stepped back a pace, wringing her hands in despair.

"You are going?" questioned the detective.

"I *must* go."

"Without untying me?"

"Juve, are you prepared to give me your oath you will let me go unhindered, without following me? Swear this, and I will set you free."

"I never swear, madame!" Juve answered dryly.

"Goodbye, then."

"Goodbye. Be it so."

"Your servant will come back? You will call out to him."

"Why, of course I shall! So kind of you to give me your advice. But I should be still more grateful if you would only add a small favor to your good advice."

"What can I do for you, Juve?"

"Take a cigarette from the box yonder, hand it to me, and give me a match."

At first Lady Beltham made no answer. It was her turn to be dumbfounded by the police officer's composure. How could the man be thinking of smoking at such a crisis? However, she walked over to the box Juve had indicated, took a cigarette from it, held it out to the police officer, who took it between his lips; then, lighting a match, she was preparing to give Juve a light when suddenly:

"No, no!" she cried. "I dare not! Perhaps it is a trap! Give me your oath it is not a trap—"

"Madame," Juve said calmly, "I take my oath it *is* a trap, and nothing else. I asked you for that cigarette in order to burn the cords that bind me, set myself free, and start tracking you down. You guessed as much? I may as well admit the truth."

"Goodbye, Juve!"

"Goodbye, madame!"—and Lady Beltham left the room, having first carefully extinguished the match she had lit and tossed it into an ashtray.

Surely now, unable to use his cigarette, which hung unlighted between his lips, to burn his bonds, Juve was left no hope of setting himself free.

Not so! Hardly had the sound of Lady Beltham's footsteps died away before the police officer broke into a short laugh.

"So there we are!" he grinned. "When it comes to matches, Lady Beltham can only think of one thing! I stake my reputation I'm on her heels in just three seconds from now!"

3. Mystery of the Châtelet

Yet assuredly Juve was not a man given to idle talking! Never in all his life had this king of police officers let fall a vain boast. Always so entirely modest-minded, he seemed to carry out the most dashing enterprises without so much as appearing conscious of doing anything out of the ordinary. But still, was he not exaggerating a trifle when he declared he would release himself so rapidly from the stout ropes wherewith Lady Beltham had seen fit to bind him? For a moment it certainly looked as if nothing could be done.

"Simply by taking his precautions does a man fight his fate," he growled to himself, and as he spoke bit at the cigarette he held between his teeth, tore off the paper, and shredded away the tobacco. This done, it grew manifest the detective would make good. Inside the roll of tobacco forming the cigarette, to all appearance a facsimile of any other cigarette, there was concealed a fine steel blade. Yes, no doubt of that; Juve knew the way to take precautions beforehand! If it was a fact that Fantômas possessed a key to Juve's rooms, it was no less true that Juve had foreseen how one day or another he might come to be tied up on his own premises.

The tiny steel blade between his teeth—its edge whetted to the keenness of a razor—he bent down his head, and, straining hard, managed to reach the rope binding his right arm.

"A second does it," he thought to himself, and as a fact it took him less than a second to have the arm free.

"Another second to tear away the other fastenings," he continued—and next instant he could conclude triumphantly:

"Just as I said! Just three seconds, and I am on the track of my vanished visitor!"

As he finished speaking, Juve reached the door leading on to the staircase. For a brief moment he glued his ear to the panels, listening to the noises of the house.

"Nothing unusual," he muttered, "so let's get to work." And therewith he opened the door and looked down the stairs. No, nothing out of the common seemed afoot in the modest building where Juve had his flat. A lady was just descending the last flight. Her hand in a yellow glove moved along the balustrade.

"Is it Lady Beltham?" the detective asked himself, but he corrected himself next moment: "Why, no. *She* is in mourning."

Thereupon, reassured and convinced that Lady Beltham must have preceded him into the street, Juve proceeded to dash four steps at a time down the stairs, torn by anxiety lest the fugitive should be out of view.

But he was only crossing the landing of the second floor when he came to a sudden halt.

"Hold hard!" exclaimed the police officer. "What have we here?"

In the dim light his sharp eyes had made out a nondescript parcel, which he picked up.

"A crêpe veil, a black skirt, gloves," he noted, making a summary inventory of his find. Obvious, of course! Lady Beltham was afraid of being shadowed, so she wore two costumes, one on top of the other! "It's a fair wager she's now in a light-colored frock!" And in an instant he had guessed the truth.

"The lady in the yellow gloves was she, by God!"—and the police officer pursued his way.

No man could match him at shadowing a suspect. No man was better qualified than this king of detectives to follow artfully on the tracks of anyone he chose, without ever drawing the victim's attention.

"It's between us two," he exclaimed cheerfully, as he came out into the Rue Tardieu, and his first glance ahead reassured him. Fifty yards from the house a lady in blue, wearing a smart, bright-colored hat, was walking quietly away.

"There we are!" cried the detective. "But it was cleverly done. Barring the chance of my habit of looking about me every way, I should never have spied the derelict clothes, and she would have slipped between my fingers. Wary now; it would be all up if she were to look round."

However, quick as thought, the detective had already made his arrangements. Pulling a newspaper from his pocket, he unfolded the sheet; then, after making a tiny hole, a quarter of an inch across, he held it at arm's length in front of his face, like a man who, as he walks on, hunts for a particular paragraph.

"To be visible and yet make yourself invisible, that's the thing to do!" he muttered to himself. "Nobody ever suspects a man planted right in the middle of the pavement. Lady Beltham, not seeing my features, will never imagine I am following her up so close." And this was exactly what did happen. It was getting very late by this time. Passersby became few in the little Rue de Steinkerque, and Lady Beltham, feeling herself secure from observation, suddenly wheeled swiftly round, evidently to see if anyone were shadowing her. Peeping through the hole in his paper, Juve could distinctly see the anxious look on her face. He was even persuaded the woman was scrutinizing him. At that moment he had come to a full stop right underneath a streetlamp. How was the fugitive likely to guess that the gentleman standing there in the full light was the police constable she had just left firmly tied up in his own house?

"Satisfied?" Juve asked himself. "Yes, she feels safe enough now, so let's go on again."

Lady Beltham had set off afresh, and the detective now followed her example, but at the same time taking good care not to keep too close at her heels. On the contrary he let her get some way ahead, all the time walking with arms outstretched, pretending to continue the perusal of his paper, stopping and starting off again, stumbling at the curbs—in a word, playing quite a capital little comedy of his own.

"Yes," he was reflecting meanwhile, "she is evidently anxious not to be followed, and that is proof positive I'm not wasting my time by keeping her in view. Now where is she bound for?"

But at that moment Juve gave a jump. Behind him a legless cripple came clattering noisily down the steep street. Arrived opposite the police constable, he hailed softly.

"Juve… Monsieur Juve?"

"Eh, what?"

"Go on just the same. Only listen here. It is I—I, Inspector Henri."

"You don't say so!"—and Juve set off again on his way. For his part the cripple pushed his way on to the pavement, and the two men began to talk to one another in such a clever fashion that nobody would ever have guessed they were in conversation.

"What are you doing here?" questioned Juve, "keeping an eye on somebody?"

"Yes, Monsieur Juve."

"And who's the somebody, eh?"

"Hmm! That's neither here nor there."

"I'm the one, I wager."

"That's to say…"

"Come, come! Never deny it. The Préfet or Havard?"

"The two of 'em are of one mind…"

"That I could play the scoundrel like Fandor, eh? Well, they're a very sagacious pair!… You hold a warrant against me?"

"No, Monsieur Juve… Only I've got to follow you."

"Very well, my man—follow me!"

"Of course I shall, Monsieur Juve, as those are my orders. But as I see you're busy—"

"Busy, Henri?"

"Why, yes! Don't try to deny it! Busy tracking the lady in blue."

"Well?"

"Well, I'm putting myself under your orders. You know very well *I* don't suspect you—that's understood… And I have a notion I may be useful to you, if you want a bit of help. But, swear you won't take it into your head to give me the go-by."

"Give you the go-by?"

"Yes, slip between my fingers."

"Not I! I give you my oath I won't. So thank you, my lad! But enough said! Join me in shadowing the woman yonder. If we get separated, we meet at the last place where we had a clear sight of one another. Understand?"

"I understand, sir. And supposing you want to speak to me?"

"I'll whistle a tune—say the 'Paimpolaise' or the 'Madelon.'"

"I understand perfectly." And three minutes later the cripple had shot ahead of Juve and was making for the outer boulevards.

Truly the general public can form little idea of the ingenuity demanded for the successful performance of the most every-day police duties. It had taken Juve and Inspector Henri but a couple of sentences to come to a satisfactory arrangement!

A little touched, though he suffered no sign of emotion to be visible, Juve thought:

"A fine fellow, Henri, anyway. *He* at least doesn't doubt my honesty. And I shouldn't be surprised if he is not going to help me succeed where I should have failed without him."

The legless man—or, to speak more exactly, Inspector Henri—gave evidence of no little activity. Thoroughly grounded in the principles governing the art of shadowing—it is veritably an art—he boldly pushed on ahead of Lady Beltham, for all the world as if he had never a thought to discover what direction she was going to take. Full steam ahead on his little go-cart, he swung round the corner into the Boulevard Rochechouart.

"A very good man that!" thought Juve as he watched him. "Yes, he's going to stop fifty yards on and see her come out. So, when I reach the end of the street, I shall be sure to see him signal to me, informing me what direction she has taken." Reassured accordingly of success in his project, feeling certain that, preceded and followed in this way—entirely without knowing it—Lady Beltham could hardly well disappear, Juve advanced at a leisurely pace. To follow too close behind might attract attention, while to keep well to the rear involved no risk; the course to take was obvious.

Five minutes afterwards, however, Juve had a highly painful surprise. He had plainly seen Lady Beltham turn the corner on the left of the boulevard. Accordingly, arrived himself at the corner of the Rue de Steinkerque, he too turned to the left—but saw no one bearing any sort of resemblance to Fantômas' wife!

"Vanished!" growled the detective. "Where's Henri?"

But the constable was no more visible than the fugitive.

"God's truth!" swore Juve in a fury. "What does this mean?"

Quite out of his reckoning, he hesitated. Should he question passersby? But the sort of wayfarers you meet, after midnight, on the Boulevard Rochechouart, in the middle of Montmartre, are quite likely to take the thing humorously and indulge in coarse chaff.

"And, into the bargain," reflected the police officer further, "there's very little chance of anybody's having noticed Lady Beltham. There was nothing about her to attract attention."

Then suddenly he gave a gasp. There, in a recess, near the post office, leaned against the wall, he had caught sight of a contrivance there was no mistaking—the go-cart Inspector Henri had employed in order to pass for a legless man.

"So then," he told himself, "it's clear he had to dash off all of a sudden in pursuit. It's equally plain Lady Beltham must have taken to flight in the same hurried fashion. What to do now?"

Juve felt at that moment that the case was indeed desperate. The more confident he had been a brief while before that his plan was going to give important results, the more doubtful was he now. By himself, and knowing no particulars of his and Fandor's new adventures, how could the inspector carry out his part successfully?

"And then," Juve added mentally, "Henri is under an obligation to follow me. He has definite orders. Who can tell if he's not going to abandon the chase in order to come back to find me?"

And thereupon he wheeled about in the direction he had come from. Frankly, in any case, he knew what he ought to do. An agreement had been come to between himself and Henri— if parted, the two officers were to come back and wait where they had last seen each other.

"I shall wait for Henri in the Rue de Steinkerque!" he decided. "I promised him I would."

But not two minutes had gone by, while he paced the narrow

pavement of the little Rue de Steinkerque, when he saw a taxi coming towards him.

"Ah!" sighed Juve, "if only—"

Then he felt himself turn pale with pleasure and relief. Right in front of him the taxi had drawn up, and already the door was opening and a friendly voice urging him to get in.

"Get in! Get in, M'sieur Juve!"

"Henri!" exclaimed the other.

"Why, yes! And mighty glad to have my two legs again!"

"But she? Lady Beltham?"

"Never fear, sir! We've got her—"

"Got her?"

"I know where she is going."

"Never! Tell me."

By this time the taxi was underway. Taking a cigarette from his pocket and rolling it between his palms to make it smokable, the worthy inspector proceeded to explain:

"See here, sir, it's a dodge *you* taught me once upon a time. I remembered it for the occasion. When I saw the lady in question making for the cab waiting for her—"

"Waiting for her? She had a taxi?"

"Number 62 A7—why certainly!"

"Go on! Go on!"

"I dashed forward—I opened the door. In the first place, that allowed me to see the old bus was empty. There was nobody inside. And then said I, 'Get in, your Ladyship! And where am I to tell the cabby to drive to?'"

In spite of himself Juve went off in a peal of laughter. By God! Henri was making a fine job of it. He (Juve) had always said he would make a capital sleuthhound, and he had not been mistaken.

"She answered you, Henri?"

"Yes, sir. But not as I hoped! 'The driver knows where I'm going,' she said, and handed me a franc."

"But so—"

"I don't know her destination? You wait a bit! The trick of opening the carriage door *you* taught me, sir! The rest I got from Monsieur Fandor. Well, I thank the lady, you see, and bang the door shut very hard, and, while the door's still rattling, I say to the driver, 'You know where to go to, eh, my man?' 'Of course,' he snaps back at me, 'middle of the Pont du Châtelet!' That was quite enough for me, eh, Chief?"

For the moment all the Chief did was to press his trusty subordinate's hand in silence. But, after all, was not this the finest mark of appreciation he could have given him? This from the great Juve made Henri turn red with pride and pleasure.

Two minutes later, however, Juve was again knitting his brows in perplexity. Now that he was sure of coming up with his quarry—to give chase to the fugitive's taxi Henri had picked out a first-rate landaulette and promised the chauffeur a royal tip—Juve was once more asking himself what extraordinary enterprise he was now starting on. If Lady Beltham was really being driven to the middle of the Pont du Châtelet, this could only mean that at this lonely spot, quite deserted at night time and so late in the night, she was to meet someone.

"But whom?" thought Juve. "*Him*, perhaps"—and he felt himself shudder.

Fantômas! For a brief while he had believed him taken, beaten, brought to his knees. But not so, he was at large, still at large, and more to be dreaded than ever!

Meanwhile, under Inspector Henri's adjurations, the taxi carrying the two police officers was making for the river at racing speed. Juve, who for some moments had sat silent, appeared suddenly to rouse himself from his torpor.

"By the by," he asked his companion, "where precisely is this vehicle taking us to?"

"Place du Châtelet, sir! I thought from there we could keep a watch on the bridge."

"Good! But—"

"But what?"

"We must be more than careful. Henri, my son, I've just had a brainwave. A bridge is a place that has two ends, isn't it?"

"Undoubtedly," Henri agreed with a smile.

"Well, I think it's as well to have both ends guarded."

"Guarded?"

"Yes. You, my friend, are going to take post on the left bank—the Palais de Justice side; I shall stay on the right bank—the Châtelet side. That way Lady Beltham, when she gets out of her cab, will be between us. She can't then escape us."

"You propose to arrest her, sir?"

"Hmm! Yes! and no! That depends! In any case let's separate. You, Henri, take another taxi and go by way of the next bridge to post yourself where I've told you. Soon as you're there, strike three matches. I shall see the light in the distance, and it'll give me a sense of assurance. If I whistle the 'Tonkinoise' march, come across to meet me; if I whistle the 'Paimpolaise,' stay where you are; and if I sing the 'Marseillaise,' well, come to my help—that'll mean there's a scrap on. Understand everything?"

"Perfectly, sir!"

"Let's to work then"—and Juve stopped the taxi, while Henri jumped out on the pavement.

"Good luck!" began the inspector, then: "By the by, M'sieur Juve, in case of alarm, or our being thrown off the scent, we're to meet at the Place du Châtelet, eh?"

"Agreed," echoed Juve. "Certain sure you're afraid I'm going to slip through your fingers, and you've not forgotten your orders?"

"Oh, Monsieur Juve!" protested Henri, who was already walking away and getting into a second taxi, after giving the driver his instructions. Ten minutes more and Juve was doing sentry-go at his end of the bridge.

"Now how long will it be," he calculated, "till Lady Beltham arrives? She'll be here, I suppose, by the time I've counted a hundred,"—and he started counting to pass the time. No doubt his own conveyance must have got ahead of the fugitive's, so he felt confident he would be able to renew his watch on his prey.

But old Juve's heart was beating hard all the same.

"What's she coming here to do?" he was asking himself, when suddenly he gave a start, then another. From far away over the bridge three little lights had flashed out. That first; then, advancing at a quite ordinary pace, a taxi had driven on to the Pont du Châtelet and halted halfway across.

* * * * *

On seeing this taxi, which came on slackening speed, and finally stopped right in the middle of the bridge, entirely deserted at this late hour, Juve had stepped back into the friendly shadow of the quay. He had no doubt—he could have no doubt—who it was. His extraordinarily retentive memory, further strengthened by continual exercise, had infallibly registered the number of the cab the fugitive had taken—and there was that very number displayed on the back of the taxi Juve was now staring after.

A minute more, however, and the police officer was like to curse and swear in impotent fury. The driver had pulled up and the door opened, but it was not Lady Beltham who got out. It was not even a woman. It was a man!

"Am I gone crazy?" Juve asked himself—and was on the point of dashing to the spot, but motives of prudence kept him where he was.

"It is a man, certainly!" he reflected, "but perhaps Lady Beltham is in the taxi with him?"

Alas! events followed fast, and each one seemed to make a deliberate mock of the police officer's suppositions. No, there could be no one else in the cab than the passenger getting out, for that individual now proceeded to feel in his pocket, extract his purse, and pay the driver, who at once drove off.

Then was it possible Lady Beltham was disguised as a man? Why, no! *She* would never have condescended to such a travesty. Nay, more than that; if the driver, after seeing a woman get into his vehicle, had presently beheld a man get out, without in the least knowing how the metamorphosis had been effected, the fellow would certainly have manifested some surprise, of which, however, no trace was visible in his behavior.

Must it be assumed, then, that Lady Beltham had simply left the taxi and that another fare, a casual stranger, had subsequently hired it? But Juve could not quite credit that.

"No, that is nonsense. It would presuppose a series of utterly improbable coincidences. Why in the devil's name should this unknown stranger also, like her, have wanted to be driven here, to the middle of the Pont du Châtelet?"

The question puzzled Juve to the highest degree, so unanswerable was it. Who could have given such an address at once so vague and so precise? Who could have had himself conveyed, after midnight, to this bridge, of all places?

"I was expecting to see a woman, and it is a man I see alight," Juve told himself. "Now what does that mean? I must find a solution—I must!"

But, cudgel his brains as he might, he could discover no plausible answer to the question he was asking himself. Once again, in fact, events were so crowding one upon another that the poor man had no time to examine the several details he failed to understand.

To see without being seen, the police officer had taken ambush on the Quai de la Mégisserie, less than half a score paces from the entrance to the Pont du Châtelet. Thereabouts, resting on the stone parapet of the sidewalk, stand the boxes of dealers in secondhand books, and it was between two of these that Juve had taken asylum. It was an excellent lookout place, and not a soul, in the darkness, could have had a suspicion of his presence.

Still, there was one undeniable disadvantage. If from this standpoint Juve was quite well able to see the one footway of the bridge, that on the right, he could only imperfectly and with difficulty keep an eye on the other, the one on the left— and it was precisely this one that the mysterious individual who had alighted from the cab was now making for.

"Hmm," pondered the detective, "should I cross over to the other side too?"

But he came swiftly to a decision in the negative.

"My word, no! better not. Henri is on the lookout opposite—I am doing the same here. It follows our friend cannot disappear without our knowing it. That's all as it should be, so we'll just await developments."

But the words had hardly left his lips ere he was trembling

again with excitement and amazement. Coming from the direction of the Pont Neuf—that is to say, following the riverside quay where he himself was in hiding—a woman, a woman of great elegance, was advancing at a rapid pace, her footsteps ringing on the asphalt of the sidewalk.

Juve turned to look at the newcomer—and his heart stood still. The woman was Lady Beltham!

"I'm going crazy!" Juve thought for the second time that night. "The thing's impossible."

But the thing was true nonetheless. The approaching figure was still twenty yards away, but Juve was possessed of too sharp a pair of eyes, and, above all, was too well used to note details of dress and appearances to feel the smallest hesitation. It was undoubtedly Lady Beltham arriving on foot, after setting out in a taxi from which an unknown man had dismounted.

"They had agreed to meet," thought Juve. "Yes, no doubt they had made an appointment! And—ah!—now I understand."

Before his eyes, in fact within a few steps of where he stood, Lady Beltham had stepped up to the parapet, and, bending forward somewhat, was looking—everything pointed to the fact—for the individual who had alighted on the bridge. It was all as clear as daylight.

"No need to cudgel one's brain," growled Juve under his breath. Lady Beltham and the man joined forces. He got into her conveyance, and she gave some information or other. Presently he had a panic, guessed the cab might be shadowed, and made his companion alight a hundred yards or so from here, thinking it best to arrive alone, to make sure there was nothing suspicious to be noted. Only, guessing as he did the truth, Juve saw that it only made the mystery deeper. Doubtless it was very possible matters *had* gone as he supposed, but this merely gave rise to another anxious doubt in his mind.

"If all this is authentic," Juve growled to himself, "it proves one thing—that at all costs Lady Beltham and this man were to make their way to this bridge. But what the devil can anyone have to do in the middle of a bridge at dead of night?"

Then, all in a moment, he felt afraid. He had designated the unknown passenger he had seen alight from the taxi as "this man"; but could he not, in fact, give him a name, admit that he knew, only too well, who "this man" was?

"Fantômas! It is Fantômas!" shuddered the police officer. For who save the Torturer could be Lady Beltham's companion? Who else could it have been who had joined her on the road, then gone on in front to make sure no danger threatened?

"Fantômas! Yes, it is Fantômas standing yonder," Juve reiterated in tones of concentrated fury. Then another illuminating thought flashed across his brain. Had not Lady Beltham come to visit him carrying a key of his flat that belonged to Fantômas? Was it not Fantômas she had joined on leaving his house? Plain then, to see that her doings had been by command of the Lord of Terror! Muttering low, like a man talking in his sleep, like a man in a nightmare, Juve resumed:

"Yes, that's how it is—that's just how it is! It was Fantômas sent Lady Beltham to tell me to arrest Fandor. And was it not his daughter Helene who was the prisoner the lad rescued? Was it not Helene he was to rejoin? Is it not she again, above all else, whom Fantômas is bound to wish to protect?"

Then he reproached himself with wasting time on these reflections. Was not the moment one for action rather? A few paces only from Fantômas, was it not his duty to spring at the villain's throat, to strike him to the earth, to kill him even, if he could not master him? A man does not hesitate when he stands a few yards from a wild beast, and he knows he has the courage to face the danger. Turning his head, half afraid he might have vanished, he looked for the figure he supposed to be Fantômas, and a sigh of satisfaction escaped him when he caught sight of the man. Recrossing from the left sidewalk to the right, he was back at the spot where he had alighted from the taxi. Standing with one hand resting on the parapet, he turned to face the direction from which Lady Beltham was advancing.

"He sees her now," guessed the detective. "He is signaling to her—I'm sure of it." In fact, the man, drawing a white handkerchief from his pocket, as if to mop his brow—though the temperature was anything but warm—had waved it in a way that might well be a signal. He felt no more doubt as he exclaimed:

"Yes, this time I am barely a dozen yards from Fantômas, without his having a suspicion of my presence! This time, I have him in a regular trap. This time he cannot make even an attempt to escape. I can make certain of his capture! I or Henri will spring at the scoundrel's throat!"

Juve had grown quite cool and composed. At this decisive moment when he was about to enter into so formidable a battle—one affecting the whole human race—he found himself able to master his nerves and force his brain to reason calmly and collectedly.

"I will let them meet," he reflected. "Together, they will get in each other's way. Then I will whistle the 'Tonkinoise'—and Henri will dash out upon them. Good! Now to prepare for the fray"—and he drew his revolver. What is police duty but a grim chase—the hunting of men? And what hunter but examines his weapons before attacking some redoubtable foe?

"Six cartridges," Juve counted, "and all well pushed home. The magazine in order? Yes, works smoothly. The safety-catch off? Capital, I am ready."

A second had sufficed for this examination. Then softly, cautiously he turned. Lady Beltham must have come level with him by now, and would pass within a few steps of where he stood. Then suddenly he saw her so close to his side he bit his lips to check a startled cry. Not a sign of agitation did she betray. Evidently quite convinced she had baffled all pursuit, convinced most likely that whoever it was she was going to meet had made sure no danger was near, she moved calmly forward with no appearance of haste.

Her face the detective did not see. He did not dare to keep his eyes fixed on her as she went by him so close he could scent the perfume that breathed from her person. He thought the fire of his gaze must attract her attention. But she was utterly unsuspicious, never dreaming that Juve was there, all ready to spring at her husband's throat.

"Dreadful," he muttered to himself. "She loves him, and she herself has put me on his track!"

But it was no time for sentimental scruples. "Yes, I will let them meet," thought the detective again. "Then I whistle. Henri is over there. I can see the light of his cigarette. But what the devil now were they coming to do, the two of them, halfway across this bridge? It's not a mere question of a meeting arranged in a safe place. They have seen each other already… What then—"

But his reflections were cut short. Some minutes are so charged with drama we can take no count of how they pass. We live them—that is enough—it is even too much. Juve, his eyes riveted on Lady Beltham, watched her every movement. Fantômas' wife crossed over to the right footway, still at the same quiet pace, and Fantômas advanced to meet her.

"The time is come," thought Juve, as he cast a last look about him. Not a soul was on the bridge—literally not a soul. In the Place du Châtelet two or three belated passengers were hurrying to the omnibus bureau before which the last bus for the night was still standing. Along the Quai de la Mégisserie, a long way off, three market-gardeners' carts were making for Les Halles. Further away still, the light of a row of taxis on a cab rank flickered feebly.

"Nobody! no one to interfere! Yes, the time is come," muttered the police officer for the second time.

Meantime Lady Beltham and Fantômas had met, and were standing stationary, talking.

"To work!" said Juve, and he took a quick step away from the parapet, plunging into the semidarkness of the sidewalk, and started a whistle. Yet he could barely hear the sounds he was himself making. A result of agitation, perhaps? For his throat was dry and his lips parched.

"Henri will never hear me at the other end of the bridge," he was telling himself; but now, from across the river, another whistle sounded. Why, yes, Henri *had* heard—heard and understood, and answered, signifying that he had observed his signal.

"Very good!" Juve nodded in approval, panting with excitement. "He is on the bridge and is bound to walk this way towards me. No need for me to budge. I shall rush forward the moment I see my colleague. Fantômas *cannot* escape us now."

But suddenly Juve let fly an oath. The whistle had no sooner sounded in reply to his than Fantômas—if it was really Fantômas yonder—had started violently. Was he giving his companion some directions? It was impossible for Juve to hear what was said from where he still stood. But, to make up, no single movement could escape his eye. At that moment Fantômas was grasping Lady Beltham's arm and dragging her hurriedly towards the foot of the bridge furthest from the Palais de Justice.

"Well and good!" calculated Juve. "Henri will bar their way."

But now Fantômas had stopped dead, and, wheeling about, was coming back towards the police officer.

"Better and better!" thought the detective. "He has seen Henri. It's for me to attack him."

But at that moment, putting two fingers in his mouth, as the street urchins do, Fantômas gave a loud, shrill whistle.

"Accomplices," thought Juve, "he's summoning his accomplices,"—and there and then started to run. If Fantômas was indeed calling to his help some of the wretches who formed his ordinary bodyguard, it was very necessary to act before these last had had time to come to the rescue. But hardly had the police officer set off running, covering the few yards that separated him from the entrance to the bridge, before he was swearing again. No doubt, hearing him approaching, Fantômas had acted at once. Still holding Lady Beltham by the arm and dragging her after him, he had leapt into the roadway, crossed it, and reached the left footway, which Juve, from where he still was, could only see with difficulty.

But he still felt confident. He could not help feeling confident. Do what he might, Fantômas could not possibly escape capture by him, or, if not by him, by Henri. He could not see the left footway in the center of the bridge, it is true, but, to make up he had a full view of the whole width of the end of the bridge near him, while Henri was bound to see, from where he was, the whole width of his end. What, then, did it matter if for a few short seconds Fantômas might be lost to view? Caught between the two officers, unable to pass either one or the other without being seen, it was out of the range of possibility for him to avoid being intercepted and captured.

It took but half a second for the detective to reach this conclusion, and his triumphant satisfaction reached a climax. The fellow was brought to bay, the monster was defeated. He yelled: "Henri, are you there? Attention!"—and next moment, in a stentorian voice:

"Fantômas, surrender! Hands up!"

Only Henri's voice answered in tones of jubilation: "Never fear, sir! We've got him!"

"Why, yes!" returned Juve. "Forward! They are between us. And fire, without a moment's hesitation, Henri!"

"Right, sir!"

Juve had now fallen back into a walk, moving right down the center of the roadway, finger on trigger, ready to fire. But Fantômas, tracked down, brought to bay, was he not going to use his weapons, open fire from his side? Indeed, he had every chance to take steady aim at his opponent. He knew exactly where the other was. He must even have seen him coming on.

But Juve paid no heed whatever to the fact.

"Fantômas, surrender!" he reiterated.

Next instant he broke into a volley of oaths once more. Twenty yards ahead of him he had suddenly caught sight of Henri's figure advancing to meet him; and Inspector Henri, just like Juve, was going at the slow march, and, like Juve again, was scrutinizing the footpaths of the bridge to right and left.

Yet neither Juve nor Henri had had one glimpse of Fantômas or of Lady Beltham. Neither one nor the other of the two officers had passed the fugitives—and lo! the fugitives were not between them.

Fantômas and Lady Beltham, in a word, had vanished from the bridge, which yet it was physically impossible they could have quitted.

*　　*　　*　　*　　*

"Juve, Juve, you saw them?"

"Henri, you let them past you?"

With one voice, at once bewildered and furious, the two police officers questioned one another, and simultaneously again, in tones of sincere conviction, came the two answers:

"I saw nobody!"

"I'm positive they didn't escape my way!" Then, as if each had guessed the doubts the other might feel, they declared:

"From where I stood I could see the whole bridge, right side and left." And, this said, both fell silent with a like unanimity. Neither Juve, in fact, nor Henri, could suspect his comrade's sincerity. They had known each other long enough to know that neither was the sort of man to talk idly.

Yet how understand what could have happened? How explain the inexplicable?

"They were on this footway," observed Juve.

"So they were," agreed Henri. "And they crossed over to the other."

"That was just when I took the middle of the roadway."

"Same for me."

"I was creeping up little by little, searching carefully to right and left with my eyes."

"I can say as much."

"So then?"

"So then—then it's just black magic."

For a few brief seconds more the two inspectors stood motionless, staring at one another with startled eyes.

Juve was the first to recover his sangfroid.

"Still, by God!" he observed, "they can't have flown up to the sky, eh?"

"Nor yet tumbled into the river?" supplemented Henri.

"Ah, tumbled into the river?" Juve caught him up. "Why, yes, *that's* possible."

"You think it was suicide, then?"

"Why so?"

"Look at the head of water, Juve. Is there a swimmer could live in those currents and eddies?"

Juve bent over the parapet.

"You're right, Henri," he said next moment. "No man could swim in those whirlpools. Besides, we should have heard the splash."

"So, sir?"

"Why, what would you have me say? I don't understand!"

Juve did not hesitate to proclaim his ignorance. Like all those who have made good, all who have succeeded again and again in making sensational discoveries, he was devoid of self-conceit. When he did not know a thing, he said so straight out and unashamed. When he was faced with an incomprehensible fact, he announced unhesitatingly: "I do not understand it!" And this time he certainly did not understand. He had seen, seen with his own eyes, seen beyond possibility of doubt, Fantômas and Lady Beltham move on to the bridge. It was barely a second they had been out of his sight, and during that brief second he had never for one instant ceased to watch his end of the bridge, just as Inspector Henri, for his part, had not for one instant ceased to watch *his* end. And yet there was the brutal, indisputable fact—Fantômas and Lady Beltham, who could not possibly have got away, were no longer there!

"Did you hear anything?" asked Juve.

"Nothing! And you, sir?"

"Nothing again, upon my word!"

"And you can think of nothing, make no guess?"

"Not I!" declared Juve, in a tired voice. "No, I can guess nothing and think of no explanation. It's just wizardry."

"The parapet?" suggested Henri.

"Well?"

"Get over it? Cling to the underside? Let themselves hang suspended in the air? Couldn't they have done that?"

Juve perfectly well understood what the inspector suggested—that Fantômas and Lady Beltham had evaded their search by springing to the far side of the parapet and staying there, suspended by their hands over the void. But Juve was already shaking his head.

"No," he replied positively. "That even is out of the question.

Lady Beltham could not have had the physical strength for such a feat, and if Fantômas had held her up—well, that would not explain their disappearance."

"But still—"

"No, Henri! No! They would only have had to come up again, and we should have caught sight of them."

"And supposing—"

"Supposing what?"

"Supposing they had let themselves down on a piece of the bridge?"

"On another bridge—yes, that would be feasible. But as to this one—"

"You are right," confessed the officer. "Only I can think of nothing else."

"No use supposing," retorted Juve. "We must find out."

"Fantômas—yes, he has found the means to make off somehow or other with Lady Beltham. We are to find out how he did it. That's less difficult, it seems to me."

Juve spoke in a constrained, quivering voice that well bespoke his exasperation. The Inspector Henri dare not offer a reply. Ever since he had been attached to the Criminal Bureau he had over and over again listened to tales of the great detective's prowess and achievements, and professed an admiration for him that almost amounted to veneration. He knew that, in principle, nothing was impossible for Juve; but all the same, he knew that, nevertheless, there were, in fact, physical impossibilities, before which, willy-nilly, a man must bow the head; and surely this incomprehensible disappearance of the fugitives was in the said category. Henri was an obstinate man, too, and kept telling himself:

"They were there. They are there no longer. And it is radically impossible they can have gone. Juve—Juve as he may be—will never explain that."

Juve, meantime, was arguing on precisely the opposite tack. The fashion, indeed, in which a man uses such powers of reasoning as Nature has bestowed on all of us—does not this form the criterion whereby genius is recognized? Faced by a plain fact, Juve never dreamed of denying it or disputing it, but simply took it as a point of departure from which to draw conclusions. That was the solid foundation on which he built up by force of ratiocination his most subtle discoveries. He was reflecting now:

"Fantômas and Lady Beltham were on this bridge—a certain fact, number one. They are not there now—an indisputable truth, number two. Thirdly, it is proved they have not left by either end of the bridge, or else we should have seen them; and still less by jumping into the river, for they would infallibly have been drowned. That much is the solid frame, so to speak, of the problem—and there is no getting outside it."

Suddenly he interrupted himself, to add:

"Ah! I was forgetting something—something important, something significant. Fantômas whistled, summoned accomplices to his help. That is a detail of his disappearance I must not ignore. It ought to be a guide."

But the fact was, this last consideration, far from being a guide to the inquirer, only involved him in great confusion. If it was established that Fantômas, by his whistle, had indeed called upon accomplices to come, it was no less certain that the latter had remained invisible. Lady Beltham and Fantômas had not quitted the bridge by either end, but neither had the accomplices come on to it by either end. Then how could they have joined the two demanding their succor?

"It is just wizardry, black magic!" the police officer repeated, angry and despondent. "The whole thing passes a man's comprehension! An airplane, perhaps?" he next muttered to himself. But that was to assume the impossible. Suppose an airplane had skimmed over the bridge and carried off the two fugitives, it was perfectly certain Juve or Henri would have seen the machine, or at any rate heard the noise of its engine, and Juve shrugged his shoulders at his own absurd suggestion.

"Listen to me, Henri," he began. "We'll lose our lives at the job, if need be, but we'll know the truth. You're quite determined, eh?"

"Most assuredly, sir!"

"Then I'm going to make you a proposal. We are going to separate once more."

"Separate? And why, sir?"

"You, Henri, are going to stop at one of the two ends of the bridge and continue your watch. I, meantime, shall be searching."

"Searching what, Juve?"

"Why, for the fugitives, the vanished couple."

"So you think they are still in the neighborhood?"

"I don't think anything, my dear man. I simply say one thing, and that is, I shall find out how they disappeared—or else I shall find them." And all the famous detective's determination rang in his words. Inspector Henri looked bewildered.

"Oh," he said. "And how do you mean to search for them?"

"Minutely. To begin with, I shall sound the stonework of the parapet, the flags of the foot-pavements."

"You imagine there's some hiding-hole?"

"If I find nothing on the bridge, I shall go under the bridge."

"Under the bridge?"

"Yes! Then, too, there may be a hollow in the stonework. Can I tell? But, anyway, you agree that, if Lady Beltham and Fantômas came here, and afterwards disappeared, there is something escapes us."

"You're right, Juve, but—"

"But what, Henri?"

"You won't be angry?"

"No, I shan't. What d'you want to say?"

"Why, yes! I do want to say something, Juve, and I dare not say it."

"Out with it!"

"Well, Juve, it's this. I think I understand now."

"Understand what?"

"How it comes about that Fantômas and Lady Beltham have disappeared."

"And you dare not tell me? Impossible, man! I'm losing my wits!"

"Or you *won't* understand."

"Eh?"

"This time, Juve, I think it's my duty to act."

"Act in what way?"

Henri seemed to get confused all of a sudden. Stuffing both hands in his pockets, he went on slowly:

"You know, Juve, they suspect you at the Préfecture."

"Well?"

"They've sent me out on your track, with orders to keep an eye on you."

"Quite true. Still, I don't see—"

"But I do, Juve! I came upon you, in a word, as you were dogging Lady Beltham's heels. You told me you were shadowing her. Were you perhaps by way of going with her, eh?—escorting her?"

"Oh, ho!" exclaimed Juve. "Very good! Pray go on!"

"After that," pursued the officer, "it's all pretty plain, eh? You throw dust in my eyes. Your plan is to clear your character. You pretend you're desperately zealous. And when you think I'm sufficiently hoodwinked, slap, bang! you pitch me into the most bewildering of mysteries."

"You are very entertaining," laughed Juve. "And then?"

"That's about all. You put me at one end of this damned bridge; *you* stand at the other. Oh, the way Fantômas and Lady Beltham vanished is mighty simple. You let them pass!" And, strong in his conviction, never doubting, in fact, that Juve was veritably and indeed the accomplice of the fugitives, entirely believing he was doing his strict duty, Henri suddenly sprang forward.

"In the name of the law!" he shouted, and, pulling his hands out of his pockets, hurled himself headlong at Juve to slip the handcuffs on his wrists.

But, alas! in all the fine story he had just been telling Inspector Henri had forgotten one little thing—that the hero of his drama was Juve.

Now Juve was not the man to let himself be caught at a loss so easily. From the very first words his colleague had uttered he had perfectly well guessed what the latter would be at, and how, in face of an inexplicable mystery, Inspector Henri had recourse to the simplest of possible explanations.

"A pretty job!" Juve ejaculated. "So now he's going to act on the suspicions they have of me! That's always the way with poor Fandor and me! Ah, well, we've got to stop the idiot from hurting me!" And Inspector Henri had barely given a hint of his intended attack before he was rolling on the ground, knocked off his legs by the most workmanlike of cross-buttocks, Juve at the same moment crying:

"Look here, young man, this is how we slip the handcuffs," and therewith proceeded to give his colleague a first-rate demonstration, clapping on his wrists the very same steel bracelets he had meant for his friend.

"Now get up!" Juve went on, and Inspector Henri did as he was bid. He was pale, but resolute.

"Very good!" he declared. "You are cleverer than I am! What are you going to do? Chuck me in the river?"

Such a show of pluck disarmed Juve.

"You're a fool, my lad!" he laughed, "but I like your spirit. Listen, and try to understand what I say. I am not an accomplice of Fantômas."

"Prove it!"

"I will. Here's my proof." And this time Inspector Henri came near giving a cry of sheer amazement. The proof he had demanded in mockery and scorn Juve gave there and then. He simply removed the handcuffs and handed them back to his colleague.

"You can have them," he said, proffering the pair. "Understand now? If I were a scoundrel, should I be doing this?"

Henri smothered an oath.

"I've only one thing more to say," continued Juve. "If I'm so magnanimous as all this, it is because I want your help." And therewith he gave a shrug, to show the very small importance he attached to the matter of Henri and his feelings, and proceeded:

"Let's think no more of it, Henri! You suspected me, and not altogether unnaturally. I've set you free—the only logical thing to be done. So now to work."

Only he too was counting without his host. Instinctively Henri had thrown himself on his neck and was embracing him, as he stammered brokenly:

"Oh, sir, sir! Such generosity! I am covered with shame."

"Bah! Think no more of it! The Préfet and Monsieur Havard think pretty much as you did!" And he laughed to hide the bitterness he could not but feel to see himself forever spied upon in this fashion, when he should have been the object of the most unbounded admiration.

"Time enough wasted!" he went on. "Let's do as I said. I may count on you, eh?"

"For life, sir! For death!"

"Oh, come, I hope there's no question of dying! There, stand where you are! I'm going on with my search."

With the same composure, in truth, as if he had not just come out of a fresh imbroglio that might easily have ended very ill for him, Juve went about the task he had set himself. Slowly, minutely, from one end of the bridge to the other, he examined, sounded, tested, and tried the ground and the two parapets. But, alas! his investigations seemed destined to be entirely unsuccessful. No sign was anywhere to be found of the stonework being hollow.

"For all that," he muttered to himself at intervals, "I *know* they were here, and I *know* they haven't flown away."

Finally, after two full hours of searching, Juve came back to Inspector Henri, who, a prey to remorse, was mounting the strictest guard, his back against the parapet of the bridge.

"Nothing yet, but I'm not done," Juve told him.

"What more do you think of doing, sir?"

"Looking underneath the bridge." And with a smile, a trifle ruefully, he added:

"You're not afraid of my taking the opportunity to vanish?"

"Oh, sir!"

"See you again presently, then."

No, Inspector Henri had no suspicions left. Possibly, however, he remained under the impression that his colleague was undertaking a perfectly useless task.

It was close on two o'clock in the morning when Juve made his way to the riverbank.

"He's good for a quarter of an hour—half an hour at most," reckoned Henri. But the minutes dragged on interminably, without the police officer having reappeared. Three o'clock struck… Then four o'clock… Then five o'clock. On the horizon a faint, sallow gleam announced the approach of dawn, but still no Juve! Suddenly Inspector Henri felt his eyes fill with tears.

"Oh, dear!" he groaned, "what am I to think? Has Juve taken to his heels? Has he fallen at the fugitives' hands? Has he come across something monstrous, atrocious?" And the poor fellow guessed some fresh mystery had developed, and that Juve's disappearance was perhaps just as incomprehensible as ever that of Fantômas and Lady Beltham could be!

4. Fandor's "Prudence"

After quitting Juve's rooms, when he had plunged his friend into the deepest of sleeps by means of the narcotic he had administered, Fandor was now hurrying away from the Montmartre district.

"Without humbug," he told himself, "the neighborhood is not good for me! I wager it will be kept under watch by the good folks of the Criminal Bureau."

Following his usual habit, Fandor was laughing; but his merriment was forced rather than spontaneous.

"Anyway," he resumed presently, "enough of imprudence! To have been to see Juve and told him my secret was, after all, a piece of folly! Juve might very well have refused my drugged cigarette and clapped hands on my collar. By God! that would never have suited my book!" And once again Fandor conveyed his thanks mentally to his friend, who, as he had not failed to note, had in no wise fallen into the trap laid for him, but had let himself be put to sleep of his own accord. Now, quickening his pace, the young man went on with his reflections.

"In any case," he thought, "I need not trouble my head about Juve. He has no clue to go upon. On the other hand, he is undoubtedly under suspicion at police headquarters. Hence to conclude he will be running no risks for a long while to come is a short step. So let us to work without worrying about him, and equally without any expectation of his coming to my assistance."

Arrived at this point, however, in his meditations, Fandor heaved a sudden and deep sigh as he added:

"Besides, will Juve *ever* give me his help where Helene is concerned?"

He was very well aware that the police officer in question felt for Fantômas' daughter the most sincere and pitying affection. He was fully convinced that his friend would have gone through fire and water to be of service to Helene. But he was no less well aware that, dreading fresh perils for Fandor, Juve only half approved the fidelity the young man still observed in his love for the girl who had been, and who continued to be, his fiancée.

"I am not deceiving myself," Fandor told himself. "Juve surely loves Helene, but he is far from wishing me to marry her!" And thereupon he shrugged his shoulders. Whether or no, in fact, his friend was desirous of seeing him contract the alliance he longed for himself with all his soul was a matter of minor importance.

"Juve loves me. He wishes my happiness," he reflected. "Once let him see me satisfied, and he will be content."

Accordingly, leaving on one side the question of Juve's future behavior, he asked himself another question:

"By the by, was it really Helene I saved?"

Fandor had indeed spoken the simple truth to Juve, and before that dearest of friends whom he loved like a father had hidden no detail of what had occurred at the dramatic moment when he set at liberty the girl who for some seconds had passed in the eyes of all present for the terrifying Fantômas.

"Was it really she?" he asked himself again.

Greatly agitated, Fandor strove once more to discover any detail that might convince him of the truth. But there was none. The girl had never quitted her hood, which indeed seemed fixed firmly to her face. So, too, she had hardly opened her lips, and had succeeded perfectly in disguising her voice. Then the few words exchanged during the pursuit by the police officers had been spoken so rapidly!

"Nay, it *was* Helene," the young man swore in trembling accents. "My heart tells me so, but I have no proof!" And he reviewed mentally the whole incident, even asking himself, in great distress, if he had not done wrong in acting as he did.

"I saw in this woman Helene. I suspected in her, not an accomplice, but a victim of Fantômas. Have I let them hoodwink me?" And he swore to himself.

"Good! I shall know at midnight."

This was, in fact, the one thing he had not told Juve, and which let loose in his heart a storm of passion at once terrible and delicious. When, outstripping the pursuit of Monsieur Havard's car, Fandor had gained the Bois de Boulogne and won freedom, his unknown passenger had suddenly bidden him stop, declaring she must alight.

"What, here?"

"Yes, here!" And with a newborn hesitation she had added:

"Now listen carefully. At midnight be at No. 120 Rue Chanez, at Auteuil. Ring three times. You have saved my life. I am asking you to save others—others of Fantômas' victims."

The words seemed still to echo in the young man's ears. In what tones had they been spoken! What agony had vibrated in her voice as she spoke the name: Fantômas!

"Yes, it was Helene," he reiterated. "It was his daughter! I swear it! She, and she only, can feel such pain in this confession that Fantômas is a monster of iniquity!"

Then he asked himself:

"And what am I to hear at this meeting that is coming? What innocent victims does it concern? Who are these other victims Fantômas threatens?"

But he was not altogether in earnest, poor fellow, in these divers questions he asked himself. At the thought of seeing Helene again, of finding at last the woman he loved, the woman he dreamed of making his wife, such a whirlwind of pain and passion awoke in him that all else was forgotten. Seriously, however, he bethought himself:

"Still, I gave Juve my word I would be prudent, and it is only right I should keep my word. Suppose I go home to get a weapon." Surely an elementary precaution! On the point of going to the most mysterious of interviews, on the point of meeting an unknown woman who might well entice him into a trap and bring him face to face with Fantômas, the young man might well arm himself beforehand.

But next moment he changed his mind. "Not so!" he thought. "That's the very thing would not be prudent. Who can say my place is not watched? A fine thing to go like a fool and get myself nabbed just when I have more need than ever of my liberty!"

Now, as ten o'clock had struck, unless Fandor went home to procure one of his own weapons, it was quite evident that he could never expect to find a gunmaker open to supply his needs.

"Annoying!" he said simply. "But prudence first! Haven't I sworn to be prudent? Very well." And, walking fast at the steady, rapid pace that was one of his characteristics, Fandor made for Les Halles, and suddenly dived into one of the wine houses that abound in that neighborhood.

"I'll be prudent—yes, and safe too!" he muttered. "I'm going to give myself a choice little dinner, and I'll pinch the landlord's knife—that's what I'll do!"

An hour later Jerome Fandor was leaving the restaurant, refreshed and, so he deemed it, armed. Concealed in his coat pocket he carried a blunt table knife with a rounded point—not surely a very formidable dagger!

"Better than nothing!" the young journalist assured himself, "a great deal better! The handle is first-rate."

He was making a joke of the thing, as his way was, but it cost him an effort to retain his good spirits. The nearer the hour approached, the closer he felt the moment when he would come face to face with the mysterious unknown he had saved, the faster his heart beat.

"Helene? Was it Helene?" The question haunted him. Forcing himself to be calm, however, and reminding himself of Juve's lessons, Fandor walked on a while yet before making up his mind to call a conveyance.

"Punctuality is the politeness of kings!" he told himself, as he hailed a taxi. "Well, I'm going to be more polite than kings if I reach the rendezvous five minutes before time." And therewith he gave the address:

"Auteuil railway station, my man, and drive hard!"

The taxi started away, but, swift as the pace was, the journey seemed never-ending to the unhappy lover, whose mind was busy with one question, and one question only:

"Was it Helene? Or was it not?"

Finally, when the conveyance turned down the Avenue Mozart and, by way of the Rue d'Auteuil, approached the Ceinture railway station, Fandor came to a definite conclusion.

"Yes! It *was* Helene! None but she could have dared to ask me to save her. None but she, in fact, could have known my identity."

But even now his conviction was by no means firmly based. Still, as he leapt from the vehicle and breathed the pure air of this district of the city that even yet preserves something of a country look, Fandor suddenly felt his mind made up. As he had told Juve, he knew he was playing a terribly dangerous game. Be the unknown who she might, she had spoken the name of Fantômas. She had even talked of doing battle with that formidable brigand.

"Come on then," Fandor exhorted himself, "the stakes are laid. Let's shuffle the cards and play up!"

He paid his driver; then, with a determined air, turned into the Boulevard Exelmans.

"The Rue Chanez," he reflected, "is a good length. No. 120 should be just about where the viaduct is—or a bit closer, perhaps." The spot was utterly deserted. It was before the time when people are returning from the theaters, while Auteuil itself shows no signs of activity whatever at night.

"Oh God!" observed Fandor, looking round to make sure there was nobody in sight, "if they murder me presently, my cries won't disturb anyone—always a comforting thought!"

A hundred yards farther on, however, his mood changed. The Rue Chanez he was looking for was before him, cutting across the boulevard, and lo! exactly at the corner stood a small private house—not a light to be seen in any of the windows— bearing, in quite legible figures, No. 120.

"So that's it!" Fandor exclaimed. "A fine house, apparently. At any rate, quite a comfortable one. If only I knew what scene is going to be enacted inside its walls."

Mechanically he pulled up, and carefully and minutely,

with the searching scrutiny characteristic of such as have often carried out police duties, he proceeded to examine the house.

"Nothing to be seen!" he told himself. "Nothing out of the ordinary! Everybody asleep, it seems, inside." And he stepped quickly forward, smothering an oath between his teeth.

"Good Lord! You might really think—"

Yes, indeed, the house seemed utterly deserted, entirely uninhabited. Was it not possible, after all, that the rendezvous given him—the rendezvous Helene had given him—was simply a blind? As he crossed the street he thought:

"That's it! I've let myself be swindled. There's no one here. Helene did not wish to see me again; she made this appointment merely to get rid of me!"

His heart was beating hard in his breast as he rang a peal on the electric bell. After all, how likely it was Helene should have declined to meet him again. She loved him? Yes, he never doubted her affection. He even felt sure the charming girl would have been only too happy to unite her life with his. But she loved her father too. Nay, more; she had reason to dread his appalling cruelty. Had she not once told her lover:

"We must part, say goodbye to one another. My father forbids me to take you as a husband. If I disobeyed his orders, I should be too terrified at the thought that his implacable vengeance might be wreaked on you"—and he had never seen her since.

He listened, trembling, to the sound of the bell echoing in the silent house, and repeated:

"Yes, that's it! Nobody within! Nobody!"

And he came near giving a cry of surprise when suddenly the door opened and was held ajar by a manservant.

"Your business, sir?" the man demanded.

For half a second Fandor hesitated what to say. Then:

"I am expected," he replied. "Take in my card, will you?"

"No need, sir. I did not recognize you at first. Come in, Monsieur Fandor—come with me." And hardly had the journalist found time to be surprised, and wonder how it was possible this man he had never seen before should know him, when he heard the other saying:

"But take care, sir! Our electric light has given out. We're hunting the whole house for candles at this very moment. This way—put your hand on my shoulder."

Fandor was glad to do so, the fact being that at that instant, his nerves torn by anxiety and suspense, Juve's gallant young friend was asking himself anxiously whatever he was to think of it all. What was the meaning of this total absence of light? Was it really due merely to a failure of current? Or did it conceal something sinister in preparation? Were they leading him into some horrible trap?

"Come, come!" Fandor checked himself. "Best think nothing without positive proof—that's the best way to avoid mistakes. Let's say no more and await developments. Yes, that's prudence—mere elementary prudence. And I've promised to be prudent."

But his guide was speaking again.

"To your left, sir, if you please. And mind the step; there's one here. I'll guide monsieur to an armchair. They'll bring a candle soon. Monsieur hasn't knocked against anything?"

No, Fandor had not, though he *had* given a momentary, instinctive start back at the thought of the plight he was in—in spite of his "prudence." To enter an unknown house in this fashion, in complete darkness—and this knowing it was Fantômas' name had brought him there—why, it was sheer madness!

"No matter! No use crying over spilt milk," the young man decided. "Best follow my guide. Ah! Here's the armchair he talked about!" And he sat down. Was not everything, in fact, to all appearance quite normal and peaceful? Failures of current do happen, and this well-trained manservant, steering the visitor to a comfortable seat and seeing he didn't knock against things, hardly gave one the impression of being a murderer.

"I'm just oversuspicious," Fandor concluded. "I'm in Helene's house; she'll be with me soon. Why go imagining all this melodramatic stuff?" And he sat up squarely in his chair, like a man perfectly confident there is nothing to fear.

But at that very moment he gave a violent start, and almost sprang up. A voice had reached him, issuing from one corner of the dark room—a calm, clear, cold voice, saying:

"There, my servant is gone, so we can talk in all peace and quietness. I am sure you will excuse me for receiving you like this."

"Like this?" Fandor repeated the words in some bewilderment.

"I mean—in absolute darkness."

"Was the darkness brought about with a purpose, then?"

"With a definite purpose—yes, Monsieur Fandor."

"But what purpose? What do you want of me?"

"I want nothing of you. I simply want to prevent your being able to recognize my face before we have come to an agreement and I have had your oath."

"My oath?"

"To forget whatever I am going to tell you the moment it shall be desirable so to forget."

"But tell me, who is it speaking? Who are you?"

"Monsieur Fandor, I can understand your surprise and curiosity, but you will understand on your side that my only answer must be: Will you give me the oath I require?"

"Yes, if it binds me to nothing dishonorable."

"It is a man of honor, sir, who requires it of you."

"You have my word in that case."

"In that case and henceforth I have no reason for concealment," and in an instant the room was flooded with a blaze of electric light. Blinded by the sudden illumination, Jerome Fandor, his eyes still dazzled by the glare, saw before him a young man of a very elegant figure, who saluted him with a profound bow.

"Let me introduce myself," he murmured, his face all smiles. "The Vicomte d'Oultremont, first lieutenant of Fantômas."

*   *   *   *   *

Surely nothing could well add to Fandor's amazement at this moment. He was counting on meeting his fiancée, the tender-hearted, charming Helene, and lo! he learned with startling suddenness how he was in the presence of the foremost of Fantômas' lieutenants. Enough to make any man turn pale! But our hero never flinched.

"Delighted," he said, with a touch of irony in his tones. The truth was that at that minute he would not have given a penny piece for his chances of life. His quick mind was piecing together infallibly what must have taken place. Without a doubt Fantômas had known of his daughter's rescue. Without a doubt, mad with rage on learning that the two young people had met—for he could not endure the very thought of a marriage between them—he must have laid hands on Helene, and, while detaining her, have delegated in her stead the most trusty of his associates to receive Fandor's visit.

What orders, meantime, had he given to this Vicomte d'Oultremont, who perhaps was no Vicomte at all, but bore some other name altogether? At the very moment he declared himself delighted to meet the pretended nobleman, Fandor thought:

"He is under orders to murder me, I suppose. Ah, well! Fantômas holds the winning cards, seems to me!"

Opposite him, meantime, his host was seating himself nonchalantly in an armchair as he proceeded:

"Delighted, eh? No, you are *not* delighted to see me; you are surprised. May I add, further, you are a very brave man?"

"You are an expert in these things?" was Fandor's instant retort in a scoffing tone.

"Enough, sir! Anyway, you will have an opportunity for judging. But that is not the point. Surely your curiosity is aroused?"

"I cannot honestly deny it," returned the journalist calmly. "But I do not know if you are at liberty to satisfy it."

"Still, ask me questions, sir!"

"You are too obliging."

In truth, the conversation was taking a piquant turn. Involuntarily, although he deemed himself in deadly peril, Fandor appreciated the situation, and, breaking into a smile:

"To start with," he said, "I will take the liberty of asking you how it comes about I enjoy the pleasure of meeting you."

"When you were expecting to see quite another person?"

"You guess my feelings to a nicety, sir."

"Unfortunately I can only partly inform you on this point. The person we speak of has asked me to take her place. That's all I can tell you."

"You can give me no proof of what you say?"

"None, sir!"

"So be it! To proceed—do you find it easier to tell me this person's name?"

"You have no luck, Monsieur Fandor. That is precisely what I must not tell you at any price."

"Even if, taking the words out of your mouth, I assert it is—"

"Hush, sir, hush! No names where a young lady is concerned."

But this time Fandor lost all patience. In his rival's tone he had divined a hidden sneer, a hardly repressed laugh, and his rage mastered him. Who was this Vicomte d'Oultremont? Who could he be? Shudderingly he thought:

"I wager he is the husband Fantômas destines for his daughter!" And instantly, in jealous fury, his feelings outraged, he sprang up.

"Let's have done with this mockery," he cried. "You refuse to answer my questions. What matter for that? Do with me what you have to do. To work!"

But lo! the frankest of frank laughs was his answer.

"Plague on it!" grinned the Vicomte. "I fully admit your gallantry, but I see your impatience is altogether a match for it!"

"You are making fun of me!" protested Fandor.

"Not at all." And the strange young man, looking Jerome Fandor straight in the face, went on:

"Friends do not make fun of one another."

"So we are friends?" stammered Fandor in bewilderment.

"If you will only consent."

"Friends? We?" protested the journalist again.

"What next? I am the enemy for all time of your master."

"Possibly, sir. But today we are serving one and the same person."

"Helene?" stammered Fandor.

"I name no names."

"To make an end, what is it you wish to tell me? What proposal have you to make? I was invited here, not by you, but by another. You are here in her stead, you say. What message has she entrusted you with for me?"

"At last, sir, you ask me a question I *can* answer. Yes, I have a message for you."

"Give it me, then, and let's make an end."

"Excuse me, sir. This message will end nothing, but, on the contrary, will be the beginning of many things. Now, will you hear me quietly?"

Fandor bowed without speaking. Ever since he had been in the room—in fact, ever since he had been in conversation with the Vicomte—he had had the impression that the latter was conducting the discussion exactly as he chose, and that his own protests, however forcible, were unavailing and would always be so.

"Monsieur Fandor," began Fantômas' lieutenant, "you spoke truth just now; you are fighting the master whom I serve. No matter! Today, this evening, if I am here in the place of—you know whom—it is in no wise because I propose to serve—I use your own expression—the terrible Fantômas; quite the opposite."

"Are you here, then, to fight him?"

"'Fight' him is a big word."

"To betray him, if you prefer it?"

"Monsieur Fandor, you are offensive; you hurt my feelings. No, I propose neither to fight nor to betray Fantômas. I merely intend to hinder his carrying out certain projects of which I disapprove."

"They alarm you?"

"They interfere with my wishes, sir!"

"I cannot, of course, know what these projects are, or in what way they—go against your wishes?"

"On the contrary, you may quite well learn in what way these plans, which I can reveal to you, interfere with me. They expose someone who is dear to me."

"Whom you love?"

"Whom I love."

"Helene?"

"No name must be pronounced between us. With the object of gratifying you, nevertheless, I will tell you this much—the name of this individual who is dear to me is not Helene, but Berthe."

"I do not understand you now!" confessed Fandor.

"Surely! You cannot understand this. But I continue. Put out by my master's projects, I was seeking, Monsieur Fandor, to dissuade Fantômas from executing his designs when, as chance would have it, the events occurred in which you bore a part. By that I mean the capture of a girl engaged in removing—I do not choose to say stealing—the treasure of Fantômas."

"Helene! Say the name! It was Helene!"

"Sir," protested the Vicomte d'Oultremont coldly, "what you are for forcing me to admit will never pass my lips. Moreover, to insist as you do is impolite. I have sworn to pronounce no name."

Under this reproof Fandor bit his lips till the blood came, but, with another bow:

"Be it so!" he agreed. "I must respect your oath, granted! You were saying?"

"I was saying, Monsieur Fandor, that chance had a great hand in this. You indeed rescued the prisoner, and I, by Fantômas' orders, made acquaintance with her. I was sent to her to demand her account of the motives that had decided her to the—the removal I spoke of just now."

"So, then, this removal was not ordered by Fantômas?"

"Monsieur Fandor, you surprise me! Do you then suppose this girl has ever bowed to my master's will? She was acting on her own authority."

"Really? Then it was He—nay, forgive me, sir!"

Involuntarily, at sight of the abashed look on the other's face, Fandor found himself asking pardon for having been on the point of uttering the name that ever haunted his thoughts!

"Well, sir," resumed the Vicomte d'Oultremont. "I was profoundly surprised by what followed. On questioning the escaped prisoner, I learned from her that the 'removal,' shall we say, that had been tried, and in part successfully, by her had had no other object save to prevent the carrying out of those very same projects I deprecate myself. I have told you why *I* do not approve these designs. It remains to inform you that the individual I questioned disapproved of them for entirely different reasons. She was troubled about the fate of the victims doomed to perish in the affair."

"Sir, I have drawn my conclusions," broke in the journalist. "I name no names, but, if what you say is true, I know who it is who desired to protect innocent victims—I know who it was attempted to carry off Fantômas' treasure in order to paralyze his activities."

"It is very possible. But I continue. The discovery of the identity of our aims, common to this lady and myself, brought about a mutual understanding. We exchanged confidences. In a word, I will not hide from you the fact that she confessed she had made an appointment with you to meet her here for the very purpose of asking your help in a tragic enterprise. She wished, in fact, to confront the gang of Fantômas' allies and inform them of the disappearance of the treasure—news that must infallibly deter them from carrying through the contemplated scheme."

"You can guess, I presume, what was the result of our interview?"

"Not yet," Fandor protested.

"Yet it is very simple. I offered my services."

"Which were accepted?"

"They could hardly be refused. The girl had a thousand chances to one of failing in the audacious step she was for taking. *I*—I had a thousand chances to one of succeeding."

"Then she placed confidence in you—you whom she knew to be a lieutenant of Fantômas? The thing's incredible."

The words were spoken in a ringing voice of conviction. This mysterious person whom the Vicomte d'Oultremont obstinately refused to name he recognized to be Helene beyond a doubt. Could he in that case believe that she had joined forces with one of the wretches who were her father's tools?

But now this amazing lieutenant of the Lord of Terror interrupted with a wave of the hand.

"She does have doubts of me," he admitted. "It is not flattering, but I am bound to confess it. I could not persuade her to rely on my help except on the express condition of having you accompany me."

"Me accompany you?"

"That is what I said, Monsieur Fandor. I had to promise, to begin with, to inform you of everything you have just learned. The narrative was, in fact, indispensable to enable you to second me effectively. Oh, let me add that of this narrative the lady in question has not lost one word. You see the telephone there? It transmits every syllable I speak."

Fandor would have darted to the instrument, but a gesture of the Vicomte stopped him.

"No, sir!" he protested, "do not try to speak into the instrument. They are gone now."

"You lie!" cried Fandor fiercely. "I cannot tell what your object is, but all this tale is past believing."

He stopped to recover breath, then went on with renewed vigor.

"It is past believing—and the girl would never have credited the possibility of my believing it! You have no proof, of course, of what you state?"

"Kindly read this, Monsieur Fandor!" And the Vicomte d'Oultremont, picking up a paper from a table, covered with some lines of writing, handed it to the speaker.

The moment was one of delirious joy for Helene's lover. "Good God!" he cried. "So it was really she who was by my side so lately!"

"Read it, sir!" insisted the Vicomte d'Oultremont; and, with a face of ashen pallor, Fandor bowed and obeyed. It was brief enough, this letter, but to the last degree peremptory:

> If you still remember the part which I cannot forget, if you are still the man I loved and whose bravery I admired, you will listen to what the Vicomte d'Oultremont has to tell you. Oh, how my hand trembles as I trace these lines. Fandor, it is into fearful danger I am sending you. And I am bound to do it. There are hundreds of human lives we can save if you consent to go with the man who will hand you this note.

There was no signature, and no word of hope or affection to conclude the message. But Fandor well knew that Helene could not, without betraying her father, show herself more confidential. Dashing away the tears that rose to his eyes, mastering the agony of mind that tortured him, Jerome Fandor declared in a firm voice:

"It is enough, sir. I am ready to second your efforts. Be so good as to inform me what I can do."

"Something absolutely and entirely simple, sir—to help me, if need be, to protect Fantômas."

"Are you mad?"

"Monsieur Fandor, I make allowance for your agitation. No, I am not mad. So listen carefully. Here is the agreement I have to propose to you, and which you are to carry out."

For a moment the Vicomte said no more, lost, apparently, in profound thought. Then he resumed, speaking slowly:

"I am going to take you, Monsieur Fandor, to a mysterious gathering to which the chief lieutenants of Fantômas are summoned. At this meeting I am to announce that the treasure has been stolen, and that, in consequence, the plans determined on cannot be carried out. This—do not forget it—will save the lives of hundreds of innocent people."

"Proceed, sir!"

"At the time Fantômas will be present. Now, do you know what scruple it is alarms the writer of the letter you have just read? She dreads the rage of these men who will then learn that they have been robbed. She fears they will accuse Fantômas of deceiving them, and will throw themselves upon him, and perhaps kill him."

"Good God, sir!" sighed Fandor.

"Thus, divided between her benevolent purposes and the fear of causing the death of... of..."

"Of her father!" murmured Fandor.

"Of Fantômas, the girl has resolved to act only on condition that you and I take our oath to protect the brigand, were it at the peril of our lives. I should likewise add that, my master once safe and sound out of the possible mêlée, you will regain your freedom, you will be at liberty to join battle with him afresh. We ourselves—you and I—will cease to know each other. Do you accept the bargain?"

Never had Fandor been in such a quandary. The thought that he was going to fight perhaps in order to defend the vile wretch he had been tracking down for years left him a prey to a very agony of paralyzing doubt. And yet, could he refuse? By appealing to him, did not Helene show her entire confidence in his readiness to fulfill her wishes? Then were there not hundreds of lives to be saved by agreeing to this unexpected proposal?

"I am bound to accept," Fandor told himself. Then, aloud:

"Agreed, sir," he announced. "Fantômas shall be rescued by me, if needs must! Continue!"

"Very good! To smuggle you into his gathering I have been telling you about, it is, of course, important that certain precautions should be taken. Once seen and recognized, you would never leave the place I am going to take you to alive. The precautions I refer to are these: I am going to shut you in—or make a pretense of shutting you in, for you will be at liberty to come out if ever it becomes necessary for you to appear and rescue you know whom—in this gigantic strongbox that was to have contained the treasure, and the disappearance of which I am going to announce. The safe in question will not be opened. They will merely weigh it. Full of gold, the weight would reach a fabulous figure. With you inside, they will still suppose it empty. You see how simple it all is?"

"Why, yes!"

"If Fantômas' men accept the story of a theft without protest, you will not even have to intervene. You will wait for the end of the meeting, and will slip out of your hiding-place without difficulty. If, on the contrary, mutiny breaks out, you will rally with me to the protection of him you nickname the Lord of Terror. The three of us, he and we, will be the stronger. Once the struggle is finished, you will, of course, withdraw. Precautions have been taken enabling you in that case to depart without let or hindrance. You agree, I may presume?"

"Yes, I agree, sir. I am not a man to go back on my word, once given."

"I am sure of it. Indeed, I summed you up from the first; you are the soul of gallantry. Will you follow me now? The time is getting on, and we must not delay longer."

"I am at your orders," declared the journalist, whose composure was by this time completely restored. Yet this mysterious, this impossible adventure, wherein he was now engaged seemed verily to be a nightmare come from the land of dreams. He was actually about to be present at a gathering of Fantômas' accomplices. He was actually to attend it because such was Helene's wish—Helene, whom he called his fiancée, and whom he would never perhaps marry! And all this was to lead him to the rescue of Fantômas from the fury of his accomplices, and to ensure his concurrence in the protection of certain unfortunate strangers he knew nothing of, whose lives were threatened by the grim Torturer!

With a firm step Fandor accompanied the Vicomte d'Oultremont, who, without another word, crossed the spacious room in which this amazing agreement had been concluded.

"This way," Fantômas' lieutenant indicated, and threw open a door.

Fandor never flinched, though beyond this door the journalist had caught sight of a man holding a revolver leveled at his head.

*　*　*　*　*

"Oh, ho!" said Fandor quickly, coming to a full stop. "A trap?"

But Vicomte d'Oultremont had instantly sprung forward,

with the order:

"Georgius, lower your gun. Why this silly mania of always wanting to guard my life? I am in no danger. Monsieur is an ally."

Then, turning to Fandor:

"An old and faithful servant," he explained to the journalist. "The man's devotion is at times embarrassing. You will excuse the incident?"

"Why, certainly!" asserted Fandor, albeit he was more and more astonished at the course of events, one surprise following on the heels of another, each more startling than the last. What was to happen before this tragic evening came to an end?

Then the Vicomte d'Oultremont threw open another door, and Fandor found himself at the entrance to an interior court-yard of the house.

"Here we have the safe you are to hide in," explained Fantômas' officer. "You see, it is loaded on a truck. As soon as you are settled inside we will be off. Please verify one detail: the lock, as you can see for yourself, does not fasten, though these seals, to all appearance unbroken—they have been faked by an expert—will convince everybody the safe is locked. But I'm forgetting the main point; you are adequately armed?"

At this Fandor could not restrain a smile. Truly the position of things was unexpected—a lieutenant of Fantômas was asking him if he was armed!

"Upon my word!" he admitted, "the exact opposite is true. This is all I possess in the way of weapons." And he drew from his pocket the blunt knife with the rounded point that was the result of his harmless bit of petty larceny.

His companion paled visibly at the sight.

"What, what?" he cried. "You came here—like that—knowing that in case of attack you could not so much as defend your life?"

"So you see, sir!"

"Let me once again express the admiration I feel for your courage. Here, take my own revolver, Fandor—an excellent weapon. You will please keep it in memory of tonight. An odd thought, eh, that one day perhaps you will be using that Browning to shoot me down?"

Fandor bowed without reply. Yes, truly, the circumstances were surprising! But was not everything fantastic the moment Fantômas came into the business? The moment the Lord of Terror intervened, were not the most unheard-of events on the way to realization? Fandor took the weapon and examined it. An initial was worked into the butt in delicate engraving—an F.

"Stranger and stranger!" thought Juve's friend. "Fantômas himself must have given this as a souvenir to his lieutenant, and now it comes into *my* hands! Very good! Let's say no more."

"Will you please hide now?" the Vicomte d'Oultremont begged. "Time is getting on."

"I am at your orders," the journalist assented, albeit, it may be, after some half-second of hesitation. Could he fail to realize the reckless audacity, the inordinate rashness of the step he was about to take? To hide in a strongbox—was this not practically to put himself in the other's power? Was it really true that the lock did not fasten? Was it true that the weapon he held in his hand was in working order? Was not the whole thing a trap? But at the very same moment that he stood trembling at his own recklessness Jerome Fandor's thoughts turned to the two beings that were the dearest to him in all the world. Had not Helene, his betrothed, in the note he held hidden next his heart, besought him to help her?

"So be it!" Fandor told himself gaily. "I cannot but keep faith. To hide in this box is to help Helene. Then as for my promise to Juve, my promise to be prudent—why, I am *not* breaking that. Is not a strongbox, after all, a place of *safe* deposit?" The Vicomte d'Oultremont never guessed, doubtless, what was making Fandor smile, as he watched the young man spring lightly on the truck and then slip into the safe.

"You are fairly comfortable?" he asked.

"I am first-rate."

"The journey won't be long, Monsieur Fandor, that's a fact, and we shall be off in a very few minutes. No doubt we shall never meet again as friends?"

"Seems likely, as you are one of Fantômas' men."

"Still, for the moment we are going to share the same dangers in the same cause. May I offer you my hand?"

"Sir," was Fandor's answer, "I scorn in you the accomplice of a villain, but I admire in you a gallant gentleman. It is to the latter I give my hand." And the two young men shook hands cordially.

But Fandor was startled. The hand the Vicomte d'Oultremont put in his was muffled in a great furred glove, sufficiently accounted for by the wintry temperature, but, for all that, he could feel it trembling with suppressed excitement.

"So the fellow is agitated!" thought the journalist, who, for his own part, felt entirely calm and composed. Be sure he entertained no illusions as to the risks he was running—it was just a touch-and-go game of chance he was playing—and he fully realized the probable consequences of his own rashness. But, for all that, he did not fail to appreciate the romantic side of the adventure, the aim and object of which was to defend Fantômas!

"Who could ever have foreseen such a thing?" he thought to himself. Then all his attention was devoted to listening. The huge metal box which he had just entered, and the door of which had closed upon him, naturally reproduced all external sounds in muffled, rumbling tones. He could now hear voices, blurred and distorted—voices of workmen carrying out their job in all haste, exchanging necessary directions amongst themselves.

"Devil take me if I can understand one word they're saying!" Fandor growled. "Are the fellows talking a foreign language?"

He was not given time to settle the point. The roar of a powerful motor soon drowned every other sound, and Fandor felt the truck under him get into motion.

"If only I knew where I'm bound for!" exclaimed the journalist, his heart giving a quick throb familiar to the boldest when they realize the imminence of the danger they are about to confront. But, for all the pains he took to guess the route followed, Fandor found himself, after a minute or two, utterly unable to get his bearings. He had noted a turn to the right, then to the left, then to the right again. After that he felt his conveyance backing, and then starting off afresh in a wide circuit—but whether a complete circle or not he could not tell, or whether he was now heading east or west, north or south.

"No matter!" he made up his mind, laughing. "Trying to find out what they don't want me to know, that'll only give me headache, and that would be the devil of a bad job." Who, indeed, but Fandor would have had the heart to joke at such a terrible moment? Who but he could have shrugged shoulders with such a fine indifference? Meantime the truck seemed to redouble its speed, and, after a long half-hour, pulled up short.

"So here we are!" he told himself. "Pity I can't take a peep outside, just to get a view of the conference hall of Fantômas' associates. I should love to see it!" Then suddenly his reflections were interrupted by the rattle of a crane. He felt the safe, his cage, swing free in the air, evidently suspended at the end of a rope or chain. Were they hoisting him to an upper story, or lowering him to the bottom of a pit?

"I don't know!" he said to himself, "but there, what matter? The one thing certain is that the dance is just about to begin." But next moment he bit his lips, with difficulty checking a cry of amazement. His prison had gone with a run down a sort of slide, and in an instant a salvo of hurrahs rang out, accompanied by exclamations he could hear quite plainly:

"Bravo for the treasure trove! Bravo! Here's the swag the police will never lay hands on now! Long life to Fantômas! Long live the best and most open-handed of masters!"

Then a short question: "By the by, he hasn't come yet, the master?"

In his cage Fandor stood, frowning with impatience. How hard it was to keep quiet and never betray his presence, now when he felt he was in the very midst of the Monster's accomplices!

"To think I only need to push open that door and hurl myself among the filthy crew, to smash up three or four at the least!" But, nevertheless, he kept control over himself. True, by springing from his hiding-place he might, by dint of surprise, have laid low some of the wretches met there in conclave, but what real gain was to be got from such an onslaught? To kill four or five of the scoundrels in Fantômas' pay? A fine exploit truly! The Torturer was much too heedless of the fate of his henchmen to be in any way affected. He would very soon recruit fresh lieutenants, and calmly continue the series of his exploits, only too glad to be rid of Fandor, who must surely perish in a mêlée of that sort!

"Let's just lie doggo!" decided the journalist, "and listen!"

More bravos rewarded his patience.

"So here you are, Eric!"

"Why, d'Oultremont, you're late!"

"When we saw the safe arrive, we all guessed you weren't far off, dear boy!"

Again Fandor found himself clenching his teeth hard to keep in an oath, for suddenly a sharp, imperious voice reached him, a voice speaking in the commanding note of such as count on instant and implicit obedience.

"Peace, you fellows!" it cried. "Is it with jests and merriment you think fit to receive me?"

"Fantômas! It is Fantômas speaks!" thought Fandor, and felt his heart beat quicker in his breast in a wild spasm of rage. To know the Arch-Scoundrel there—so close to him! To grip in his pocket the butt of a pistol, and not to spring at the throat of the monster, not to dare, on penalty of breaking his pledged word, to reveal his presence and throw himself upon this man who had forfeited all claim to be called a man!

"I have given my word! I have given my word!" he warned himself over and over again.

Amid the deep silence that followed the master's words, Fantômas resumed:

"Eric, Vicomte d'Oultremont, I see that, as agreed between us, the safe is here. So you have carried out the order I gave you?"

"Yes, master."

"That being so, I take it we shall be able, all of us, to share the treasure the police thought to rob us of."

"It shall be done, master, as you choose to decide."

"So be it! But first there is a formality remains to be ful-filled. Gentlemen, you remember the last words I spoke at our meeting of last week? You are aware of the stupendous scheme I laid before you?"

His ear glued to the walls of his prison, Fandor felt his face turn yet paler than before. What, was the strange adventure in which he was engaged actually unfolding on the lines indicated? So it was true that Fantômas was once again planning one of those bold strokes that had rendered him the most abomina-ble of human monsters?

"Oh! if only he would speak out plainly!" thought Fandor. "If only I could guess from his words the purpose he contem-plates! Tomorrow I shall be free to resume the struggle."

But it really seemed as though Fantômas was suspicious, and purposely avoided uttering any phrase that might have betrayed his secret intentions. Again the master's voice spoke.

"Yes, you know what is the enterprise, as daring as it is easy of accomplishment, that is to occupy our attention. It is to carry out this successfully that we are going to share out the gold in the safe yonder, which the Vicomte d'Oultremont, your comrade, has forced a thief to restore—a thief who shall be duly punished. Well, gentlemen, before going further, it remains for us to exchange the oath guaranteeing our mutual reliance one on another."

Fantômas' voice took on a deeper note as he proceeded:

"This oath, gentlemen, I now recite, pledging myself to observe it as I do so. 'I swear on my honor as a murderer and a true man, on the crimes I have committed and whereof justice knows nothing, to obey implicitly and blindly the master I have adopted as mine. I swear to sacrifice my life for my fel-low-workers. I swear to devote all my strength and all my ener-gies, and my very existence if needs be, to ensure the success of the enterprise now in hand.'"

For a moment Fantômas was silent, then he resumed:

"One after the other, gentlemen, say: 'I swear!'"

Paler than ever, Fandor strained his ears. Alas! by the gravity of Fantômas' tones could he not guess with more and more certainty that the Lord of Terror meditated some stroke of daring of exceptional enormity, a conviction yet further confirmed by the terms of the oath proposed by the master? Did not the very wording adopted indicate that, for once discarding the poor vagabonds, the wretched apaches who usually formed his bodyguard, he had gathered round him a band of criminals belonging to the higher ranks of society? Were not all these accomplices of the brigand's whose voices Fandor could hear, though he could not see their faces, apparently men of education on a par with that of the man Eric d'Oultremont, who had first received him?

But now the journalist's attention was again concentrated on the swiftly moving incidents of the scene. No sooner had Fantômas ceased speaking than a hurricane of eager voices broke out, each man crying louder than his neighbor the words: "I swear!"

Then, suddenly, one voice rang out in caustic tones:

"*I* do not swear!"

Instantly a mad hurly-burly was let loose.

"Death, death to the traitor! Kill him, kill him, the false-hearted brother!"

But once more the Chief's powerful voice imposed silence.

"Ho there! be silent, all of you!… Vicomte d'Oultremont, you refuse to take the oath?"

"Yes, I refuse, Fantômas!"

"Your reason?"

"It is personal to myself."

"Personal? Nay, confederates of our sort have no personal motives. Swear the oath, or prepare to die."

"I do not fear death, Fantômas. But you will not dare to kill me!"

"I not dare to kill you? Vicomte d'Oultremont, say your prayers!"

Fandor could bear to hear no more. From the moment the Vicomte d'Oultremont had definitely refused the vile oath he felt his rage choking him. He thought:

"The fellow will be torn in pieces, not a doubt of it! Why does he not proclaim that the treasure chest is empty? Why should he wait? That said, Fantômas will have something else to do than force him to take this infamous pledge."

Next moment he was asking himself, as he thought of the Arch-Villain's last threat:

"What! Am I to leave the poor fellow to be murdered? He is a brigand, true, but what of that? Once I appear, all will guess the safe is empty. In one body they will rush for Fantômas. The d'Oultremont will fly, while *I* protect Fantômas. And Helene—yes, Helene will be grateful!"

Bound by his pledged word—a promise once given is inviolable—Fandor could hesitate no more. He had entered into a solemn pact whose object was to save life—the lives of innocent victims Fantômas was plotting to destroy. Now, by his unexpected appearance, he would be fulfilling the pact. How, then, should he fail to act—above all when he saw, into the bargain, the possibility of protecting a man whom—he knew not why or wherefrom—he found to his liking?

"Stand back, Fantômas!" yelled Fandor. "Back, and run for your life! The safe is empty! Your accomplices are the victims of a cheat!"

It may be that, in his rage, Fandor rather overplayed his part in thus inciting Fantômas' accomplices against their master. But no such trifling scruple could restrain him. Revolver in fist, he threw open the door of his prison and sprang forward.

For one brief lightning flash Fandor beheld a great hall where half a score young men crowded round a grim apparition—an apparition that caught and held the journalist's gaze. It was a fantastic, an appalling figure, a man with features hid beneath a black hood, body molded in a close-fitting suit of black silk tights, shod and gloved in black.

"Fantômas, I—" began Fandor, but the words died on his lips. He had a clear perception of the Vicomte d'Oultremont darting towards him. He saw Fantômas lift his arm and heard him laugh. There was a sharp report, and the unhappy Fandor fell fainting to the floor, streaming with blood, shot full in the chest!

5. Juve's Fate, and Fandor's

"Henri is the best lad in the world—when he doesn't see in me the worst of scoundrels; but he is a bit heavy-witted. I'd just as gladly think out things alone, but, think as I may, there's no very brilliant notion occurs to me!"—and Juve went off in a peal of laughter that surely betokened rather a growing sense of nervous strain than any real lightheartedness. He stood solitary on the embankment that extends on either side of the entrance to the Pont du Châtelet, leaning his arms on the stone parapet, as calmly thoughtful, to all appearance, as if he sat at his own desk in the Rue Tardieu.

Not for long, however, did the police officer remain in this passive attitude, one little suited to his active temperament. Craning his head to look down on the boiling waters of the flooded stream, he pulled a face expressive of anything but satisfaction.

"Yes, Henri was right after all," he remarked in thoughtful tones. "A swimmer would stand a poor chance among those whirlpools." And Juve relapsed into his brown study. For a mind like his, capable of flights of fancy, yet at the same time well-balanced, the problem to be solved was of absorbing interest, calling upon all his powers of observation, all his sagacity as a detective, no less than all the varied knowledge he had acquired in a life of never-ending experiences.

"Come now," he muttered at last, "let's look things in the face. However inexplicable a thing seems, in reality it can always be accounted for. Let's think a bit. It's no time to give way to despair."

But say what he might, Juve found himself compelled to summon up all his energy not to yield to despondency. Never had he felt so sorely tempted to throw up the sponge. Reviewing the whole situation, forcing himself to believe nothing of which he was not positively certain, he had to admit that all circumstances combined to render the sudden disappearance of Fantômas and Lady Beltham in the very highest degree incomprehensible.

"I saw them plainly in the middle of the bridge," he told himself once more. "I was at one end of the bridge there, and Henri at the other. They were in the middle, therefore, between us. Well, it is as certain that they never came off the bridge by either of its two extremities as it is a positive fact that we could not find them on it when, marching one directly towards the other, Henri and I met in the middle. So—so what became of them?"

A problem clearly stated, folks are fond of saying, is half solved; but at this conjuncture Juve found himself forced to confess himself persuaded of the falsity of the said axiom. He saw quite clearly where the mystery lay; he was even well informed of all the details; *but* the solution completely baffled him.

"Still, there's no paltering with the truth," he told himself next moment. When a person vanishes from the top of a bridge, without coming off it by either end, the logical conclusion is he threw himself into the water. No, logic could find nothing to say in contradiction to Juve's conclusion. Only logic is not always adequate to clear up a confused situation. Juve thought on:

"Granting they climbed the parapet and threw themselves over, what are the possible hypotheses?"—and, grave as ever, the police officer counted on his fingers:

"Hypothesis number one: a boat is on the spot. Yes, but a boat can be seen and heard. Oars make a noise. An engine rattles. And we saw nothing and heard nothing. Besides, how should a boat have come to be just there? No, the boat hypothesis must be rejected."

Then he went on:

"Hypothesis number two: having mounted the parapet and thrown themselves over, well, the pair go plump into the river. But, good Lord! this is no explanation either. Plunging into the water, two bodies make a noise again, that to begin with—and then… Hmm, the state of the river makes any escape of that sort incredible."

The fact is Juve could suffer no illusion on this point. No doubt a swimmer like himself, a swimmer absolutely fearless, might, at the peril of his life, have defied the swollen torrent of the river; but, though the exploit might at a pinch be held possible for Fantômas, it was utterly beyond the powers of Lady Beltham.

"And then," Juve continued further, "there are indications convince me nothing like that took place. In the first place, it is pretty well proved that it was by no mere chance Lady Beltham and Fantômas met on the bridge. Now I cannot admit anyhow that they arranged a rendezvous there simply from the wish to enjoy a cold bath at that hour of the night. Besides that, at the moment Fantômas found himself pursued, he gave a piercing whistle, and this whistle could be nothing else but a signal calling up accomplices. But what accomplices did he need to summon if he had made up his mind to escape by swimming? On the contrary, he would in that case have taken good care not to notify his presence and give the alarm."

Juve was frowning with perplexity and annoyance, entirely forgetful of his weariness and the cold that grew more and more biting as the dawn approached.

"Upon my soul! yes, I am logical"—he sighed—"and it leads nowhere." But even as he uttered the despairing words, of a sudden he rubbed his hands.

"Oh, ho! It's not everything to be logical. We must be thorough, too"—and triumphantly he proceeded:

"Hypothesis number three—perhaps the true hypothesis! Fantômas sees himself in danger of being captured. He whistles to warn his accomplices who are a long way off; and then, laying hold of Lady Beltham, he throws himself into the water. Oh God! not a pleasant job, but still feasible. Is his object to swim for the bank? Not a bit of it. All he wants is to grip hold of one of the iron rings that are fixed under the arches and cling on to it—cling on without ever shifting his position till Juve is gone, till it is possible for his accomplices, warned by the whistle, to come up with a boat of sorts."

Juve stopped to think. As he had first admitted, when propounding his explanation of the inexplicable disappearance of Fantômas and Lady Beltham, this procedure had nothing agreeable to recommend it, but, to make up, neither had it anything particularly impossible against it. Indeed, faced with so imminent a danger, might not Fantômas very well have attempted the impossible without a thought of anything save to discover a means of escaping instant arrest?

"To hang on without stirring to one of the rings embedded in the piers of the bridge was within his powers," reflected the detective. "The villain's energy is notorious. Yes, the Lord of Terror is capable of such a feat, and even capable of supporting Lady Beltham. Besides, he may have found means to tie her."

But even as he pondered this third hypothesis, the intrepid police officer again felt himself trembling. Supposing Fantômas had acted in this way, it was manifest that, far from having disappeared, far from having made good his escape, he was still there. Involuntarily, though the night was far too dark to let him distinguish anything whatever underneath the arches of the bridge, Juve strove to penetrate the gloom.

"He is there! He may possibly be there!" he repeated to himself in tones of indescribable rage, and set off pacing to and fro with an angry tread.

"How to find out?" he kept asking himself. "How to make certain?"

But next moment he broke into a laugh, and, his voice once more well under control, "Very well," he said, "when a man thinks something is happening in a certain place and would like to be sure, the only way is to go there and see!"

No doubt of it, Juve's heart was set tonight on being strictly logical. Nobody could have been more so, but if he proposed to visit one after the other the different arches of the bridge to make certain Fantômas was not under one of them, holding on by one of the rings fixed in the stonework, it was unfortunately a matter of endless difficulty to realize the project. Should he call a boat? But how find a boat at two o'clock in the morning at such a spot?

"Of course," thought Juve, "there's the police boat moored at the old sluice by the Mint; but, given the time to go for it, wake up the watchman in charge, get them to put it at my service, it won't any longer be worthwhile looking for my fugitives. So,"— and again Juve knit his brows in perplexity.

"Bless my soul!" he exclaimed, "but I'm forgetting one detail. Whether they swam ashore or whether they caught on to a pier of the bridge, it's certain they must have made a noise in plunging in. That way my hypothesis of 'catching on' does not get over the difficulty."

Who but Juve would have thus argued with himself, showing such stern precision in drawing his deductions? But here was just one of the admirable characteristics of the police acumen possessed by the famous detective. He was a man never satisfied with coming near the truth. He was determined to grasp the whole facts down to the smallest details. And lo! at this point he suddenly shrugged his shoulders, crying:

"Lord! I think I'm going silly! Why, of course they made no noise. Supposing they slid down a rope hung there beforehand"—and this time a broad smile irradiated Juve's face.

Yet surely it was a wild conjecture Fandor's friend was making. To suppose that Fantômas, and Lady Beltham with him, had let themselves down to the surface of the water by means of a rope was to assume—as he had but now observed— that this rope had been made ready beforehand. But with what object could such an arrangement have been made by the Lord of Terror? Juve was not slow to ask himself that very question. Still, though it may be almost impossible to discern a first scintilla of the truth, it is quite on the cards that this gleam of light, once discovered, the consequent deductions are very easily drawn. In an instant the detective had drawn his.

"Now suppose all this had been got ready for the very purpose of breaking short a pursuit they deemed dangerous, whenever that pursuit might occur. Suppose every day, directly night fell, the rope was hung in position by accomplices.

Suppose Lady Beltham had become aware of my shadowing her and had gone to warn Fantômas. Suppose, in fact, they had come here, the two of them, of set purpose to put me off the trail."

Then suddenly he realized the impossibility of carrying his conclusions further, and resumed:

"One thing is certain, that if I have guessed right, if they have caught on to a ring under an arch, they are there still." So—so it came back to the necessity of undertaking an immediate search, but alas! this in no way determined how it could be feasible to carry out any such search.

"Ah, well!" declared the police officer sharply, "if I succeed— well and good. If I am deceiving myself, I shall catch a cold, that's all. As Fandor is so fond of saying, 'Nothing ventured, nothing gained!'"—and deliberately Juve began his preparation for the maddest of enterprises. Shedding his topcoat, taking off his boots, then discarding jacket and waistcoat, in a word, three parts undressing, he approached the brink.

"Damned dangerous currents!" he muttered. Then without a moment's hesitation he sprang in. The first sensation was one of paralysis. So icy cold was the water the blood seemed to freeze in his veins, and for the moment he felt incapable of the slightest movement. But he was far too energetic, too vigorous, for this to last long.

"Oh, but this is too silly," he told himself, and with a violent effort forced himself to strike out. After that he quickly recovered his wonted suppleness of limb, his marvelous address as an incomparable swimmer. For sure the river was in a dangerous state, full of treacherous back-eddies, and was running with the strength of a mountain torrent. Still, he managed to hold his own. Slowly at first, then more swiftly, for the difficulties only gave him redoubled strength, he left the bank behind and made for midstream.

"The whole point," he told himself, "is that I may get a sight of them. Once I see them they are taken. I will drown with them, if it must be, but I will *not* let Fantômas escape me!"

He was utterly and entirely absorbed indeed in his quest.

That he was himself in danger was of small account. One thing, and one thing only, mattered—to succeed.

When the swimmer reached the first pier of the bridge, he had to do vigorous battle with the current before he in his turn could get a hold on a ring and secure a moment's breathing space. And now he began to doubt his own hypothesis.

"No, no!" he told himself, "I have been imagining an impossibility. They are not there—they can't be there! To stay more than five minutes in such a place would be something beyond human strength."

But he was an obstinate fellow, was our good Juve. Never in his life had he given up a search once undertaken, without carrying it to completion, and this time too he was resolved to go on with the thing.

"To proceed," he encouraged himself. "Now for the second arch!" Again the struggle was terrific, and twice over he thought he *must* give in. In this confined space the force of the current was prodigious. The strength of the stream was so overpowering he feared it was impossible to make a single inch of headway.

"Fandor would make fine fun of me if he saw me carried off downstream," he thought. "By heavens, I *will* get forward!"—and get forward he did. He reached the second pier, but it was with despair in his heart. This time doubt was no longer possible—the explanation he had for a moment deemed capable of accounting for the disappearance of Fantômas and Lady Beltham must be abandoned. The current was too swift for it to hold good. Neither Fantômas nor Lady Beltham could have held out against the raging torrent, even by clinging to a ring.

"And yet," Juve reflected, "they haven't flown up to the sky!"—and as he muttered the words the police officer mechanically raised his head to look up. Next instant a cry of utter stupefaction escaped him. Immediately above him, dangling from the parapet, fixed at a point that evidently marked the middle of the bridge, hung a rope—an entirely unexpected, but no less obvious, confirmation of the hypothesis the detective was at that very moment abandoning.

"I'm going crazy," thought Juve. "My wits are leaving me!"

But, clinging with one hand to the ring that enabled him to resist the down-rush of the stream, he was able to convince himself that he was in no wise a victim of hallucination. It was veritably and indeed a stout rope that dangled over his head. The end hung barely a few inches above the water, just clear of the ripples that rose and fell on the troubled surface of the river. "I can't understand! I'm further and further now from understanding!" he wailed. He had realized the impossibility of Fantômas and Lady Beltham having escaped the way he had supposed. Then what use had they made of this rope—if, indeed, they *had* used it?

"Yes, they got down that way, very likely," Juve reflected. "The rope had been fastened there after nightfall by an accomplice—quite likely again. But that's not explanation enough. One gets down *onto* something or *towards* something—well, then, onto what or towards what did they come down?"

So convinced was Juve of the impossibility of guessing the riddle that he simply gave up all attempt to solve the problem. Besides, what did it matter? By this time one fact was proved beyond dispute—the fugitives were now far away, so far that any search was from the very beginning doomed to failure.

"Nobody," growled Juve in a tone half of amusement, half of vexation. "No, there's nobody. I've nothing left to do but take my departure"—and he left hold of the ring.

Again the current bore him away with fierce, overmastering strength, and it was then, as he was making a supreme and desperate effort to escape from the grip of an eddying whirlpool, the unhappy man knew the agonizing torture of a long-drawn, cruel death. Suddenly he felt his right foot seized and held.

"A snag?" he asked himself. "A rope's end carried down by the stream?"

But next moment his other foot was gripped. Yes, gripped, that was the way it felt, and in bewilderment—or was it delirium already beginning?—he thought of a hand emerging from the foaming waters, grasping him by the ankles, and pulling him down to the bottom of the river with irresistible force.

"Great God! I am going to drown," he groaned, and struggled with all his might to clear himself. It was a grim struggle truly—the struggle of a man paralyzed by the cold and exhausted by fatigue, but who *will not* die—a struggle that lasted whole minutes.

Yet he was fully conscious all the time. "A hand! It is a hand that holds me," he growled—and he felt this hand that gripped him master his resistance, drag him down slowly, inevitably, and knew the horror a swimmer experiences who finds his last convulsive efforts vain, and is sinking… sinking.

Juve expended the last remnants of his energies to see at least who was the assailant he owed his death to. He tried to bend his body over, but in vain. In a flash he had disappeared below the surface of the flood that swallowed him up.

The poor wretch had had no time even to cry out—and if another eddy showed amid the whirling waters of the river, that was all. A man drowning is so little a thing—even when that man's name is Juve!

*   *   *   *   *

"Am I dead, or am I not dead? I don't think I am dead. But I'm upside down, heels over head—most uncomfortable! Here goes to right myself. A funny way to deal with a wounded man! I shall surely have a fit, if I'm not stifled first." And Fandor gave a laugh, though certainly he had small cause to feel merry. The situation he found himself in, and was treating with his usual reckless nonchalance, seemed indeed a terrible and desperate one. He had opened his eyes in an odd place he could make nothing of. He felt worn out and exhausted, as is always the way after a long spell of unconsciousness, and, into the bargain, he realized he was at Fantômas' mercy. Any one of these facts might have sufficed to break down the journalist's resolution, but his sense of humor did not desert him.

"Anyway," he told himself, "as I can't very well go out walking, suppose I try to think things out."

Then, still smiling, he went on:

"Only, I *should* like to know just where I am"—and indeed

the poor man had good reason to be perplexed. It was something worse than a prison where he was, it was a veritable cage! All round him, confining his person so closely he was quite unable to move, were walls of iron. These were curved, and enclosed so diminutive a space that, crouched together as he was, bent double, his head actually touched the top of the villainous contrivance. A cage? Nay, something worse than that—a sort of metal barrel, a cylinder of iron or steel.

And it did not keep still either! Fandor could feel his prison going up and down, heeling over, now on one side, then on the other. Yet not a sound to be heard—absolute silence save for a slight rustle at intervals as of silk rubbing against the exterior.

"Where am I?" the journalist asked himself after a short pause. "I'm hanged if I know. So suppose I try to discover how I come to be where I am."

Nor was it unlikely that the young man's reflections and recollections might lead him to the truth without much delay. To begin with, he had a quite clear and distinct recollection of the final moments he had passed inside the safe where the Vicomte d'Oultremont had secreted him.

"Yes, I gathered that gentleman was going to get his face bashed in, and I sprang forward to stop it. Yes, so far my reconstruction of what passed leaves nothing to be desired. So, to proceed"—and proceed he did without any difficulty.

"At that, Fantômas, who never expected to see me emerge from the safe, I imagine, did not hesitate one second, but out with a revolver and let loose at me. Hmm! Now the plot thickens. Two points call for explanation. I saw—or thought I saw—the Vicomte d'Oultremont spring forward as though to throw himself in front of me. Was he for saving my life, the gallant scoundrel? And then, as a matter of fact, how did I come not to be killed?"

This last question being, as may be supposed, of special and personal interest to the inquirer, Fandor began by seeking its answer.

"A ball full in the chest—and I can feel no wound. That's a bit extraordinary!"

But next moment he burst out laughing, as he muttered:

"My pocketbook, by the Lord! Capital notion that of mine to have it always stuffed full of papers. It acted as a breastplate. The ball must have flattened on it. Papers, as a rule, are very difficult to pierce with a bullet. Evidently mine saved my life." He concluded with an air of conviction:

"Naturally that didn't hinder my receiving a terrific blow just over the heart. The ball, in fact, reproduced precisely the effect of a 'straight left' from the fist of a champion bruiser, and it knocked me out in a second—"

But suddenly he stopped dead, looking disconcerted.

"And that might easily lead me to suppose they actually believed me wiped off the slate of the living. Devil take it! Perhaps I'm in my coffin, what?" But he quickly recovered his assurance, and, with a shrug:

"No, no," he corrected, "that can't be. I am being a deal too much shaken up. It feels more like being in a vegetable basket jogging to market!"

The other question the undaunted journalist had put to himself proved yet harder to solve—had the Vicomte d'Oultremont really tried to save his life?

"For a murderer," he reflected, "it would be a pretty stroke; but there, perhaps I flatter him. When I thought he meant to spring in front of me, no doubt he was just simply trying to make good his escape."

However, a moment's more thought sufficed to convince him that the problem was really too unimportant to merit further consideration. Whether the Vicomte d'Oultremont did or did not mean to safeguard him against Fantômas' attack did not prevent his being in the hands of the King of Terror and liable at any moment to lose his life.

"Devil take it!" growled Fandor, fully convinced by now of the risks he ran, "no chance even of calling in a lawyer to draw up my last will and testament!" And he made a face of consternation, as he groaned: "And, by the Lord! it's suffocating in this palatial residence of mine, and I'm positively feeling seasick."

The next moment, intrepid as he was, the young man shuddered. As he noted the fearful temperature that grew momentarily worse, he had suddenly realized a dreadful fact.

"But how am I to breathe in this precious barrel?" he asked himself, and no sooner had he put the question than he actually seemed to be struggling for breath. The narrow iron box in which he was confined was hermetically sealed; never an opening allowed the air to enter. Without a doubt, if he remained but a few moments more he must succumb to asphyxiation.

"To die—well and good," Fandor said to himself, making fight against the instinctive anguish he felt overcoming him, "but still, before entering another world, I should like at least to know where I have the privilege of being imprisoned! Can't well be so, but one would swear I'm suspended from the car of a balloon."

All the while, in fact, he experienced again and again the unpleasant, sickening sensation that his cage was lurching giddily in every direction. True, it would stay motionless for minutes at a time, only to start afresh swaying and dipping, causing him to bump against the walls and bruise himself.

"I can't make it out! I can make nothing of it," Fandor had to admit. Nothing whatever, in truth, could he think of capable of such swaying to and fro, at once wild and wide.

"A vessel—is it a vessel's hold I am in? But no! No matter how heavy the sea, no boat or ship ever sails head downwards—if a ship ever has a head!" And he proceeded more cogently still:

"Then a rowboat makes a noise with its oars; a sailing vessel heels over before the wind, always the same way; and as for a motorboat, the hull always vibrates a bit. No, I'm not in a vessel of any sort."

He glued his ear to the walls of his prison, trying hard to catch some sound to explain the mystery. But the silence was unbroken, save for the light, almost continuous, rustling made by some unknown substance sliding past the iron plates of this strange kind of barrel.

"Bah!" Fandor decided presently, "I'm not going to cudgel my brains anymore to guess what's evidently past finding out.

More by token, my brains are pretty much addled with the infernal pain in my head"—and he gasped under the dread influence of the ever-increasing heat and the ever less-breathable air.

"Did Fantômas suppose me dead already when he shoved me in here?" he asked himself, "or did he count on my dying a hideous, lingering death? Bah! it is just as likely he simply meant me to perish in such a fashion that my body would never be found. Perhaps too, while getting rid of me, he was planning some way by which he could entice Juve into a trap and master him as well."

At the thought Fandor lost a portion of his nonchalance. To die was nothing to him. For years he had grown accustomed to the idea that one day or another he might fall into the hands of the Lord of Terror, who would wreak a terrific vengeance on the man who had defied him. But, though he was resigned to meet possible defeat for himself, he could not acquiesce in any such defeat for Juve. Had not Juve earned victory? Did not the great detective by his self-devotion, his ceaseless struggle against Fantômas, deserve a hundred times over to triumph over the monstrous villain? As he thought of the gallant police officer, Fandor felt the tears rise to his eyes.

"Bah!" he growled again, "I'm never going to be chicken-hearted, surely? A dying man must avoid all self-pity, all regret for the past. But *am* I going to die?" He answered his own question unhesitatingly in the affirmative. The agony in his head was worsening from instant to instant. It felt as if his forehead was clamped in a vice, as if a heavy round-shot was rolling about inside his brain, knocking against the walls of his skull. He was panting. The heat was suffocating. His breath whistled between his teeth.

"Yes!" muttered the sufferer in sudden despair, "no doubt this is asphyxia beginning. I shall be delirious in another three minutes—and after that it won't be long!"

He tried to laugh, but could not. His weakness was overpowering. The sweat poured from his brow.

"Done for!" he told himself. Then, next instant, he burst out laughing.

"Die? Not a bit of it! There's somebody coming to the rescue, I say."

For now he could hear a low, dull, rasping sound, going on steadily all the time—the noise of a file worked at tip-top speed.

"Yes, they're come to rescue me," he repeated aloud. "The locksmith is there to force my door."

He gave a laugh of triumph, that broke off suddenly.

"Oh, but it's fancy—delirium, that's all it is!"—and he strove to reason it out quietly. The dread of approaching madness, the fear of the hallucinations that attack men dying of asphyxiation, made him distrust the evidence of his senses.

"No!" he decided. "I don't hear anything!"

But, do what he would to reject the mistaken notion of hearing a file at work, his ears insisted obstinately on conveying it to his brain.

"Yes, I do hear it!" he was forced to admit, and he listened with passionate eagerness. At times the noise was very distinct. Evidently it set up a vibration in the metallic walls of his prison, and this in turn vibrated all through in sympathy; at others, again, the sound seemed to stop altogether. And every time the silence was renewed the journalist was tempted to think he had never heard anything at all.

"Oh, the bitterness of this slow suspense," he groaned. "Why can't I be left in peace? And then, even if I do hear a file biting into iron, what is there to show the thing has anything to do with me?" But for the last few moments, since he had first heard the sound of filing, his prison, so it seemed, had been tossing about more violently than ever, taking great leaps to right and left, making great bounds upwards, followed by sudden dives into the depths.

"If only I knew what it is I'm in," he wailed. "It strikes me I'm like one of those little figures they show in scientific experiments, which the slightest pressure sends plunging to the bottom of a bottle or shooting to the top."

However, his breathing had become so difficult, his head was so heavy, he almost abandoned the effort to reason logically. Only flying, fragmentary thoughts were now possible.

"I do hear something," he stammered. "No, no, I don't—I don't hear a sound." But by this time the blood was thundering in his ears, and the frantic beating of his pulse cut him off effectively from external sounds.

"They've come to rescue me… They're trying to rescue me… too late… they'll be too late!"

It was his last lucid thought. Indeed, he barely realized, poor wretch, how his prison suddenly quivered under a terrific shock, how it seemed to leap up bodily in the air, then, coming to earth, rolled over and over, bumped lightly, then appeared to slide along with a motion at once swift and easy, powerful yet gentle—and unceasing.

Fandor's eyes were now closed. He was bleeding at the nose. The death-rattle was in his throat.

But he was not dead. He was not even absolutely unconscious. He had fallen into the state of torpor that heralds the last breath in cases of death produced by the lack of air to breathe.

6. A Desperate Adventure

If Jerome Fandor could have known Juve's fate when he was fighting against asphyxia in his hideous cage, he would at least have been spared the anguish of thinking of his beloved comrade's lot. It seemed, indeed, that Juve was never more to be troubled by Fantômas' machinations, for at that same moment, or very nearly the same moment, he was sinking to the bottom of the Seine, caught in the grip of an assailant he had not so much as been able to identify.

Yet the police officer was not to die. He had done what every swimmer does—he had, at the moment he felt himself being dragged under the eddying waters, instinctively inhaled a deep draft of air, and then held his breath. It was indeed no matter of yesterday that the detective had trained himself to breathe in this way without breathing. He had, in fact, been accustomed to take regular, daily practice in the art, and had thus come to rival the pearl-fishers of Ceylon, who, as we know, are able to stay two whole minutes underwater without losing consciousness.

Quite well aware of what was happening, Juve felt himself sinking slowly to the bottom. Then presently the hand that grasped him seemed to grow heavier and its grip more brutal, and his descent quickened.

"Well, anyhow," he told himself, "the Seine is not a hundred yards deep. I'm going to touch ground, surely."

At that moment with a sudden jerk of the body, he managed to turn and look upwards, and his amazement was beyond words. Yes, it was a hand that held him—but a prodigious, a monstrous hand—the hand of a giant, it seemed.

"Deuce and all! Am I going crazy?" Juve asked himself.

But, unlike Fandor, who had to put the same question to himself, Juve was instantly convinced of his own perfect sanity.

Indeed, the struggle he had to make not to breathe, to keep his lips shut tight, was too painful a one to leave any doubt in his mind on this point. Agony such as this in a nightmare wakes the dreamer.

Then, with lightning rapidity, in less than a fraction of a second he had grasped the truth.

"The grappler of a diving boat!" he told himself.

But next instant his brain seemed to stop working. So extraordinary was the sight he beheld that he had not a thought left for anything else. Suddenly the turbid waters of the Seine were lit up. A pencil of dazzling light, the cone of illumination cast by a searchlight, shot through the gloom, and lo! in the glare a black mass became visible, a mass of metal of enormous, fantastic bulk, that lay its length apparently on the bed of the river.

Juve was still trying to discern more clearly this amazing piece of jetsam when suddenly he was struck a terrific blow that caught him right on the back of the neck—a blow that might well have been expected to stun him. But at that decisive moment the police officer exhibited a supreme proof of his inimitable coolness, his astounding presence of mind. As a matter of fact, he had barely felt the impact. Safeguarded by the curtain of intervening water, he had only been aware of a slight knock. Yet he fell as if mortally hurt.

Knowing as he did all resistance to be vain, realizing that in a fight against the mechanical monster that had dragged him to the bottom of the river he was doomed to inevitable defeat, was it not best to play cunning?

And his artfulness was fully rewarded.

Hardly had he dropped before he felt himself lifted by his assailant, then quickly borne away. Then he had the impression of being deposited in a great pipe or tube, of some mechanism being set in motion, then, in a moment, a current of fresh air blowing about him.

Surely any man but Juve would thereupon have sprung to his feet and inhaled a deep breath with a delight proportioned to the length of his submersion. But he took good care not to act so imprudently. What, reveal the fact that he was alive and unhurt? No, indeed, Juve was not so foolish as all that. What he did was just to breathe lightly and cautiously between his clenched teeth and stay absolutely still.

"Dead, is he? Yes or no?… You don't know?" cried an imperious voice. "Ah, well! Carry him to dungeon No. 3. I have more urgent work on hand than to trouble about that policeman fellow! I must get away and find out where Helene is."

And the voice that had uttered the words in tones of concentrated fury was one Juve unhesitatingly recognized. It was the voice of Fantômas!

*   *   *   *   *

Recognizing that voice, and guessing that the brigand was close beside him, Juve had to make the most tremendous effort of will to remain motionless, as he had resolved to do. He was quivering, in fact, with mad rage, and a frantic longing to hurl himself at the scoundrel's throat. But Juve was not the man to act in any such madcap fashion. Where he was he did not know, or if Fantômas was alone or no. At the slightest movement on his part he would be seized and held, and rendered incapable of getting at the villain.

"Merely to open my eyes," reflected the police officer, "means my instant death. Nor is it at all certain that by so perishing I can deliver humanity from the ruffian. Patience, I say. All things, even the hour of vengeance, come to him who waits!"

Juve was shamming dead, and now he took even more pains to do the thing thoroughly. Without giving a sign to show how it hurt and bruised him, he let them take him by the feet and drag him along the ground towards the dungeon where Fantômas had ordered them to deposit him. Surely in this he showed proof of a type of courage of which not many brave men, not many heroes even, would have been capable. To master the nerves, to go on pretending, when death is certain, when it seems that nothing can stave off the fatal moment— this is perhaps the purest form gallantry can assume.

As they hauled him along, the detective was thinking:

"Funny sort of ground, eh? One would swear it was a sheet-iron floor. Now where the devil am I? And how the devil did I get here?"

Indeed, he began to ask himself if he had not, without knowing it, actually lost consciousness.

"I was at the bottom of the river," he reflected. "Then suddenly I felt I was out of the water and could breathe. It is just bewildering! I had no sensation of coming up to the top again."

Still, for all his use of the word "bewildering," Juve was speaking with perfect coolness. He continued his soliloquy:

"True, I saw a wreck. In fact, it struck me it was one of those huge lighters that carry petrol and are near two hundred or three hundred feet long. Can it be aboard this lighter the diving vessel has conveyed me?"

But at that moment a violent shock cut short the police officer's efforts to solve the mystery of how he came to be fished out of the water. The man, or men—there were evidently two of them—who were carrying him head first, without more ado, sent him rolling across the floor, and Juve took good care to make no attempt to stop himself.

"Michael Strogoff," he remembered, "let himself tumble into a ravine rather than let out that he was not blind. I will suffer my skull to be cracked before I confess I'm still alive. Ho, ho! Am I not as good a man as Jules Verne's hero?"

Then he heard a door shut to with a ringing, metallic clang there was no mistaking, and then the noise of bolts being shot home one after the other.

"Alone at last!" he told himself, seizing the opportunity to breathe freely and fully.

Then, still without stirring, he went on:

"Yes, that's it. I must be aboard the lighter, and—" But there he broke off short, and, forgetting all caution, let out a great sounding oath. A sudden light had flashed across his brain and left him panting with excitement. Granting he had guessed right, and was on board a lighter sunk in mid-channel of the river, why, he knew instantly and completely the solution of all the mysteries he had been vainly striving for hours to elucidate.

The lighter—why, of course, it was just a huge diving bell. After that, how fail to realize the fact that it served as a haunt and refuge for Fantômas—an inviolable, undiscoverable asylum? In a flash Juve had hit the truth, staggering in its fantastic improbability. In the very heart of Paris, where no police raid could ever track him or trouble him, when he was safe against all investigations—there, beneath the waters of the Seine, Fantômas had contrived the most extraordinary of homes.

Yes, there was his den, this vessel beneath the waves! Truly the Lord of Daring must be possessed of an amazing ingenuity to have had recourse to such a strange device. For sure, he must have had to surmount tremendous difficulties to arrange this extraordinary abode.

"But is the thing really impossible?" Juve asked himself, and answered his own question: "No! It is feasible after all!"

Nor was he deceiving himself. In these days they build submarines that can stay for hours together underwater. Was it not infinitely easier to construct some sort of vessel fitted with reservoirs of compressed air, such as the *Nautilus* in one of Jules Verne's incomparable stories, and sink it once for all at the spot where it was to remain?

"At night," Juve thought it out, "a tug steams by towing a string of barges. Fantômas owns all the needful material. On the way the tug drops the particular lighter fitted to take up position underwater; the ballast tanks are opened and fill with water, and down she sinks—and who the wiser?"

Nor again was there any greater difficulty in contriving means for entering and quitting this strange dwelling. All that was needed was to utilize the cellars of some house standing on the riverbank. To pass from these cellars into the river itself by donning a diver's dress, to walk along the bed of the stream, reach the vessel, and enter by way of an airlock, from which the water is exhausted and atmospheric air then admitted—the way the crew can leave and re-enter a submarine—all this was in no way impracticable.

"And what advantages to gain!" Juve thought admiringly. "The certainty of eluding all investigations, the power to defy all search, the ability in an emergency, as tonight, to throw off the scent any pursuer. Oh, Fantômas is veritably a genius!"

Loathing the vile monster, Juve yet found himself for the moment admiring the grandeur of some of his ideas. Who but he would ever have resorted to such a habitation? Who, in one word, could have contrived it all, save Fantômas? And the famous police officer gave yet another proof of his contempt of danger and at the same time of his modesty. He forgot the danger that menaced him from all sides. He even forgot that he was at any rate Fantômas' equal in having divined this underwater refuge and guessed its existence. No, all he felt was a twinge of fear.

"My God!" he sighed, "will it ever be possible to master the man who has realized a scheme such as this?"

Then, by a quite natural reaction, he started up, more intrepid than ever, more determined than ever to fight to the bitter end. For now he knew; he had discovered the refuge of the vile King of Terror. Should he not use this advantage to win the day? Was he to confess himself beaten at the moment when he had such a trump card as this in his hand?

"I see it now. I understand now," he muttered. "Everything grows clear. Yes, Fantômas and Lady Beltham suspected I was on their track. They would not run the risk of my discovering the usual passage by which they slip in here. That is why they had themselves driven to the middle of the bridge. Then with a whistle Fantômas warned his companions in their underwater dwelling. This done, he let himself slide, with Lady Beltham, down the rope they had left ready. No doubt both had put on diving suits. Possibly, indeed, there existed some other way of getting aboard. No matter for that! Why yes, they were sure of making their escape!" And he gave a sardonic laugh as he added:

"Still, a lucky thing, after all, they thought to baffle me! A lucky thing they tried to drown me! Otherwise we should never have known what this place was the Torturer had chosen for his refuge." It was truly Juve's inmost nature that was revealed in the words. He was a prisoner. He was shut up in a dungeon of such a sort as put any possibility of escape utterly and absolutely out of the question. Death was already at his throat. He knew no mercy. No pity was to be looked for, and lo! he was positively congratulating himself on his good fortune in being there, because his being there was an advantage gained in the battle the world was waging against the hideous brigand.

But these reflections were soon abandoned, and, panting with fierce excitement:

"To work!" he cried suddenly. "Now or never!"

What did he mean? The detective knelt down. No doubt his captors were so sure no attempt at escape was possible—or they had so entirely believed him dead—that he had been left completely unbound. He got to his feet without let or hindrance.

"To start with, let's reconnoiter the localities," he decided, as cool-headed as though he were not about to undertake the most nerve-racking investigations that were to inform him as to his chances of life or death. But this examination, as he told himself, could not take long, and he soon assured himself that he was in a sort of narrow closet or compartment, a yard wide by fifteen or eighteen feet in length. All the walls were of iron, floor as well as ceiling, which latter he could touch with his hand.

"First-rate!" he exclaimed then. "Things will go of themselves."

Now what things could he be speaking of? However, he went on:

"The whole difficulty resolves itself into this: to know whether Fantômas is on board. I should certainly like to know that before setting to work."

But, again, what did that speech mean? Even supposing anyone could have read Juve's thoughts, they would never have guessed what he proposed to do. If Juve was filled with admiration for Fantômas, was not he, too, worthy of admiration, and for precisely the same reason—viz., for his fertility of invention? Suddenly he broke into a short laugh, the laugh that invariably rose to his lips whenever he was well pleased with his own notions.

"I'm a noodle!" he grinned. "Fantômas himself announced he was going away. I shall know when he returns by this—that he will inevitably come to view my corpse. It surely shows no excess of vanity on my part to assume that he will make a point of being posted as to my fate, and will even insist on verifying this detail in person." And, prisoner as he was, in the condemned cell of this sinister jail, Juve rubbed his hands with satisfaction.

"Better and better," he growled. "The whole thing runs on wheels. I have time enough for my preparations, and there's every chance I shall succeed in my purpose." And the police officer set to work on certain odd-looking proceedings. Removing his braces, he stripped off the woolen vest that was the only piece of clothing he had retained when he sprang into the river.

"A capital precaution this I took," he laughed. "They did not search me, evidently because they thought I was dead. True, but it might have been otherwise. Now, even in a minute search I wager they would never have spotted these." And as he spoke he calmly tore off the buttons of his undershirt.

"Five, six, seven, eight," he counted. "Quite a pretty total. Enough to blow any ordinary house sky-high; enough, anyway, to shatter the door of my cell and kill Fantômas, if he thinks of coming in—and to kill me, too! Bah! We shall feel no pain."

The buttons, in fact, were nothing more nor less than little capsules, each a marvelous piece of workmanship from the hand of an expert craftsman. For all their appearance, they were actually made, not of mother-of-pearl, but of steel, so that each formed a species of small, hermetically-closed box.

"So now to open our cartridges," said Juve, "and prepare our artillery." And, calmer than ever, he hastened to do as he had said. He unscrewed each of the buttons he had just torn off and emptied out a pinch of a brown powder, carefully piling the whole in a little heap against the door of his dungeon.

"The last word in high explosives," he grunted. "A happy discovery to make war a little more terrible. It fires at the lightest shock, and possesses such prodigious force that with a few pounds all Paris could be annihilated at one blow. Yes, it will serve my purpose well to rid the world of Fantômas."

Then, with a smile, he added:

"And to make Fandor my heir. Oh, if only I knew what he's busy about, that damned young rascal!" And Juve heaved a deep sigh. Like Fandor, he too was indifferent to his own fate. Firmly resolved to blow up Fantômas' underwater dwelling as soon as the Lord of Terror should be back in it, no less firmly determined to destroy himself while accomplishing that act of justice, Juve grieved only when he thought of Fandor.

"Bah!" he cried next moment, in an effort to drive away these dismal thoughts, "Fandor will weep for me. But what of that? Anyway, I am not going to give way at thought of the sorrow my death will cause him." And he shook his head and forced himself to think of something else.

"Well, I wonder, am I going to have long to wait? Hmm! Fact is, I'm far from warm, and a man of my age soon catches a chill! Truly the hospitality of the house leaves something to be desired!"

Indeed, the poor man was beginning to shiver. "And then I've every chance of being bored," he grumbled on. "Not so much as an illustrated paper to glance through! Upon my word, Fantômas, your welcome is worse than at a dentist's."

Suddenly Juve checked his forced merriment, and started violently.

"What's that?" he cried, and listened with all his ears. "Surely I'm deceiving myself?" he faltered. But no, he was not mistaken, as he very soon assured himself. Low and trembling, full of an ineffable pain, a voice was calling: "Juve! Juve! Juve!"

He was opening his lips to answer, but closed them again.

"Juve!" the voice went on appealingly. "Juve, do you hear me?"

But the detective was thinking:

"A trick, perhaps, to find out if I am still alive—a trap. Who, otherwise, could be wanting to communicate with me?"

But the appeal became more urgent: "Juve, for pity's sake, answer!"—and Juve's heart was touched.

"After all, what risk do I run?" he asked himself, "and if, by any chance, it were—" He left the words unfinished. Suddenly he had pictured the fair form of Helene. Doubtless Fantômas' daughter detested her father's crimes, but still she felt a filial affection for her parent. Was it not possible that at this moment she was in the accursed place? In a hoarse whisper he demanded who was there.

"I, Juve—I, Lady Beltham!"

"Lady Beltham! What, Lady Beltham! And you dare—"

"Juve, by all the feelings that are most sacred to me I swear I had no hand in your capture! Willingly would I give my life to save yours."

"Instead, madame, of dreaming to save my life, it would have been a better deed not to have warned Fantômas I was following you!"

"But I did not warn him, Juve! All I told him was that I had been to beseech a favor of you. It was he, and he alone, who guessed you were bound to be on his track. He could not believe I had been able to throw you off the scent."

The words brought a smile to the detective's face in spite of himself. Fantômas' dread of him as a sleuth-hound—was not this equivalent to a compliment?

"Let it pass!" he conceded. "This is hardly the time to dispute about the past. The present is troublous enough. What have you to tell me?"

"To tell you, Juve, an appalling thing."

"Oh God! I can do nothing to avert it; I would rather know nothing of it!"

"Juve, you *can* avert a fearful calamity."

"I? Why, what calamity?"

"This very night, Juve, Fandor attacked Fantômas. Yes, in the very midst of a gathering of confederates, over which the master was presiding, Jerome Fandor sprang up before his eyes—"

"Oh, the gallant lad! But what became of him? Speak! Tell me!"

"I cannot, Juve. I do not know Fandor's fate. I have besought

Fantômas to tell me, but he refused to answer."

Then, as Juve said nothing, too much overwhelmed to speak, the noble lady continued:

"Oh, Juve, if you but knew! Fantômas is near mad with fury. Helene—yes, Helene I say—has disappeared. It was she who stole her father's treasure. It was she whom you arrested, she whom Fandor let escape. But Fantômas believes her still in the hands of the police, and he swears to be avenged. If she is not released, a hundred thousand, two hundred thousand Parisians are to perish! Juve, Juve! From this spot where we are Fantômas can throw floods of poison gas all over the city. You understand? Say you understand! Fantômas *must* recover his daughter. Oh, in mercy's name, if you know where Helene is, tell me! Juve, I swear I have no power to save you. If I could I would. But think of all the unhappy creatures who are to die ! Speak! Speak!"

"Madame," retorted the police officer, "I shall not speak—for three reasons. The first might suffice, but the other two have their weight, I assure you. I shall not speak because I do not know where Helene is. I shall not speak, madame, because I fear Fantômas is by your side, and it is he who forces you to question me! Lastly, I shall not speak—my last and final reason—because a man holds his peace to commune with himself when he is about to die."

Then he raised his voice, to add the brief words: "In one second's time!" And, as he spoke, over the little heap of cheddite he had piled up, deliberately provoking the terrific explosion, Juve clapped his hands sharply together.

*   *   *   *   *

Instantly on this decisive action, that was bound to explode the brown powder the police officer had extracted from the buttons of his vest, followed an appalling catastrophe. A volcano seemed to have burst into eruption. A whirlwind rent the air, succeeded by the fierce roar of flames and a tearing and rending of everything in its path.

As is well known, the effects of modern explosives are tremendous, and the more so if their blasting force meets with any solid resistance. Cheddite going off in the open air produces a hundredfold less devastation than if it meets with an obstacle—a wall or a building—to check the expansive forces of the fumes. In the closely confined space where Juve was, in this strange underwater construction, the explosion was bound to be at its maximum of destructiveness.

Barely had Juve time to look around him. He heard the crash, he saw the flames—and that was all! He felt himself whirled about, seized and lifted from the ground by an irresistible cyclone. His whole body seemed bruised and broken. His brain refused to act.

And then, in an instant—he knew not how it came about, how the thing was possible—he found himself once more swimming in the tossing waters of the Seine.

"I—I'm alive!" he stammered, but could not yet gather his wits or make a reasonable guess as to the course of events. He struck out instinctively—a swimmer falling into the water has no need to think to make the movements needful to support himself.

However, the icy chill of the river soon restored the detective to a knowledge of matters. Under the nipping cold, that for once was to have the most salutary effect, Juve felt his nerves calm down. The blood boiling in his veins flowed more sedately. He said, without breaking his stroke:

"Why, yes! Water is not compressible!" And he broke into a laugh that still showed some traces of hysteria.

But a man of Juve's caliber could not long remain passive. He was of those men who invariably rise superior to circumstances, who are bound to find a way of escape out of the worst predicaments.

"Yes!" he continued his reflections. "That is what saved my life! The explosion produced an overpressure inside the sunken lighter, and it flew to flinders. But the actual force of the explosion acted on the walls of the construction. And I, for my part, had merely to withstand an enormous atmospheric pressure—but for an infinitesimal space of time." Of this we see perfect examples in the case of explosions on board submersed submarines. The little vessels are reduced to scrap iron, while members of the crew are recovered safe and sound.

But it was really no time for Juve to be studying the laws of dynamics. Putting aside all thought of scientific explanation for a phenomenon only the net result of which apparently was of importance, the swimmer struck out more vigorously than ever.

"Very little wreckage," he observed next. "And the noise, occurring underwater, has attracted nobody's attention. Well, I shall be able to get ashore quite unobserved. By the by, I should very much like to know what has happened to Fantômas. I presumed he was by Lady Beltham's side. Was I mistaken, I wonder?"

Still, as it was quite impossible to win any certainty on this point, the detective left off troubling his head about the question.

"Confound the current!" he growled. "I am drifting downstream monstrously fast. Where the devil am I going to land?"

But next moment he ceased to give a thought to the question of reaching the bank.

"God's mercy!" he swore suddenly. "A victim of the crash!"

Entangled in an eddy, he had caught a distinct, if momentary, glimpse of a body floating half out of the water.

"Fantômas?" he asked himself. "Oh, but I *must* know!"

Heedless of the weariness that was growing upon him, fighting off the cramp that was stiffening one leg, Juve quickened the rhythm of his stroke.

"The body can't be far off. I'm going to have a look at it. I must recover it from the water."

As yet the only light was that of a pale, overcast, stormy dawn, but the surface of the stream was, nevertheless, lit by some straggling gleams, and suddenly Juve again caught sight of the dark patch where the lifeless body tossed like a straw on the tumbling waves, and, with an involuntary cry of "There! There it is!" Juve, swimming might and main, reached what he took to be a corpse.

No, it was not Fantômas, that much was certain! Instantly he saw it was a woman—it was only her skirts, in fact, that had kept her afloat.

"Lady Beltham?" Juve asked himself. "Yes, Lady Beltham beyond a doubt!" And, turning to swim on his back, he gripped the unhappy woman with both hands. Be sure the police officer had to exert every ounce of energy he possessed not to let go. In this flooded river, amid these strong and dangerous currents, where Inspector Henri had declared no swimmer could live, Juve was trying an apparently hopeless task.

"I will do it! I will!" he swore to himself, and once more his inflexible will carried the day. Slowly but steadily he progressed. Small matter to him where he came ashore, sooner or later, here or elsewhere, but chance brought him to land by the extremity of the little peninsula below the statue of Henri IV on the Pont Neuf. He touched the quay, clung to the stonework, at last felt the steps of a stair under his feet; this he managed to climb, dragging after him, all but exhausted, the lifeless form he still grasped.

"Saved!" he cried. "But only just in time! I'm getting old, that's certain!"

But in this Juve was surely overcritical of his own powers. How many young men, indeed, could have survived the experiences of this night of horror?

Once on the bank, utterly deserted, as was to be expected at such an hour, Juve was forced to sit down, overmastered by sheer fatigue. Then, too, exposed to the icy wind, he felt the cold gripping him, the awful chill that supervenes on complete exhaustion.

"Come, come!" he chided himself. "I'm never going to faint, surely? This is no time to play the woman!"

He pulled himself together, and, bending over Lady Beltham, took her wrist and checked the beating of the pulse. A purely instinctive movement this, a mechanical impulse quite independent of conscious volition, for at that moment he was convinced the woman was dead. Not so! The pulse was beating! The shock of the discovery brought him sharply to his feet.

Fantômas' wife had swooned, but she was still alive.

"Poor woman! Poor woman!" thought Juve. "And I have no means of helping her; I can barely drag myself along."

Still, something must be done, and done quickly. Doubtless Lady Beltham—for the love she bestowed on Fantômas, for the affection she bore him despite his crimes—was she not indeed blameworthy? Yet surely she deserved some pity. Unworthy, vile as may be the object of passion, she who feels that passion in her heart burning like an incurable wound, is not such an one deserving rather of commiseration than of censure?

"I ought—ought to shout for help," Juve faltered, but to shout from where he was, to cry out in the darkness, which was still intense, would have been utterly in vain. The police officer made yet another almost superhuman effort. He got to his feet and moved off, staggering as he went. To tell the truth, his mind was still far from clear. Shivering, stumbling, he swayed feebly on his legs. He kept telling himself:

"I must get upon the bridge. There's a constable on duty at the cab rank in front of the Palais de Justice. I'll give him the word—"

But all the while he was asking himself:

"Have I the strength to get so far? Bah! If I do fall, a passerby will find me. Paris is on the point of waking up."

The next moment he halted in bewilderment. In his half-dazed state he had turned, not towards the bridge, but in the direction of the point of the island.

"Oh, luck's dead against me!" he groaned, and, wheeling round, he made, by way of a shortcut, for the little square contrived at that spot. But he had not taken fifty steps in that direction when a fresh surprise brought him to a full stop. He had just reached the cabmen's shelter in the square. The lights were burning inside. The door stood open.

"Upon my word!" he exclaimed. Then his eyes glittered with delight. On the little table that in summertime serves as a desk for the official in charge, a loaf of bread and a lump of cheese lay on a crumpled piece of paper. Close beside them was a bottle of red wine, uncorked and half full. Over the back of a chair hung a heavy cloak with many capes, such as roadmen and cabmen wear.

"Upon my word!" cried the police officer for the second time, and felt no scruples about taking advantage of the windfall. Lifting the bottle, he drank a copious draft. Seizing the loaf, he bit off a great chunk. Laying hands on the cloak, he threw it about his shoulders. Instantly he experienced a novel feeling of well-being, and his mind cleared.

"No doubt," he guessed, "there are some building operations in progress nearby. Evidently all this belongs to a watchman in charge of the stores."

But his conscience was already pricking him. What of Lady Beltham? He was forgetting her. How could he leave her without succor? He felt ashamed of his own cowardice and selfish greediness. Already the wine he had drunk, the warm cloak he now wore, had given him fresh vigor, and now his duty lay clear before him. He picked up the bottle clumsily in hands still numbed with the cold, and hurried back to the riverbank.

"I will make her drink a few drops, and then try to carry her here. The watchman will be back presently, for sure."

Fatigue and distress were on the wane. He was now burning with feverish heat, and was conscious of renewed strength—fictitious, perhaps, and merely due to the reaction, but nevertheless effective.

"Quick! Quick!" He spurred himself on, and found himself able to break into a run. Reaching the bank, he muttered:

"It was here, surely, I left her? It was just about here." But he could see nothing of what he sought.

"Can I have made a mistake? I could have sworn—"

The next moment he stood rooted to the spot, petrified with astonishment. At his feet, on the flagstones of the quay, he discerned the wet splash, the mark left where the woman's body had lain. But Lady Beltham had vanished!

"Have I blundered?" Juve asked himself. "Am I crazy? She simply can't have made of!"

But next minute the conviction was forced upon him that no mistake was possible. A yard or two away was the stair he had climbed on emerging from the river. The steps also had had no time to dry yet.

"Why, then," concluded the detective dreamily, "then she must have come to her senses and taken to her heels!"

But the supposition struck him as so fantastic he could hardly accept it.

"She was less fatigued than I was, that's true," he reflected. "But cold, fear—"

He turned his head to scrutinize his surroundings, and a stifled cry forced its way through his lips, a cry of amazement and satisfaction. A hundred yards or so away a shadowy form was visible, that with staggering steps was making for the steps that lead up from the little peninsula Henri IV to the roadway of the Pont Neuf.

"Lady Beltham!" cried Juve. "It is Lady Beltham!"—and instantly he felt his energy redoubled. If Lady Beltham was taking to flight, making all haste to disappear, did not this mean that she too was moved by overmastering motives, reasons that forbade her to succumb to her exhaustion?

"Perhaps," thought the detective, "she imagined herself to have been carried here by the current." Then he shook his head at the absurdity of his own supposition.

"I'm talking nonsense! The current might have cast her up on a shallow shore flooded by the river; it could not have lifted her on top of an embanked quay."

But now another possibility occurred to him. Might it not be that, on coming to on the flags of the quayside, Lady Beltham had guessed she had been recovered from the water, and her rescuer had believed her dead? That being so, was it not plain that, dreading to incur the risk of police investigations, she had, naturally enough, hurried away? She was a woman well capable of mastering any physical distress when Fantômas' interests demanded it.

"Yes, that's it! That's how it is!" Juve declared. "She makes off before her supposed rescuer can get back in company with a police constable"—and a shudder ran through him. For Lady Beltham to have given proof of such energy, for her to have had strength left, in her half-drowned condition, to contrive an escape—was this not proof positive she was acting in the service of the man who was master of her whole heart, in the service of Fantômas?

"Yes, it is clear evidence I cannot have gained my object, I can have done him no hurt; that I was mistaken, and he was not in the lighter when I fired the charge."

He ground his teeth, poor Juve, in rage and disappointment. He had risked his life, faced a fearful death, without the satisfaction of winning the smallest result! But presently, chiding himself for this fit of discouragement:

"Why, no!" he resumed his reflections. "I am wrong. I have not wasted my time. To begin with, did not Lady Beltham tell me that from this vessel Fantômas could throw clouds of poison gas over all Paris, and produce a hideous catastrophe? His game is stopped now, anyway. I defy him now to carry out the threats embodied in his letter to the Préfet of Police. And that's not all. His retreat is cut off, his refuge is destroyed! More than ever he will feel me dogging his footsteps. Who can say he will not lose his head? that he will not commit some act of imprudence that will deliver him into my hand?"

Then Juve gave a sudden exclamation:

"But I'm crazy, by the Lord! Whatever's wrong with me? I'm losing my wits, surely!" And, forgetting cold and weariness, the police officer dashed off at a good speed. He was resolved that more than ever Fantômas should feel him at his heels. He was determined to track down the brigand in spite of every difficulty to recover the scent, even as the sleuth-hound pursues his prey.

"Lady Beltham," he cried, "why, of course Lady Beltham is going to join him. Sooner or later she will find him, or he will come to see her. I have only to follow *her* to discover *him*."

This was obvious enough. If the detective could close in on Lady Beltham, and shadow her without betraying his presence, it was a thousand chances to one this course would put him once more on the scoundrel's track.

But was it not too late now to catch up his quarry? Juve

quickened his pace, though he dared not run for fear the noise of his footsteps might attract the other's attention. Following Lady Beltham's example, he made for the stone stairs leading up to the level of the bridge, and mounted them four steps at a time. He was very soon reassured. Lady Beltham—at the cost of how fearful an effort!—had gained the opening into the Place Dauphine. Once there, thinking herself safe from all pursuit, she had dropped on a bench at this spot so far remote from the busy traffic of the city—one which no vehicle ever passes at night.

"Where can she be going?" the detective asked himself. "She is in such a plight I defy her to walk three steps without a constable arresting her. For myself, I'm in no very presentable state, and I shouldn't get very far without some unpleasant encounter. Ah, but look ! She's off again already."

And so she was. Suddenly the poor woman had risen and quitted the bench on which fatigue had forced her to rest for a few moments. Yet she did not seem at all afraid of being followed. Not for one instant could she have supposed her rescuer was actually Juve. She marched straight before her, without taking the smallest precaution, like a person whose one thought is to reach his destination.

"Perhaps she is going to take a conveyance," thought her pursuer. "In that case I should be in a pretty fix. My pocketbook I left on the quay. I haven't a sou to bless myself with. Bah! We shall see what we shall see!"

At the moment Lady Beltham was passing alongside the Palais de Justice, going in the direction of the Châtelet. Juve broke into a short laugh.

"Oh, ho!" he grinned, "it's as plain as plain! I'm an idiot not to have thought of it straight off. Lady Beltham knows Fantômas was not on board, but that he was to return there. Not a doubt of it, she's now bound for the house where Fantômas would have to get into his diving suit if he wanted to enter his underwater dwelling."

As he reflected thus, the police officer could not refrain from a chuckle of satisfaction. If such was really Lady Beltham's intention, was he not assured, by following her, of gaining a piece of information of incalculable value?

However, two minutes later, the worthy man was singing a different song. Heedless of the bitter cold, quite unconscious apparently of the wet clothes that still clung about her shoulders, Lady Beltham had reached the Quai aux Fleurs. Arrived there, she leaned her elbows on the parapet overlooking the Seine, and remained motionless.

"The devil!" growled Juve, who had for his part taken cover a few yards away in the angle of an entrance-doorway. "It would not be good manners to disturb her. All the same, she's going a bit too far. She's on the road to give herself a chill—and me too. And when I remember my clothes are just over yonder, staring me in the face! It's a regular torment of Tantalus."

But the famous detective was of a sort to endure far worse hardships than this when the success of his police investigations was involved. Lady Beltham never budged, and Juve faithfully followed suit.

He felt pretty confident now he had run his quarry to earth, and he was not the kind of officer who lets a prisoner escape, once he has him in his toils.

7. What Talking Means

How long Fandor remained in his state of lethargy and semiconsciousness he could not himself have said with any approach to certainty. The lack of air to breathe, producing as it did a sort of half-swoon, left him, in fact, in a condition of torpor that precluded at once thought and the sensation of pain. He had just sense enough left to gather that his prison was pitching and rolling more and more violently, and to realize that it was moving forward at a pace comparatively rapid. At the same time he was entirely incapable of drawing any conclusion from the fact, or indeed experiencing any surprise at this succession of strange sensations.

Yet, as a matter of fact, the young man had little reason to complain of this loss of full consciousness. Confined in a box of sorts hermetically sealed and of very small dimensions, he would infallibly have perished by asphyxiation in a much briefer space of time if actually this state of partial coma into which he had fallen had not, as it were, slowed down the process of living and lessened in notable proportions the volume of air his lungs demanded.

In a word, he experienced a phenomenon precisely similar to what occurs in mining disasters, when such of the victims as have been lucky enough to faint away are rescued still alive, while the unfortunates who have continued conscious are asphyxiated and have died hours ago.

Fandor, however, was in no condition to speculate on such matters, or to feel either satisfaction or the reverse, when suddenly he came back to complete consciousness. A new sensation, in fact, had roused him from the comatose condition in which he lay—nothing more nor less than his being hurled with terrific force against the walls of his barrel.

"What!" he ejaculated. "Am I off the rails now?" Then directly after: "Why, what? I'm come to a standstill this time!"

He was still half dazed, and found it hard to get his wits properly together. Nevertheless, his memory was clear enough. He remembered perfectly well the series of adventures he had lived through.

"I'm not moving anymore!" he went on to himself. "That's a fact… Follows I've arrived somewhere, eh?"

Then he began panting for breath again. The mere fact of having uttered a few words, of having come awake again, was accelerating his heartbeat, forcing him to take quicker breaths. In a moment he felt the same oppression. Again the sweat poured off him. He was literally stifling.

"Oh, dear!" he thought, "this is bad—very bad! I suppose it's the beginning of the end for me!"

Not a doubt of it, if Fandor remained but a few seconds more in his present sorry plight, asphyxia would complete its fatal work. Yet hardly had the young man thus summed up the situation before he was striving instinctively to make a fight of it. The fact was that, despite the increasing lethargy that oppressed him, Fandor had received the strangest and most extravagant impression. He seemed to have caught the sound of someone speaking, to have heard a careless voice saying:

"See, there! There's a buoy just come bumping into the old hooker!"

A buoy? Fandor corrected mentally: "No, no—a barrel—my barrel!" And suddenly he started to yell, albeit so great had been his amazement at hearing human voices he had lost a whole second before trying to attract attention. Alas! had the thought perhaps come too late?

No sooner had he given tongue than exclamations of alarm broke out close by.

"Hi, mate! did you hear that?" came from the same voice he had already heard.

"Why, sure! Someone's bawling a good 'un!" The expression was not choice, but Fandor never dreamed of taking offense. On the contrary, he redoubled his efforts, and yelled louder than ever:

"Here!… Help, help!… Quick, quick!" And, as if he deemed these appeals still insufficient, he supplemented them by a series of kicks and thumps on the walls of his prison. But, alas! his hearers could not realize the miserable plight of the prisoner.

"Where does it come from?" said the same rough voice.

"Don't know!" replied a second speaker in a tone of bewilderment.

By this time Fandor's breath was failing altogether. He had begun to bleed at the nose again, and his temples were throbbing so violently he thought the veins must surely burst. He reflected in terror:

"If once I lose consciousness, goodbye everybody!"—and he fought desperately to stave off the giddiness that was mastering him.

"Open! Open!" he vociferated again. "I am stifling."

"It beats me!" went on an indifferent voice. "What d'you think to it, Eugene: small boys having a lark, eh?"

"Likely enough. But still—"

Without a moment's cessation Fandor went on drumming at the metal walls of his barrel. Would they come to understand at last? Would the pair who had heard his shouts guess whence they proceeded? As a fact, the men who had heard Fandor's cries were just two laborers on the job of hurriedly removing materials piled on the Quai de Javelle, which the flooded river threatened to sweep away. They quite failed to locate the exact point from which came the muffled thumping that still went on and on.

"Small boys likely?" one of the men, the one called Eugene, again suggested. "But, no, it can't be them. There ain't none on the prowl at this time o' day. Why, it's only five o'clock, old man—"

"Then, by God, could it come from the sewers?"

"From the sewers, eh?"

"Why certainly! A fellow as has got trapped in 'em, and the water's like to overtake him?"

As he spoke the man was approaching the riverbank. Not three steps had he taken when he let fly an excited oath:

"Oh, blast me! Listen, man! Look! It's from the buoy the noise comes."

"From the buoy? What buoy? You're loony!"

"No, I'm not. Listen, listen!"

The man waved frantically to summon his mate, and pointed to a big buoy of the sort used to moor vessels in harbor, which the current held tight up against the quay wall.

"I tell you it's from inside that they're calling."

"You're crazy!" repeated the other fellow.

"I ain't crazy! And I ain't drunk! I heard—"

"You thought you heard, you fool! To start off, there ain't naught there. And if so be there was, are there ever folks inside them sort of things?"

It was Fandor's fate that lay in the scales at that moment. Exhausted by the efforts he had made, the unhappy man had swooned away once more. If the laborer continued skeptical and persuaded his companion to look elsewhere, it was all up with the journalist. But fortunately chance would sometimes seem to be deterred by the very horror of certain catastrophes, as if realizing the hideous cruelty involved. The man who had heard Fandor's cries shook his head.

"Maybe there *ain't* never folks in them sort of things," he retorted, "but I'm dead certain someone was yelling inside that there buoy."

"You were dreaming, I tell ya!"

"Give me my pick… We'll soon see."

"You mean to smash up that there buoy?"

"You're right there."

"Well, old man, if ever there *is* anyone inside, you'll break his head—that's all!"

The objection was not without weight. But so convinced was the man of the truth of his supposition that he never hesitated:

"Give me a hand, mate!" he demanded. "We'll hurry up things a bit, eh? Now, heave ho!" And by their united efforts the two laborers did not take long to haul up high and dry on the quay the iron cylinder within which lay Fandor in a swoon and now quite unconscious. Thereupon a panic seized the two men, for as they shifted the buoy they could distinctly feel Fandor's body bumping about inside.

"Oh, hell!" swore laborer number one.

"There, you see," came from number two.

"Now are we to open or not?"

The quays were still quite deserted at this early hour, but a short way off a tug was puffing up and down, maneuvering to get a rope aboard a barge they had to tow out of danger from the flooded river. One of the men ran towards the vessel.

"Yo, ho!" he hailed. "Quick, send us over an engineer. There's someone we've just fished out—in a buoy—and we don't know how to get the door open."

But, naturally enough, nobody on board the tug could make head or tail of this odd statement of events. Five good minutes were wasted before finally one of the engine room hands from the tug hurried up to the scene of action, attended by a cabin boy carrying a bag of tools.

"Quick! quick! Ain't nothing moving now, but just this moment—" And the argument was likely to start afresh.

"Why, God bless me, lads!" began the engineer, "you're thinking it's a submarine, anyways! It's called a 'deadhead,' and they use 'em to tie up to—"

"Oh, open it, open it, if you know how!"

"Oh, that's easy enough," the man declared. "Three bolts to loose, and there you are. The cover unscrews, o' course, to let 'em now and again swab out the bilge as leaks in." And in a leisurely way, without any sort of hurry, the man set to work to pry out the safety-bolts.

"See here," he explained meanwhile, "it's a buoy that's been torn loose from its anchor-chain. Look, there's a couple o' links hanging on it still. Oh, look, and it's had a pretty tidy knock too, I can tell ya. One would think it was an explosion belike…"

But the poor man never finished his sentence. With a last blow of the hammer he had knocked off the bolt-heads and the cover of the iron cylinder flew open. Then, as he saw Fandor, he was struck dumb with alarm and amazement. Beside him stood the two laborers, equally staggered.

"A man, by God!"

"A dead man!"

"Nay, perhaps he ain't dead! Come on, give a hand, do!" And all pressed forward to help the mechanic, who was dragging Fandor's lifeless body from the barrel. Instantly questions and answers and explanations broke out afresh.

"Why, he's dripping with blood!"

"Oh God! Don't you see his nose is bashed in?"

"A crime, for certain sure!"

"Or may be an accident, eh?"

"See here," put in the engineer in a voice hoarse with excitement, "the fellow ain't dead, I say. Must get him aboard and look after him—he wants warmth, he does."

Truly Fandor had good reason to bless the whole race of seamen, hard-working, honest, handy fellows as they are. He was right well looked after on board the tug, so well indeed that by dint of the repeated drops and thimblefuls of "grog" they forced between his teeth he came to himself dead drunk and laughing fit to split his sides!

"Pity's sake, stop tickling!" he screamed.

The fact is that, applying the treatment usual with the apparently drowned, they were just then busy tickling the soles of his feet.

"Let me be, do! I can breathe all right."

This time they were working his arms energetically up and down to facilitate the play of the lungs.

"I'm feeling very well. And it's just a screaming joke what's happened to me. I… I…"

But there the patient stopped. His terrors allayed, knowing himself safe, he fell in an instant into such a profound sleep that his rescuers, good people little versed in the normal effects following on great crises of agony, began to feel renewed alarm.

"What say? Is he going to slip through our fingers?" asked a voice.

"We'd be in a guilty fix if he did!" observed the master of the tug.

"For sure, it would be best to go for a constable," suggested the captain's wife, and her opinion was unanimously approved.

Less than five minutes later a constable was informed of the surprising discovery of a man found half dead in a buoy drifting downstream. And thereupon a whole complicated mechanism, as it were, got underway. While he still lay asleep, weak and worn out with the utter exhaustion of persons rescued from great catastrophes, the journalist unknowingly was occupying the time and energies of an endless series of officials. The constable, to begin with, dumbfounded on hearing the amazing details, returned to his station and reported to the sergeant on duty. The latter immediately decided he must telephone to headquarters to ask instructions. But at this time of day a new secretary was in charge of the office, and was no less prompt in deciding on the line of conduct to be followed. For is it not the invariable custom of bureaucrats, whenever anything occurs out of the ordinary routine, to make every effort to throw the alarming responsibility onto somebody else's shoulders?

"They'll know what to do at headquarters," the secretary phoned back to the sergeant-in-charge, and without a moment's delay the news was communicated—again by telephone—to the Prefecture of Police.

"A man inside a buoy? Whatever are you getting at?" demanded the Prefecture of Police by the mouth of a district inspector. "Damn it, there are no buoys in the Seine."

"But still—"

"Oh, well, let the Criminal Department know! It's their business to look into anything savoring apparently of crime."

Now at the Criminal Bureau, it has never been the custom to refuse the investigation of anything sensational. Very far from it. Is not every inspector all agog to undertake an inquiry that may set him in the limelight and win him the kudos of being mentioned in the papers? The particular inspector, a young man who was on all-night duty there, jumped with joy when he heard the news.

"Oh! Yes!" he answered instantly. "Keep an eye on the man! I'm coming—time to get there in a taxi, and I'm with you."

Yes, Fandor was still sound asleep when already the intricate wheels of the administration of justice were in full swing—and the result could not fail to follow in due course.

"It's here they've rescued a man from the water?" asked the inspector as he stepped on board the tug.

"Yes, here! Yes, Doctor—"

"I'm not a doctor, Captain—"

"Oh, I thought you were. They'd asked the station to send one."

"Really? Well, the police are here first."

"The police?"

"The police. Why, yes, my good sir. But I'm in a hurry to see the individual."

"He's asleep."

"Don't care for that. I'll wake him."

"We can't do that. Shake him, and he grunts, but don't so much as open his eyes."

"Very good! We'll soon see. Will you lead the way?"

"If you wish." And two minutes more and Juve's youthful colleague entered the cabin where Fandor lay. Followed a scene words fail to describe.

"God almighty!" swore the detective.

"What's up?" queried the tug master.

"Why, I know him!"

"You know him?"

"Know him, rather! You do too."

"I...? I...?"

"Of course you do! It's Fandor, Jerome Fandor."

"Fandor the journalist? The enemy of Fantômas?"

"The enemy of... Why, no, not just that... Oh, a pretty business! a mighty pretty business!"

Under the astonished eyes of the gallant seaman, who, like everybody else, was familiar with Fandor's name and felt for him an admiration almost approaching veneration, the detective was searching his pockets.

"The enemy of Fantômas," he repeated. "You think that? Well, you're making the mistake of your life. Look here, best just notice what I'm after!" But there was little need to urge the seaman to watch the police officer's movements. He had, in fact, seen the young detective haul a pair of handcuffs from his pocket, and turned pale with horror.

"You… you… you're arresting him?" he stammered. "But if it's Jerome Fandor…"

"My dear sir," was the detective's quiet reply, "it is just because your man is named Jerome Fandor that I'm clapping the bracelets on him. Oh God, sir! you don't know what the villain has been at? Well, I'll tell you. He contrived Fantômas' escape—yes, Fantômas, when Juve had captured him, and…"

But the young officer never concluded his explanations. Behind him Fandor had just exploded in an uproarious fit of laughter. He was awake at last, and had heard what was said.

Could he possibly regard seriously this grotesque arrest?

It may be, nevertheless, Fandor did wrong in taking it so lightly. He should have known how the most undoubted police blunders are precisely the ones it is most difficult to disprove and set right.

* * * * *

Two hours later, perfectly rested and in the best of good spirits, Fandor was conducted to the Court of First Instance—in other words, before the examining magistrate—whose duty it is by law to hear the case of all persons arrested in order to decide whether the arrest is to hold good or no. Smiling more genially than ever, the young journalist bowed to the judge.

"Sir," he began, "I think I shall waste the least possible fraction of your time—my name is Jerome Fandor."

"Hold your tongue," the magistrate interrupted him roughly. "Give me time to read the report."

Still smiling, Fandor observed pleasantly:

"Excuse me, sir, but I thought my name would ensure my being treated politely."

But his irony failed of its effect. The other simply waved his hand, enjoining silence, and read out:

"Found in a buoy wrecked in harbor…"

He did not trouble to finish. "You were in a buoy?" he

interjected.

"I was—so they told me."

"And what were you doing there?"

"I was dying, sir."

"That's no answer!"

"Really? Well, it's the only one I have to give you."

"Well, you'll explain in court later on."

"What?" cried Fandor, with a shout. "It's serious?"

"What's serious?"

"You keep me still under arrest?"

"You fancied, possibly, I was going to set you at liberty?"

"By God! I did imagine I might entertain that hope."

"Why?"

"Because to arrest me is against common sense."

"You think so?"

"I do—and I'll prove it. Come now, what do they accuse me of? Of having worked Fantômas' escape? Well, if I did let Fantômas go, you must allow he's not over and above grateful, seeing he is trying to murder me."

"I am not bound to believe you…"

"Sir," observed Fandor gravely, "it's just as well. If you shared my feelings, you would hold a very low opinion of yourself!"

"Insolence, eh?" stormed the judge.

"No, frankness!" corrected Fandor. "However, that's not the point now. Can I legally claim to summon a witness?"

"Claim, no! Ask, yes!"

"Well, I ask to be taken before Monsieur Fuselier."

At the name of the erstwhile examining magistrate, now advocate general, and soon to be promoted higher, the judge's face took on a worried look.

"Very good," he said eventually. "I will have you taken before him, if he will condescend to see you." And, ringing the bell, he handed an envelope containing a short message to an officer of the court, telling Fandor to await the answer.

He was never the most patient of men, was the worthy journalist, and this time he lost his temper completely.

"It's simply too idiotic," he growled. "A man risks his life, takes the risk of being murdered ten times over—and the reward the law and the police give him is a pair of handcuffs. So much for judges and their intelligence!"

Ten minutes later, however, the journalist had recovered his equanimity.

"Monsieur Fuselier asks us to send you at once to his room. The officer will show you the way."

"Excellent!"

"It will be excellent for you if Monsieur Fuselier sees fit to let you go. I only hope he will. Till we meet again, sir!"

"Oh, if it's all the same to you, I will say goodbye for good to you. I have no wish to prolong our relations." And, leaving the magistrate a trifle abashed at this lack of consideration, Jerome Fandor set off for the room occupied by that lifelong friend of his known as Germain Fuselier. At that moment the journalist found himself possessed of all his wonted cheerfulness. He was completely recovered from all he had undergone, and felt no anxiety whatever about the future, so far as concerned his own personal safety, at any rate.

"Fuselier is no fool," he reflected. "I shall explain my adventures to him and he'll set me at liberty. By the by, where the devil shall I get hold of Juve? What has he been after since last I saw him?"

Then, under his breath, he sighed:

"And Helene? Shall I ever get on her track, I wonder?"

On entering the imposing room allotted to the Advocate General, Fandor called up an ingratiating smile to his lips.

"Monsieur Fuselier," he greeted the great man, "good day to you!"

The magistrate rose hastily, and came forward to meet his visitor.

"You again!" he exclaimed.

"Yes, here I am as usual—and, as usual, handcuffs on wrists. You see, I'm growing into an incurable sort of habitual criminal, eh?"

"But why? What have you done this time? I cannot believe what they tell me."

"No more can I. The cock-and-bull stories I hear about myself make me think they're all lunatics."

"Still, there are facts…"

"Oh, facts!"

"Why, yes, facts. You can't deny that!"

"Monsieur Fuselier, I deny nothing, but I'm going to explain everything."

"Everything?"

"Everything—from A to Z. See here, will you request my escort just to take a turn in the corridor? I think our talk is going to be a serious one." And, as a matter of fact, Fandor was quite right in his surmise. Always hitherto he had been cordially welcomed by Germain Fuselier. Now, on the contrary, he observed in his friend's bearing signs of embarrassment, marks of constraint, that spoke volumes as to his sentiments. It may be he did not believe him guilty, but all the same he had been impressed, and very unfavorably, by this story of an escape which was evidently going the rounds among the magistrates no less than among the police.

"I will do what you wish, Fandor," the judge agreed. Leave us, officer. Stay in the corridor. I will call you in case of need."

Fandor gave no sign of noticing the terms of this order, eloquent of distrust as they were. He was beginning to realize more and more clearly that Monsieur Fuselier considered him suspect. Still, was it not up to him to explain, as he had promised, the events that had made his behavior appear ambiguous?

Helene was far away by now. Juve, on the other hand, had no longer any cause to fear a reprimand from his superiors for the very good reason that he had no doubt already received it. What motive was there left to make him keep silence?

"I'm waiting for you to speak," Monsieur Fuselier prompted him. "Where have you come from?"

"From some very odd places. I'm just returned, my dear sir, from a mooring buoy… from the bed of the Seine… from paying a visit to Fantômas… from a strongbox… from driving in a car with my fiancée."

"You're speaking seriously?"

"Most seriously."

"You don't realize, however…"

"That I look like a madman ? Oh, yes, I realize that perfectly. But I'm *not* mad…"

"I hope not. Still…"

"Wait a bit! Don't interrupt. I am back from these different places. Now listen carefully. It is absolutely untrue that I ever connived at Fantômas' escape—for the good reason that Fantômas was never a prisoner."

"But Juve…"

"Reported this to the Préfet of Police? That is so. Only Juve made a mistake."

"You are certain?"

"Yes, dead certain of that much! Now I proceed. I did not let Fantômas escape, but I am quite ready to admit that I did risk my life to defend him."

"To defend him? Defend Fantômas?"

"Precisely so—to defend Fantômas. Moreover, he rewarded me by firing a revolver shot at me which effectually prevented me from knowing whether one of his lieutenants, the Vicomte d'Oultremont—"

"The Vicomte d'Oultremont?"

"You don't know him, Monsieur Fuselier? That's a pity! A charming young man… I was saying how the shot my friend Fantômas fired at me prevented me from knowing exactly whether the gentleman in question is a blackguard…" And at this point, observing Germain Fuselier's scared look, Fandor could not help going off into a wild fit of laughter.

Nevertheless, the magistrate's alarm was not at all to be wondered at, and no doubt Fandor would have been quite ready to admit as much, if he had not for the moment been tempted to give play to his usual boyish sense of mischief. As a matter of fact, the journalist had not stated a single fact that was not strictly true. Everything he professed to have done, everything he related as having befallen him, was absolutely authentic. Yet could he for one moment suppose this series of astounding events possessed the merit of being possible or probable in anyone else's eyes?

At sight of the journalist's uproarious merriment Monsieur Fuselier rose. He too was smiling, but his smile still betrayed a constraint suggesting something like annoyance. Noticing this, Fandor checked his mirth.

"Come now!" he said in a conciliatory tone, "I'm going to throw a light on the subject. Indeed, I'm not sorry to put my ideas a bit in order. Presently, when you have restored me to liberty, I'm off to my paper to write a sensational serial, and I mustn't get myself mixed. So, you see, Monsieur Fuselier, I'll start afresh from the beginning, and go over it all again—this time in chronological order. Well, I contrived Fantômas' escape, and I met my fiancée. You know, of course, who my fiancée is?"

"Helene? Fantômas' daughter?"

"Yes, Helene."

"But she is dead."

"You mean she is supposed to be dead? That's not precisely the same thing."

"But—"

"Monsieur Fuselier, you are going to say something silly."

"Look here, Fandor, I really feel my brain's giving way!"

"I'm extremely sorry!"

"Your adventures are so terrific I can't but ask myself if I'm not dreaming."

"Many and many a time, my dear sir, I've asked myself the very same question."

"Well, I'm going to take my precautions accordingly."

"Precautions?"

"Why, yes. I want to have some evidence by me of what you say. You understand, I feel bound to supplement my personal impressions by a written report."

"I don't see any objection. You are going to take notes, eh?"

"I should never get done in that case. No, I'm going to call in a clerk of the court. You have nothing to say against that?"

"Not a word, my good sir! Do whatever you think advisable."

"Well, I'm going to send for a collaborator of the sort." And Monsieur Fuselier got up and, crossing the room, went out, shutting the door after him.

"Ah, well!" thought Fandor, "he's not so difficult as I thought. It must be allowed, indeed, I may have startled the poor man."

Then suddenly he felt a shock of surprise.

"Why, what? Why on earth didn't he ring for an attendant?"

Jerome Fandor's mind worked at express speed, and with him deeds quickly followed on the heels of thought. The instant he had noted this detail he felt a twinge of alarm. Surely it was odd that, instead of summoning one of the attendants allotted to his service, this Advocate General had troubled to see to the matter himself. In a moment the journalist was on his feet and in his turn moving to the door, heedless of any sort of scruple or any thought of his own dignity. Reaching the door, he did not open it, but simply put his ear to the keyhole.

"Whatever is he after, my worthy friend?" he muttered. Nor was he long in finding out.

Not for a moment suspecting that his odd behavior had induced his visitor to spy upon his doings, Germain Fuselier never even thought of lowering his voice. Addressing an usher, he was issuing orders:

"You are to go down at once to the Prison Infirmary, and give a message to the doctor on duty. Tell him to come to my room without wasting a second and to bring four hefty attendants with him. You'll tell him Jerome Fandor is with me. Yes, don't stare at me like that! You'll tell him Jerome Fandor is with me, and he has gone mad!"

"Mad?" the startled usher exclaimed.

"Mad as a hatter! He's telling a whole string of nonsensical tales. Off with you at once! I shall wait five minutes before going back to him. We mustn't have him get impatient, but I've no mind to be overlong in the same room with him."

"Damn the fellow!" swore the journalist as he heard this treacherous order. "He thinks I'm mad, and wants to have me locked up. Hmm, lucky I've got sharp ears!"

For the moment Jerome Fandor turned pale. Albeit a man whom nothing daunted, the notion of being hauled off to the Prison Infirmary did not strike him as altogether agreeable.

"Five minutes!" he repeated. "Oh, yes, I know that sort of five minutes. It lasts exactly three. So, I've got three minutes to clear out—and I'm handcuffed!"

Anyone else would have despaired, but not so Fandor.

"Bah! Time enough!" he calculated. "A careful little arrangement of scenery, and I'll be off." And thereupon he set to work with feverish activity. To start with, he pushed shut the bolt that secured the door of the Advocate General's room.

"There!" he grinned, "that will delay them a good ten minutes, what with fetching a workman and having the door forced. And when he is inside, he'll be convinced I'm far enough away."

Jerome Fandor chuckled as he went on: "A chair by the window—and the window open—capital! When folks find things like that, they think instantly of an escape over the roofs. Now I'll strengthen their suspicions a bit. Those curtains yonder—in two seconds they're twisted into a rope—that's always done."

No sooner said than done. To tear down the curtains of the big window, tie them together end to end, then lash them to the crossbar of the casement was the work of a moment.

"And now to vanish!" he proceeded. "I've fixed up all the details to make 'em think I've escaped. All that's left is not to budge, and I shall be in perfect and complete safety. Where the devil am I going to hide, by the by?"

Then he looked at the fireplace, and gave a smile of satisfaction.

"Just the very thing! It is as big and wide as even I could wish."

Lifting the register quietly, he scrambled into the space above it, and smiled with renewed satisfaction. The flue over his head was so wide he could easily stand upright inside it.

"I'm going to have a boring time up here," he grumbled. "But better that than going for a spell to Bicêtre! Anyway, the afternoon's getting on, and I shall slip off quietly tonight when nobody is thinking about me." After which he let down the register again, and waited, quite unperturbed.

The fact is Fandor had profited right well by the lessons Juve as a police officer had many a time given him. He had learned that the best hiding places are always the simplest. Above all he knew that sundry signs of heedlessness cleverly faked are all that is needed to bamboozle the average policeman. Accordingly he felt little or no doubt that the false trail he had laid by leaving these indications of an escape by way of the window would infallibly appeal to his pursuers.

"By the by," he exclaimed suddenly, "I wonder if the chimney draws well."

It seemed an idiotic remark, but it was nevertheless pertinent. At the very moment when Monsieur Fuselier was shaking the door and storming to find it shut against him, Fandor left his hiding place as bold as brass.

"I saw a packet of cigarettes and a box of matches on our friend's desk," he murmured, "and I'm going to borrow those indispensable articles. Borrow? No, no! I have some small change on me. I can pay him for them."

By this time they were shaking the door furiously, to the sound of a torrent of angry exclamations, while hurried foot-steps could be heard outside. Meanwhile Jerome Fandor calmly counted out a little pile of sous, which he arranged neatly on the Advocate General's desk.

"No need to make my case worse than it is!" he told himself, with an ineffable look on his face. "From now on I'm an escaped lunatic; that's sufficient. I don't want to make myself out a thief." And solemnly he wended back to his chimney, and, his conscience at ease, struck a match and lit a cigarette.

*   *   *   *   *

"The chimney draws to perfection," thought Fandor as he watched the smoke of his cigarette going straight upwards. "A piece of luck! Fuselier won't notice any smell of tobacco. Poor man, what a face he'll be pulling presently!"

At that moment the door gave way, and Fandor's ears convinced him he had in nowise exaggerated the lively effect his conduct was having on the temper of the worthy magistrate.

Catching sight of the journalist's little arrangements, the Advocate General immediately fell a victim to the ruse.

"By the window!" he cried. "Fandor has escaped by the window. Why, he's a very devil! And, into the bargain, mad as he is just now, he's bound to have all the unnatural cleverness of sleepwalkers. We shall never catch him."

"I accept the omen," thought Fandor, beaming with satisfaction. Poor innocent! And he had to bite his lips not to burst into a guffaw as he heard the manifold and multifarious orders the Advocate General was issuing.

"Warn the police guards… Send out men on the roofs… We must telephone to the Criminal Bureau!"

"So," was Fandor's next thought, "so perhaps I'm going to see Juve turn up? Hmm, I'd just as lief he didn't, though. He'd soon see through my little game."

Meantime Monsieur Fuselier was still storming:

"He was shamming mad, I'll wager. He was just set on humbugging me with his preposterous rigmarole. Oh, curse it all! curse it! I ought to have guessed what all that talking meant."

It was too much for Fandor—the notion of Monsieur Fuselier calling himself an imbecile in his despair diverted the young man to the last degree.

"So that's that!" chuckled the undaunted journalist. "But there, to understand just 'what talking means' is not within the compass of everybody."

Another five minutes, however, and he was beginning to find things a great deal less agreeable. As a matter of fact, he was exceedingly uncomfortable in his chimney flue. True, he could smoke, but, to tell the truth, he would much rather have been able to sit down!

"I ought to have taken a chair with me," he said gravely. "True, I could never have got it in. Now, aren't they ever going away, these damned policemen?"

In truth, a never-ending procession of police was defiling through Germain Fuselier's office. No sooner was the alarm given than the inspectors one and all came hurrying up. No doubt to a man they found the thing diverting—this adventure in which the Advocate General had anything but the best part to play.

Toward six in the evening the prisoner began to suffer veritable tortures. Forced to remain absolutely still, he felt his limbs growing numb and cramp running through every part of his body.

"A pretty go," he groaned, "if I have to shift. I can just see myself kicking out the register!"

Yet shift his posture he must. If it remained unchanged but a few seconds more, it was quite clear he must go off in a faint. After all the dreadful predicaments he had been in, he was still too weak to dispose of his normal powers of resistance.

But once again luck stood him in good stead. Unexpectedly a fresh visitor, the last, entered Monsieur Fuselier's room—no other than Monsieur Havard in person.

"Well?" the magistrate inquired.

"Well, my dear judge, nothing! Nothing at all!"

"But he can't have vanished into thin air, I suppose."

"He may have managed to hide. The palace is enormously extensive. My men have searched everywhere without seeing anything."

"Well, sir! your inspectors don't know how to set about their job."

"Say rather, Monsieur Fuselier, they are not accustomed to be running after criminals the Advocate General deals with as lunatics—and lets 'em escape."

"Oh, come, Monsieur Havard, you are poking fun at me?"

"Heaven forbid! I'm only come to tell you that, under the circumstances, I have just stopped the search!"

"Stopped the search? Oh, that's capital! The department confesses itself incompetent! Delicious! Upon my word I no longer wonder how Fantômas can continue his exploits!"

"But—"

"Not another word, Monsieur Havard. Enough said! You stop the search—well, I'm going out to dinner. Good night to you, sir!"

Meantime, in his chimney, Fandor felt fatigue and pain

and cramp fly like magic. The quarrel he caught the echoes of
filled him with such glee he had to stuff his handkerchief in
his mouth to smother his frantic merriment. The joy of this
wrangle whereof he himself was the direct cause!

"And so it goes!" he chuckled. "Havard will be off to protest
to the Préfet of Police; Fuselier will lodge a complaint with the
Procureur General; and I—I'm going to cut my stick!"

The door of the room had banged, and Fandor guessed what
that meant. Without more ado, or open variance now, Germain
Fuselier and the Chief of the Criminal Bureau had parted, each
going his own way. The journalist forced himself to wait a few
seconds more by way of precaution, and then, heaving a sigh of
relief, quitted his hiding place.

"Oh, but it's good to have a stretch!" he cried, suiting the
action to the word with no little satisfaction. "I was feeling horribly messed up. Decidedly I'm past the age for playing at little
chimney sweeps."

The next moment he grew serious again: "And my handcuffs! I must get them off. That's certain, but devil take me if I
know how!"

As much at home as if in his own house, Fandor strolled up
and down the Advocate General's official room, glancing about
him on every side.

"Not a trace of tools!" he growled. "Not a blessed thing to
drive a hole with. Not so much as a file to be found! Why, what
a fool not to have thought of this difficulty! He's confoundedly
badly provided, this magistrate. He can't possibly have foreseen
a man would be wanting to break off a pair of handcuffs in his
office."

Still, if Fandor, as was his way, spoke lightly of the difficulty, this did not prevent his being badly disconcerted. To make
off through the corridors of the Palais de Justice with hands
tied together was practically an impossibility; but how, without
tools, get rid of the embarrassing encumbrance?

"It cannot be I've lost all my powers of invention. I can't
think of anything. I *cannot* see any way out."

But at this point he stopped short to tell himself: "Ah, but there's a cupboard I haven't examined—though I should be very much surprised to find what I want in it." And, crossing to the wardrobe he had noticed, and opening the door, he pulled a wry face.

"Just clothes!" he remarked, "Fuselier's traps. I'm getting on fine!"

He had just, in fact, come upon the place where the Advocate General, like the careful soul he was, used to hang his ordinary garments along with his official robes.

"It might prove useful for going to a fancy-dress dance," the young man thought, "but that's about all. Oh, ho, the old fellow doesn't care much about following the fashions, it appears."

This last reflection was easy to account for. Holding up the Advocate General's robes with his bound hands, the journalist had noticed a voluminous cloak that was quite out of date from the point of view of the taste of the present day, being in fact one of those caped greatcoats—very convenient garments, be it said—which men of a former generation were fond of wearing, as is evidenced by old daguerreotypes.

"No, anything but elegant!" Fandor criticized, "and of no earthly use to me."

He turned away, then presently strolled back towards the magistrate's desk.

"A fine scheme, truly, to think of—the getting away with the handcuffs still on! I shall have the crowd at my heels before I've gone fifty yards."

Then suddenly he broke off, and actually cut a caper of joy.

"Why, I'm going mad, upon my soul! What's the odds if I do keep the handcuffs on, so long as I fix up so as nobody can see them?" And, dashing back to the cupboard, he threw the ponderous garment about his shoulders, folding his arms underneath the cape.

"There we are!" he laughed. "Out of sight, out of mind! Handcuffs clean out of view! On condition of not shaking hands with a soul and never wanting to roll a cigarette, I defy anyone to suspect me of wearing these pretty bracelets."

This was perfectly true. By keeping his arms closely crossed on his chest inside the loosely fitting cape he could easily hide the telltale handcuffs.

"More by token," he went on, "yet another advantage! If one of the palace guards sees me in the distance, he'll take me for Fuselier. There can't be so many magistrates in the habit of wearing cloaks of the sort."

Lighting a cigarette—the last he would have a chance of smoking before he was back home—Fandor strode deliberately to the room door.

"Provided I don't meet anyone in the corridors," he told himself, "I'm all right. Once in the palace itself, nobody will pay the smallest attention to me."

The young man encountered no official in the corridors immediately outside. Nay, more, on going down into the purlieus of the Palais de Justice proper, he saw nobody, official or other, who seemed to notice him.

"Yes," he thought, "Havard has evidently done what he said. Furious at Fuselier's sarcasms, he has made up his mind to stop all further perquisitions. There's never an inspector on the premises! Well, I've no reason to complain, eh?"

He had still less when presently, without let or hindrance, he found himself crossing the vast Salle des Pas Perdus, and reached the doors that divide in two parts the stairs leading to the Boulevard du Palais.

"Once across that threshold, I recover all hope—just the opposite of Dante's gate of the Inferno."

But the words froze on his lips. Hurried footsteps sounded behind him. Was he being pursued? He felt a wild impulse to dash away at a run, but this was the very way to attract attention. Hurrying, without risking too great an appearance of haste, he pushed open the door with one knee and passed out.

"If you please, sir, will you help me?" a voice was appealing to him from behind—a woman's voice. And, turning round, Fandor saw a young mother who, carrying a doll in one hand and with the other holding up a tiny toddler barely able to walk, found it impossible to open the heavy door.

"Why, of course, madam," Fandor agreed, and instinctively

reached out an arm.

Imagine the look of horror that followed on the other's face. "But—but—" she stammered.

One of the Palace guards stood not twenty steps away, at the foot of the stairway. The faintest cry might be fatal. The journalist found his tongue without an instant's hesitation.

"Madam," he begged, "don't be afraid, and don't give the alarm. It is true I am a prisoner trying to escape. But perhaps you know my name—Jerome Fandor?"

"Jerome Fandor? The journalist Jerome Fandor?"

The young woman drew away, saying over the name she had just heard with growing terror.

"Why, certainly!" Fandor assured her. "Yes, I am Jerome Fandor."

"But Fandor is not—"

"Is not a man to be afraid of. I am entirely of the same opinion. See here, madam, read *La Capitale* these days. Then you will see how it is. By the by, I mustn't wait. Excuse me, madam. And goodbye!" And full steam ahead now, in terror lest the woman should give the alarm, the journalist tore down the stairs four steps at a time.

"So there," he thought to himself, "a man, for sure, would have shouted and bellowed—kicked up a shindy to rouse the whole Cité. But a woman's so much more gentle! Dear little body!"

At that moment he looked round, and turned livid. The young woman he deemed so gentle had made straight for the guard and was talking to him excitedly, pointing in the fugitive's direction.

"Damn the little baggage!" Fandor swore. "But the air's not good for me hereabouts—let's get away." And in two strides he was across the broad footway. A prowling taxi drew his attention:

"Cab?"

Fandor eagerly accepted the offer, and dashed for the vehicle.

"Where to?" demanded the driver.

"Just where you choose!"

"Eh, what?"

"I tell you you've got to open the door for me. No need to stare at me that way. My hands are hurt."

"Should have said so, mister!"

"Should have guessed it, my man. Now, straight ahead!"

"Straight ahead, what?"

"Why, yes. Get a move on, do! Can't you see my wife over there, with a bottle of vitriol handy?"

"Oh, ho?" the man grinned knowingly, "you're out from the Divorce Court, eh?" And at last the fellow got underway.

Seated inside, the journalist heaved a great sigh of relief.

"A warm corner!" he admitted to himself. "And to think I could find nothing plausible to tell that fellow. I'm on the downgrade, that's certain. My wits are leaving me."

Then, still holding his cloak close about him, the undaunted journalist leaned out of the window.

"Driver!"

"Sir?"

"Montmartre way. Does that suit you?"

"Must make it! What part?"

"Rue Dancourt."

"Righto!" And Fandor fell back in the seat.

Rue Dancourt? So he was bound for the Rue Dancourt—for home? The young man had, in fact, come to a rapid decision, thereby affording definite proof that, in flat contradiction to what he had just declared, he by no means lacked intelligence.

"Now, it's very certain," calculated the journalist, "that the police will be hunting everywhere for me. Fuselier has no doubt lodged his complaint. Havard, on his side, will be keen on the game. In one word, all night long Paris will be patrolled by men whose one ambition it will be to lay hands on me. Well, I've no wish to come across these gentry. So the best thing I can do is to go and rest a bit, get my handcuffs removed, and think."

But Fandor had a well-founded conviction, however unfounded it might appear, that it was still at his own house he ran the least danger of being discovered.

"My address is known," he reflected. "It is such a bold stroke to go back home that the idea will never enter any policeman's head to look for me at the very place I ought by rights most carefully to avoid visiting. And then about getting quit of my handcuffs."

A quarter of an hour later the taxi brought Fandor to his own front door.

"Got to open the door for you again?" inquired the driver.

"If you'll be so good, old man."

"Well, there you are. Seven francs twenty-five is my fare."

Fandor made to put his hand in his pocket, but stopped in time.

"Good Lord!" he muttered, "I was just going to make another unlucky show of how things are with me." Then aloud:

"I'm out of change. My concierge will settle with you." And he effected a headlong entrance into the house.

"Hello! So there you are at last, M'sieur Fandor," cried the concierge in surprise, as she recognized her lodger. "Why, I've been reading in the papers—"

"Must never believe what the papers say, madam. Haven't I often told you so? And I know what I'm talking about, as I'm a journalist myself."

"Granted, M'sieur Fandor, but—"

"Just a moment. I have a taxi standing outside. Would you have the kindness to pay the man? I haven't a sou left in my pocket."

"Certainly, M'sieur Fandor. I'll see to it."

That was all the journalist wanted. He thanked the good woman, and darted for the stairs.

"Safe at last! Safe at last!" he was telling himself when a voice hailed him from below.

"Hi! you're upstairs already, M'sieur Fandor?"

"Yes! Why?"

"There's a letter for you."

"A letter?"

"Marked 'private' on the envelope. Wait a moment and I'll bring it you."

"No, no! Don't! Chuck it up on the first landing. I'll come

and fetch it. I'm coming down now."

Fandor could not help smiling to himself. Could he, even to get his letter and merely before his concierge's eyes, run the risk of letting his handcuffs be seen?

No sooner, however, had he picked up the letter on the first-floor landing, where the woman had thrown it, than he knew instantly by the writing on the envelope from whom the message came.

"Ah!" he sighed. "Helene! It is Helene's writing!" And walls and floor and ceiling seemed to be whirling giddily round him.

8. Hot on the Scent

Many a time in the course of his adventurous life had Fandor encountered dramatic surprises. Again and again had he found himself confronted with the most astounding events. Always hitherto in such cases he had preserved his composure intact. But now for once, as he pressed between his manacled hands the envelope that bore the handwriting of his fiancée, he confessed himself overmastered by the stress of his feelings.

"Helene!" he cried, and again, "Helene! Ah! what can she be writing to me about, what secret can she be confiding to me?"

He had to exert a violent effort to win a real mastery over himself, and throw off the torpor that had overtaken him, to continue his way upstairs and enter his rooms. The door scarcely shut behind him, without giving another thought to the handcuffs he still wore, and which still impeded his movements, he threw himself into a chair, tore open the cover and read the missive, the sight of which agitated him so sorely.

Helene! Ah, yes! still as always he cherished for her a hopeless love. Hopeless, for how many atrocious deeds built a fatal barrier between himself and the girl he had met in former days in Natal and whom he knew to be the daughter of the terrifying brigand whose undoing he and Juve had sworn to bring about. She was the child of Fantômas, but she was horrified at the crimes of her scoundrel father. But how could she, without proving herself an unnatural daughter, deliver him up to justice? Juve himself, zealous as he was in his work as a police officer, would not have wished it, would have deemed the act a monstrous one.

And how well did Fandor realize, how ardently did he admire the heroic life of self-sacrifice Helene lived. Was not she also waging a grim struggle against Fantômas—the only one she could carry on with a clear conscience? In hidden ways she was ever working to checkmate the vile designs of the Lord of Terror. It was she who would stealthily save the victim threatened by her father's machinations. And Fantômas, who loved her but was driven on remorselessly by the mania of crime, had wreaked on her cruel acts of vengeance.

Helene! But when Fandor thought of Helene, he felt his whole being flooded with a soft wave of tender emotion. Would he ever have the right to wed her, the fond privilege of calling her his wife?

"I know," he reflected. "Doubtless Fantômas has forbidden her to marry me. He has made this the price of sparing the life of many a foredoomed victim. But such a sacrifice as he has forced on her, is it not beyond the strength of a human being?"

Again it was only by a cruel effort Fandor could check the tears that welled in his eyes. The letter shook in his hands, as he read with mingled anguish and tenderness the poor phrases Helene had written to heal, if it might be, his wound.

> You have sacrificed yourself for me, Fandor, and I grieve to think of the hideous result that has followed for you.
>
> You recognized, Fandor, who I was and realized how it was a duty there was no shirking that had led me to adopt a costume which, as you also know, I hold in profound abhorrence.
>
> You helped the pretended Fantômas to escape, and just now when the Vicomte d'Oultremont, my father's lieutenant, was receiving you, I shuddered to think of the danger I was about to make you incur.
>
> Tell me, Fandor, did I do wrong? I count on you as a friend. I know you are a brave man, chivalrous and prepared for any act of self-devotion...
>
> And even now my father is planning an awful thing. Oh, Fandor, how it pains me to have to write to you in veiled phrases, taking heed not to utter a word that might guide you to the wretched man my affection as a daughter forbids me to betray.
>
> I have learned, Fandor, what happened. How? No matter for that. I have heard of your dash to save this same Vicomte d'Oultremont's life. I know how you were shot down and fell unconscious into the hands of Him I must not name.
>
> Oh! my terror then, my despair, when I heard from Him

what he had done with you, how he had destined you to a fearful death in the buoy to which his ruthless cruelty condemned you.

Yet I was able to save you. You are alive. You are out of danger. With all my soul and strength I thank heaven for that!

Yes, no doubt there are monstrous accusations hanging over your head—and that by my fault. It is because they think you saved Fantômas that you were arrested. But I cannot believe these suspicions are seriously entertained... You are a hero. Justice will be done you.

And now, Fandor, I have but to say farewell... Farewell... The word hurts you? It wounds *me* to the heart. Yet must I write it—and mean it... Be sure, Fandor, it is a grave reason that parts us. By giving my father my oath that I would never be your wife, I have won a precious boon from him, an oath that he respects and will respect so long as I remain and continue to remain faithful to the reciprocal pledge I have given...

Farewell then... farewell forever.

Never seek to see me again. Forget me.

I am going away, very far away, to the other side of the ocean, and I do not tell you where—must not tell you where.

My task, Fandor, is not finished. The incidents that marked your arrival with the Vicomte d'Oultremont did not avail definitely to deter Fantômas from his purpose to realize the project that terrifies me. But I can go on fighting. I can, yes! weak woman though I be, I can hinder the abominable catastrophe. It is for that I am crossing the seas.

Oh, Fandor, never doubt my sincerity! Never doubt my affection! Never doubt that to my last breath I shall do the impossible to be worthy of the love I have inspired in you.

I am leaving the country, Fandor. I am going overseas, and it is to do my duty in hindering Fantômas from perpetrating a frightful crime. I write you these lines that I may at least be sure your thoughts will go with me and you will never doubt that an imperative motive, a dreadful motive, has forced me to see you no more.

And in a bold unfaltering hand Fandor saw she had signed the touching letter, "Helene."

"Oh, God!" the young man sobbed, his head dropped between his hands. He was at one of those moments of self-abandonment even the strongest natures are liable to, and which in the horror of their deep discouragement come close to the very border of despair.

"Helene is leaving me," he groaned, and as he reread the letter, at certain passages he ground his teeth to keep in a scream of pain and rage.

"She saved my life," he murmured. "It was she sawed through the chain that held the buoy I lay dying in… And she is going!"

The thought haunted him. Was not the certainty of her departure the assurance of an endless series of moments devoid of joy or happiness? Should he ever see her again? What was behind this farewell? What further peril was the undaunted girl about to confront in order to checkmate her father's plans?

"She is going away, and I cannot tell where," he groaned. Then suddenly he sprang to his feet. Was he to confess himself beaten like this? Was he to accept her farewell thus tamely?

"No, never!" Fandor swore. "I mean to see Helene again. I will know, at any cost, what this oath she has given Fantômas means—this oath that condemns us to remain strangers to one another. Who can say this oath is not based on some scruple I might relieve her of?"

Then after a moment's thought he added: "And so Fantômas contemplates some new and infamous enterprise. For Helene to be attempting to counteract his designs, these must be signalized by special and exceptional atrocity. So be it! my duty is to join the battle too. My duty is to stand at her side in the struggle she is undertaking."

With a nervous step the young man began to pace his room, the wildest thoughts, the most contradictory surmises, surging through his brain. Helene was going to a foreign land, that was all he knew. She had confided no detail to him that might have made it possible to guess her intentions. Ought he not at once and above all things to take measures to join her?

"Tomorrow for regrets and complaints," Fandor swore to himself. "Today calls for action—and act I will."

With renewed energy he forced himself to forget for the time all the reasons for tender sorrow that still moved him. His mind must be free, unclouded, decisive.

"So then," he told himself, "Helene is going overseas. What conclusion to draw from the information?" But the indication was so vague that at first Fandor despaired of gaining any valuable hint from it.

"Ah, yes," he said regretfully, "Juve perhaps might be able to make something of this." But he could not go to look for Juve, as he instantly perceived with renewed vexation. A slave of duty, unable to transgress the legitimate orders given him by his superiors, Juve would be bound to arrest his friend at sight.

"So I must not go near him. I must keep out of his way," was the journalist's conclusion. But next minute he was smiling again. Was he not assured that Juve was hard on the track of Fantômas? Then what need to give him a piece of information he did not require? Surely Juve was capable of managing things for himself.

"*He* will be on the alert to arrest Fantômas. *I* propose, to begin with, to protect Helene and overthrow the scoundrel's plans. We two shall meet, never fear!"—and again he applied his mind to the solution of the apparently insoluble problem before him. Helene was departing overseas, but where was she bound for?

"Come now," he exhorted himself with the icy coldness of one who is resolved to impart no trace of passion into the investigation of a mystery. "Let's be logical. Logically Helene is bound to have written to me at the last available moment, when she was on the point of taking ship. Yes! No doubt of that, else she would have been afraid of my getting track of her. Ergo, either she is already on the road, or is just going to be."

At this point the young man granted himself the gratification of another cigarette. This simple piece of reasoning, this frank appeal to logic, seemed already to throw new light on the problems exercising his mind.

"On the road or on the point of going," he repeated. "In that case, it seems to me, there is a possible means of eliminating certain routes. I have merely to consult the list of vessels sailing"—and he ran to pick up the day's paper, which his concierge, an excellent housewife, had duly deposited on a table that same morning when she was "doing" his rooms.

"List of sailings… yes, here we are!"

But next moment his cheerfulness was dashed, the fact being that the list of names of liners preparing to leave port was a very long one. From Marseilles, from Cherbourg, from Bordeaux, from Le Havre, steamers were ready to put to sea. On which of them had Helene booked a passage? Some were bound for the Indies, others for the East, others again for the faraway African settlements or the remote parts of America.

"I cannot so much as make a guess," the journalist groaned. But, at the very same moment he was bewailing his inability to divine the destination Fantômas' daughter could be making for, he set to work to reread his fiancée's letter, wanting to make sure there was no phrase in it that might possibly reveal her plans. Suddenly his face paled, as he ejaculated in a shaking voice:

"Ah, by the by, what about the stamp?" And he fell to examining the envelope with a fascinated scrutiny. The postmark had, as often happens, been stamped on Helene's letter with heavy ink from a greasy pad. It had marked badly and was only partially legible.

"Date and hour of posting—I don't care a hang for them. But these letters—'Tr,' and after that 'tra' and again 'ue.' It's not a mark one usually comes across—the letter had not been posted in Paris; a Paris letter invariably bears the word 'Paris,' followed by the number of the arrondissement and underneath the name of the particular office."

The journalist broke off, panting, the veins on his forehead swollen under stress of his excitement. Surely he could manage to reconstitute the imperfect letters, and so discover where the letter had come from, when the information would be of such inestimable value to him. He devoted many minutes to the search, but could arrive at no reasonable conjecture. There was no post office he could think of with a name fitting in with the three or four letters the thick ink had alone marked legibly.

"I must check this with a list of offices," he thought, and took down a directory, which he examined minutely for anything likely to help him, but no name appeared to correspond.

"Nevertheless," he protested to himself, "I'm bound, surely, to get on the scent this way"—and he forced his jaded mind to continue the quest.

"Now where else can one post a letter? At a railway station? In a train?" But at this point he started up, swayed by the excitement of a new idea. In a train! Why, yes! All the important trains have postal vans on them, and some of these, attached to certain special expresses, have particular stamps of their own.

"Oh, I'm getting warm!" he cried, and, picking up the envelope again, examined it afresh. He thought:

"'Train,' why yes, that's obvious. 'Train' is the word cut down to 'Tr'—just the last three letters missing. But then what do these other letters mean—'tra' and 'ue'?"

Like a flash of lightning the explanation burst on him. "'Train Transatlantique,'" he shouted, almost stunned for a moment by the joy of the discovery. Here was the scent lying before him, clear and pretty well unmistakable. He knew perfectly well, in fact, that connecting Paris and Le Havre, in order to give passengers traveling by the great liners the opportunity of avoiding a troublesome transshipment from the railway station at Le Havre to the harbor, special trains are run, going direct to the quayside and known as transatlantic trains. Yes, it was all coming clear now. No doubt Helene had suspected the postmark might betray her. At the last moment, therefore, in the act of boarding the train, she had tossed the letter into the box, calculating that it would arrive after her boat had sailed.

But now Fandor knew the anguish of soul due to a fresh apprehension. "After her boat has sailed," he groaned. "So the letter comes to hand after she is gone. So then…"

Then he hesitated. Perhaps he was deceiving himself. With feverish hands he took up the paper again, and looked up the sailings under the heading "Le Havre." "Friday morning," he read, "at four a.m., the *Paris,* for New York."

The sheet dropped from his fingers. "Too late!" he cried, and was filled with an intense disappointment. He had pictured himself joining Helene, fighting by her side, working to relieve her scruples. But she was far away. Already at sea, she was dreaming of him.

"I am under a curse, it seems," the unhappy young man told himself.

His doubts were removed, at any rate. He had discovered the actual truth. Helene had embarked on the *Paris*. Everything went to prove it.

"Come, come. Courage!" he exhorted himself. "Perhaps all is not yet lost. I will start for New York by the next boat. Perhaps I shall come upon her there."

He was doing his best not to despair—not to abandon all hope. Yet was he not perhaps deceiving himself? Deeply dejected, he got up and went to a cupboard. Opening it, he took out the necessary tools, and at last freed himself from his handcuffs.

"Good!" he exclaimed, "and now I'm going to have some dinner and buy the evening papers. Possibly I shall find news about my escape in some of them."

He sallied into the street in such a condition of weariness and discouragement he never once remembered the risk he ran of some unlucky encounter. Newspapers in hand, he entered an unpretentious restaurant.

"Monsieur's order?" asked the waiter, and at the customer's request handed him the menu. Carelessly enough, for he was no gourmand, the journalist cast his eye down the long list of dishes.

"The fried trotters are first-rate tonight, but we have kidneys," the waiter was advising, when suddenly Fandor rapped out a big oath, and, paying no heed to the other customers finishing their dinners, and regardless of the waiter's terror, who had hurriedly sprung away from the table, he demanded:

"This is today's menu?"

"Why, yes! of course!"

"Thursday? Today's Thursday? Can't you answer? Today's Thursday?"

"Of course it is, sir!"

"Then pay yourself out of this! Good night to you!" And flinging down a note on the table, he took incontinently to his heels.

It was Thursday. The *Paris* was to put off on Friday at four in the morning; Fandor had mistaken the day!

"And I never remembered how, to save travelers from going aboard at night, the transatlantic trains *de luxe* generally start in good time to arrive at the quay before nightfall. Yes, Helene is on board the *Paris*. She took train this morning about eleven—later perhaps. Why, the *Paris* is still in harbor at Le Havre."

Dashing home, he pitched clothes and toilet articles into a suitcase, collected all the money he could lay hands on, and went down into the street again.

"Gare Saint-Lazare!" he ordered the driver.

But, alas, a fresh disappointment awaited him at the station. The first train for Le Havre reached there well after the *Paris* was due to sail—in fact, after six o'clock.

*   *   *   *   *

For some minutes Jerome Fandor felt literally stunned by the staggering blow. So fully persuaded had he been that he would be able to overtake Helene that his disappointment was indeed cruel on finding himself up against this uncompromising material fact. There was no train—and there was an end of it. Still, the young man was too energetic, too well used to fight and overcome fate to remain for long in this state of mental prostration. Soon he pulled himself together.

"There's no other train? Well, there's always a road leads to Le Havre, eh?" The idea of a journey by motorcar had naturally enough occurred to him.

"It's as simple as A B C!" he laughed. "A couple of hundred kilometers is no great distance."

But next minute he sang a different song. No, of course there was nothing impossible about getting to Le Havre by car before the steamer sailed, but there had to be a car—and Jerome Fandor did not possess one.

"Damn it!" was the journalist's simple comment as, suitcase in hand, he took a seat in the Café Terminus. The waiter came up.

"Monsieur's orders?" the man inquired.

"A forty horsepower," was the unexpected reply. But no sooner said than the journalist burst out laughing at his own silliness.

"A glass of beer," he corrected, "and a sandwich."

Fatigue could get little or no hold on the young man, but all the same he was for once feeling pretty well at the end of his tether, and it was no time to do anything injudicious and needlessly run the risk of a collapse.

"Yes, I ought to have a forty horsepower," Fandor went on to himself, "but I can't see how I'm going to get one. Apply to the swell drivers on the rank by the Opera House? Hmm! too dangerous! If they are looking out for me, the place is watched to a certainty. Then their charges are ruinous, these fellows, and I'm bound to be careful with the small bit of money I have in hand." This last argument was very much to the point. For weeks now he had not drawn a centime at the pay office of his paper, *La Capitale,* and the state of his finances was far from brilliant. Pulling out his pocketbook, he counted over the contents.

"Eight… nine… ten… eleven hundred francs! I'm no Rothschild. And I can hardly dip very deep into this capital just when I'm off to the United States. A bad job, not a doubt of it!"

Mentally he reckoned up the fare a chauffeur would ask him. At the lowest estimate he must expect an outlay of four hundred francs with another hundred for a *pourboire.* "And even then," he concluded ruefully, "I'm not sure of getting hold of a car."

Straight before him, meantime, the great clock of the Gare Saint-Lazare was ticking on inexorably, each little jerk forward of the hands seeming to strike a blow on his heart. Altogether he was in a pretty fix!

"Ten o'clock very soon," he groaned, "and I ought to be at Le Havre by three at latest. Hmm! It's about time to do something definite. Certainly 200 kilometers is nothing out of the way, but we must allow for breakdowns and punctures."

Like all experienced drivers Fandor never compared the theoretical speed of cars with the actual speed they can keep up overall, stoppages included.

"No," he reiterated, "I have not a second to waste." Then, springing to his feet: "And I'm not going to waste one! To work! The luck's on my side. After all, what do I risk? After the crime I am accused of, it would be no more than a peccadillo!" Had the journalist already conceived a feasible scheme, then? With a brisk step Fandor left the terminus and made for the Madeleine. Passing that fine building, he took a seat outside a fashionable restaurant at the upper end of the Rue Royale.

"An up-to-date crowd," he sized up the customers. "Wealthy young men, and, what's better, dealers in motorcars. It will be the devil's own luck if I don't carry out my little plan." And this time addressing the waiter who presently appeared with a grand air, and setting down his suitcase well in view, he ordered a cocktail, and: "Hurry up!" he added. "I'm in a hurry. I've a long way to go."

Gulping down the potent beverage he proceeded to take careful stock of the row of automobiles standing before the café.

"How about that one?" he asked himself. "Hmm! a good make—but one never knows what condition it may be in! That other there? First-rate machine—but there's only one spare wheel. Ah! the last in the line, there's what I like. For the price I'm going to pay, I can always treat myself." And he examined more minutely the car that had attracted his attention. Undoubtedly it was a very fine car, built both for speed and durability, with an engine that should knock off its eighty an hour without pressing. Moreover, it was fitted superbly.

"A perfect beauty," Fandor decided. "And now for our little gamble," he added, his heart, if the truth be told, beginning to thump hard. The fact is he had not the faintest notion who the car in question belonged to. He had quite made up his mind to steal it—or, more strictly speaking, to borrow it, for he quite intended to restore it to its owner—but he wondered if this bold stroke was really going to come off. A single slip, a single silly blunder might spoil everything and lead to an arrest that would be the more disastrous, as it would definitely stop his leaving Paris.

"Supposing the owner is known to the doorkeeper, I am

done for right away," he thought. "Supposing by any chance the fellow has removed some electric gadget or other, I am just as badly off. Bah! Nothing ventured, nothing gained—and I have no car of my own."

He hailed the doorkeeper in an authoritative tone.

"Yes, sir!"

"Just put my suitcase in the car."

"Which car, sir?"

"The last in the line, my lad, as I was the last to arrive."

It was now or never; but the man obeyed without a word.

"Can one wonder after this," thought Fandor, "that motor-cars get stolen by the dozen! I'll wager the young fellow is going to open the door for me."

He paid for his drink and, getting up, marched off in the wake of the obliging official, who, as he expected, threw open the door of the car.

"Here's something for yourself"—and Fandor dropped a handsome tip in the man's hand. But, in the very act of doing so, he felt himself turn pale.

"No luck!" he muttered. "Just as I thought—the key has been removed from the starting-up gear on the splashboard." His brain reeled with the giddy rush of his thoughts. At all costs, he *must* get started now; but how to do it without this confounded thing necessary to make contact.

To gain time, he wrapped the rug carefully round his knees. A scrap of metal—all he needed was a scrap of metal, a bit of old iron or anything, and instinctively he felt in his pocket, while the doorkeeper stood by, bowing obsequiously.

"I've got five seconds to find—I don't know what!" he told himself. But it took him less than that time to decide on his course of action. His fingers, groping in his waistcoat pocket, had touched one of those brass pencil cases often given away gratis as an advertisement. It might suffice if only the slot or keyhole in the starting-gear was approximately of the same bore.

"I've lost my starting-key," he said casually, turning to the doorkeeper, "but this will do instead"—and he applied the pencil case to the aperture in the starting-gear with a hand that never shook, though feeling like a gambler throwing his last desperate stake.

Would it fit? It did, and instantly the starting dynamo began to hum, while in another moment the main motor followed suit in a louder key.

"Saved!" Fandor ejaculated, and threw in the clutch.

But, just as he was pulling out from the line of stationary cars, a tall young man suddenly issued from the café and halted thunderstruck in the doorway.

"The owner!" thought Fandor, but, mastering his panic, he threw back a jeering: "Too late, sir!"—and, swerving round the refuge to his left, taking the nearest corner with the adroitness of a professional, he was off full speed ahead. Yes, too late in all conscience! By the time the unfortunate victim had given the alarm, he would be far enough away. Moreover, he took the precaution to make a show of following the Rue de Rivoli in the direction of Vincennes, then with a sharp turn by the Tuileries to double back along the quays, and so into the road for Mantes, direction Le Havre.

"Now let 'em look for me," grinned Fandor. "They'll never catch me. Oh, Helene, will you ever know what I'm doing for you?"

However, this was no moment for sentimental reflections. The time had flown swiftly. It was now close on midnight, and it was only barely possible to reach Le Havre before the steamer sailed.

"Tomorrow for useless dreams," he told himself. "Now to go ahead, and at a tidy rate!"

But Fandor's conception of a "tidy rate" was nothing less than a wild stampede that turned the head giddy. A driver tried and trained, at once cautious and daring, knowing all the ticklish places on the road, but on straight stretches affording extended views ahead never hesitating to let her rip at the most frantic speeds, he simply devoured the distance, his wheels covering the kilometers with an undeviating regularity. He passed Nantes, Bonnières, Gaillon, dashed through Rouen like a thunderbolt, and half-past two had not struck as he drew near the outer suburbs of Le Havre.

"Punctual on the clock," he laughed to himself, "and now let's slow down and drive like a man of sense"—and ten minutes after he pulled up in the central square of the Norman capital.

"Yes, upon my word," he chuckled, "there's a police station close by. I could not wish anything better," and, stopping his engine, he took a letter-card from his pocket and scribbled a few hasty lines.

> Sir,—I have been compelled by imperative motives to steal your car at the door of a café. I am taking the necessary steps to have it returned to you with the least possible delay. On the other hand, as my action shows a neglect of the most elementary courtesy, I hold myself at your disposal—or, rather, I shall do so on my return to Paris—to offer you whatever satisfaction you may deem adequate. We can fight—it is for you to choose—with revolver, big gun, or *mitrailleuse*—or enjoy a good dinner together! To conclude, should you consider you have a right to compensation—petrol consumed, wear and tear of tires—I undertake to fix the amount at a liberal figure. If you care to receive such payment, and will present the blank check endorsed herewith at the pay office of my paper, *La Capitale*, I have no doubt the manager will honor it. My signature is not unknown.
>
> JEROME FANDOR.

"There!" he ejaculated. "Now for a word or two of postscript, just to ease my conscience, and that will be all"—and he wrote without a smile:

> P.S.—Your engine is a beauty, but your oil supply wants regulating. Shorten the stroke of your pump by a tenth. Yours sincerely.

"The face the fellow will pull," spluttered the journalist, taken with a fit of uncontrollable laughter. "Bah! If he's a gentleman, he'll be amused at the little adventure"—and by way of finishing off his queer letter, he signed a blank check and, slipping it into the letter-card, stuck down the edges.

"Excellent!" he chuckled. "And now for the gentleman's address. "Examining the plate which every motor is bound by law to bear, he copied the name, "Hervé de Chancelieu," and the address, "3 Avenue du Bois."

"So, ho!" he thought, "he must be a rich man! But there, what matter?"—and he tossed his missive into a mailbox close by.

"And now," he proceeded, "for the garage. Tomorrow, when they find I don't come back, they'll write to the owner, who will by then have my letter. Not a chance of their doing anything else, and no fear, if they do act so, of my movements being traced too quickly. Fact is one must think of every possibility nowadays with this confounded wireless. I've no mind to be arrested on board."

In another quarter of an hour Fandor was free to do whatever he chose. He had left the car at the best garage in Le Havre, one he had long been familiar with, taking care to have it put in a locked compartment, in other words, safe from any possibility of damage.

"And now for the *Paris!*" Making for the outer harbor, he hired a boat and was rowed across to the wharf where the floating giant still lay moored.

"Oh, to think," sighed the young man, "that Helene is on board; to think she is asleep in one of those staterooms without a suspicion I am here!"

But he had to deny himself all unpractical reflections. The moment of departure was approaching, and both the wharf and the wide decks of the huge vessel were crowded with a hurrying mass of men. Passengers' luggage brought by the last train was being got aboard. The last consignments of provisions required by this floating city were piled on the quay and the company's men were carrying them in hot haste across the narrow gangways. All this amid the puffing of steam-cranes, the screech of windlasses, the shouts of the officers of the ship, already busy with preparations for casting off.

"I'm only just in time," thought Fandor. "In another ten minutes they would have refused to take me, I suppose."

He stepped up to an official stationed at the end of a gangway connecting ship and shore.

"To take a ticket?" he asked.

"A ticket!" cried the man in a startled voice. "A ticket for where?"

"For New York," was the journalist's unperturbed reply.

"But they don't issue tickets here. They don't issue anymore tickets. All the places are booked in advance."

"I'm quite aware of that, my good man, but I'm also aware of this: there are always passengers turning up at the last moment. Can't I speak to the purser on board?"

"But—"

"Here's a couple of louis for you."

"Hmm!—fact is… What class when you are on board?"

"Third," said Fandor unhesitatingly.

"Third! It's a third-class passenger asks… Well, of all the impudence."

"Call it fifteen louis for yourself," announced Fandor in the same quiet tone as before.

"Say, if you offered me a thousand francs…"

"I couldn't do it."

"If you did, I couldn't take it to go and worry the purser for a 'third-class.'"

"Why?"

"Because he'd tell me, when a fellow of your sort comes asking a passage at the last minute, it's best to give a word to the police. You understand me?"

"Why, certainly!"

"Then take yourself off!"

There was no more to be said. As a matter of fact Fandor had all along been very doubtful of the reception he would get, for he showed no trace of surprise at this curt dismissal. He just grumbled as he made off:

"He takes me for a deserter or an international crook, perhaps. Quite naturally, too. But I was bound to try my luck. As the fellow won't let me on board, why, what odds does it make his taking it into his head I'm a bad lot?"

It was now half-past three, and suddenly the steamer's siren sounded.

"That means she's off," thought the disappointed Fandor. "In five minutes they'll be casting off the ropes and hauling in the gangways. Time to roll a cigarette, anyway."

Then, calmly as ever, after performing that operation, he removed his hat, stripped off coat and waistcoat, and took off his collar.

"So there we are!" he observed. "Now I look like a man of his hands, manager of a third-rate hotel or something of that sort."

His reflections were cut short by another blast of the siren.

"Good!" said our hero. "Stand by!"

Along the bulwarks crowded a throng of passengers, still awake for all the lateness of the hour. The company house-flag was broken at the masthead.

"Haul away gangways!" shouted a voice.

Then in a flash, quitting the patch of shadow where he was hiding, Fandor dashed up to the men standing by to drag ashore the fragile bridge of planks still joining the vessel with the wharf.

"Stop! stop!" he bellowed. "Another piece of luggage to go aboard! Cabin 137"—and he shot by. In vain they tried to seize him; in vain a sailor barred his way; jumping lightly on one side, Fandor dodged the man, and plunged down the main companion leading to the first-class quarters.

"Stop him!" cried a chorus of voices. Easy to say that, but already the flying figure had darted down an alleyway, sprung up another stairway, and come out again on deck. In the hurry of departure, when over two thousand people, all more or less excited, are elbowing each other, how should anybody worry about him?

The captain, turning to another officer, growled:

"Passenger aboard us without a ticket, by God! Damn the fellow! He's made good anyway. You'll have him hunted down tomorrow, eh? and clap him on a job?"—and the great man troubled his head no further about such a trifle. Every time a big liner crosses the Atlantic, are there not poor devils who manage in this fashion to slip on board and secure a free passage? And does not a harsh law in these cases authorize ships' captains to utilize the labor of these undesirables in the cuddies and storerooms?

It is even laid down that on making land the poor wretches are not to be allowed to disembark. To punish their audacity, the company conveys them back again to the port from which they set sail.

But for the moment Fandor was not so much as dreaming of coming back. Down in the tweendecks, among the unfortunate crowd of emigrants, he was now laughing triumphantly to himself. The *Paris* was sailing, was actually underway. What did aught else matter? Over and over again he kept repeating:

"Am I not aboard the same ship as Helene?"

9. Good Old Juve!

"Is she going to take root there, I wonder? I don't know if *she's* cold or not, but *I'm* shivering worse every minute!" And Juve, if not quite so desperately chilled as he made out, was indulging in an unbroken string of curses. In front of him, her elbows still resting on the parapet overlooking the river, Lady Beltham stood awaiting something or somebody—he did not know what or whom.

"It's not common sense!" resumed the police officer after a few more minutes. "There she stands staring at the water. Thanks to me, she's just come out of it. Seems to me she must know what it's made of, eh?"

He shrugged, and made a movement as if to go on his way, but, of course, never stirred from his corner. Here was one of those detectives who would choose rather to be killed than abandon a scent once started. But in this case his patience was to be sorely tried, for it was a full hour before Lady Beltham, bending pensively over the foaming waters, at last woke from her long fit of abstraction.

Not far off was a street lamp, and, never suspecting she was the object of so strict a watch, she moved directly into the circle of light.

"Poor woman!" Juve could not help exclaiming. For a moment he had seen the beautiful face clearly, and, in spite of himself, he was touched with pity. Such an agony of distress was depicted on her pure, delicate features that, short of possessing no heart at all, a man could not fail to be strongly moved by the sight.

"She is no miscreant," thought Juve, "only a woman who loves. True, she loves the most atrocious of villains, but can she command her passion?"

Then, foregoing these sentimental reflections, the detective muttered:

"But where is she off to now? Surely she cannot dream of calling anywhere in the state she is in?"

This, indeed, was pretty obvious. After the involuntary bath Lady Beltham had just taken, she could not even have passed through any frequented street without attracting the attention of passersby. Nor, in fact, did Fantômas' partner seem to intend anything of the kind. Quitting the quay, she was making for the maze of ill-famed alleys that border on the Rue de la Harpe.

"There's plenty of shady resorts thereabouts," thought Juve, "but I can't believe she would dare to visit one of them."

But suddenly he felt both amazed and anxious. At the door of a shabby café stood a superb automobile, and Lady Beltham was making directly for it.

"Very good!" the police officer observed to himself. "Madam has been paying a visit to Fantômas' underwater dwelling, and her car is waiting for her. Upon my word! I only see one difficulty, and that is, how the devil I'm going to shadow her any farther."

Indeed, it appeared highly improbable that the detective could follow up successfully the swift car the lady had at her disposal. To stop a cab in the state he was in would have been to the last degree imprudent. No driver would have consented to take a fare of such dubious respectability. Yet how otherwise procure the conveyance he must have?

"But it would be just too silly to be thrown out now!" growled the detective. Obviously any piece of trickery such as Fandor was going to indulge in a few hours later—collaring, that is to say, a car at the door of a café—could never commend itself to the honest police officer. While the journalist, with his easygoing ways, was always ready to run a perilous risk, Juve, for his part, as a responsible official, could not possibly adopt such methods. He growled:

"And to think I am within a yard or two of the Prefecture of Police, where I could find all the chauffeurs ever I wanted!"

But this very thought was to end his embarrassment. Hardly had he pronounced the words before a brilliant notion occurred to him.

"After all, what is it I require?" he asked. "Why, just ten minutes' grace, that's all. Unless Lady Beltham's car were to start off with her at once, I should have time to recover my clothes on the quay in front and get myself another car."

He had taken hiding in an entry leading to a dubious-looking tavern while Lady Beltham was engaged with her chauffeur, apparently giving him a host of explanations.

"Then," he went on, as he watched the lady get in, "if the car starts off, as is likely, in my direction, I think I may make sure of scoring my point."

Yes, Juve's mind was just as fertile in expedients as Fandor's. The ruse for which he was claiming success was admirably thought out. A few minutes more and Lady Beltham's car was passing the spot where he stood, going at the reduced speed necessitated by the narrowness of the lane. Juve seized the opportunity to spring on to the petrol tank, slung under the back axle, and cling on behind.

"Quick! I must be quick," he muttered. "Passersby might see me."

Already the car, as it swung round on to the quay, was gathering speed. But Juve cared nothing for that. With a suppleness of limb hardly to be expected of a man of his age he succeeded in stooping over and unscrewing the stopper of the tank. At once the pressure fell, and the petrol was no longer forced up to the carburetor. The engine began to misfire, and ended by stopping altogether. By that time, of course, Juve was far enough away. The instant he held the brass stopper in his fingers he had dropped to earth.

"There!" he muttered. "Having once started, they'll feel quite sure the stopper's not far off, and so the chauffeur will set to work hunting for it everywhere. That gives me just the time needful to do what I've got to do. When I'm ready—well, I'll see to it that the stopper's found all right—and there you are!"

It was, indeed, an admirable bit of contriving. Could Lady Beltham's driver come to any conclusion save one? Having once started, and that without any difficulty, he could not for a moment suppose the stopper he found missing had been stolen beforehand. On the contrary, he was almost bound to believe it had come unscrewed *en route*.

Meantime, Juve, for all he imagined he had plenty of time, set off at a run, and reached the Prefecture panting for breath. Over there, far from going upstairs to the official quarters, he hurried to the covered galleries where the service cars stand ready for all emergencies.

"A driver?" he panted, and "Here!" came a voice in instant response.

"Off with you, my man!"

"But who are you?"

"Juve!"

"Monsieur Juve? Oh! that's another thing. And where to?"

"Pont du Châtelet first."

"And then?"

"Can't say."

"Good!" said the fellow. "With you I don't care a hang, Monsieur Juve. To the other end of the world, if you like."

"Not so far as that, I hope."

"I'm always good for a couple of hundred kilometers."

"Not so far as that even. I've reason to think…"

Still talking, the driver had got underway. The man had been a bicycle agent, and, when appointed an official driver to the police, had fancied himself as good as gazetted Marshal of France! Starting off with a swing, running up the speeds with a masterly touch Fandor would have appreciated, he was off and away at a record pace.

"Pont du Châtelet, you said?"

"Yes, that's the place. My coat and waistcoat, my boots, all my traps ought to be there still"—and it was with no little satisfaction he resumed possession of his warm, dry clothes and waved to the driver to go on.

"Go easy," he ordered, "from now; but speed up again if I give you the word." Gesturing his orders to the driver, he steered his vehicle back into the lane where he had left Lady Beltham's own car. As he approached, he could see the unfortunate chauffeur searching, light in hand, the gutters and narrow pavements of the alley.

"Poor devil!" he chuckled. "How he'd be cursing me if he knew."

He quickened up speed, and, as he passed the man, simply tossed the metal stopper on the ground.

"Go ahead!" he directed his driver. "Take a turn to the left and stop at the corner of the first cross street."

Ten minutes afterwards the police officer was still laughing. Hearing the stopper fall, Lady Beltham's chauffeur, of course, soon found his property, which he supposed had been struck by the wheel of the car that had just gone by. Thereupon, to pick up the stopper, put it back in place, give two or three strokes of the pump to restore the proper pressure, and start afresh was the work of a few seconds.

"So there," observed Juve to himself, lying back comfortably in his own conveyance, as he followed less than a hundred yards behind that of Lady Beltham, "there we see another good reason for never using a tank under pressure. If only Fantômas kept up-to-date machines with exhaust action, I could never have…"

But there he stopped. Quickening up as he drove up the Champs-Élysées, the driver of the car the detective was shadowing had wheeled into the Place de l'Étoile, circled the Arc de Triomphe, and now turned with little diminished speed down the Avenue de la Grande Armée.

"Where is he off to?" Juve asked himself. "Are we going to leave Paris altogether?"

It seemed like it, for the car shot past the Barrière du Roule, never stopping to make its declaration of petrol in hand.

"Oh, ho!" growled Juve. "So we're making for the country, are we? Evidently Lady Beltham doesn't intend to return yet awhile, as she is not taking a way-leave for petrol."

A few minutes more and the much-tried detective was to experience a still greater surprise. After reaching the Défense and circling the *rond-point*, the car had struck off for Nanterre, and was now pulling up at Bougival for fresh supplies. The road was straight just here, and Juve had had time to have his own car stopped.

"Halt at that petrol dealer there," he ordered, "as soon as the other car has gone on again." And, ten minutes afterwards, the detective was questioning the startled tradesman.

"Criminal Department duty. There's my card. Now, how much petrol did you sell that car just gone?"

"Fifty liters, sir."

"They didn't tell you where they were bound?"

"Why, yes, they did. Le Havre it was. The chauffeur asked me which was the best route to Rouen, by the upper road or the lower."

"God Almighty!" thundered Juve. "Going to Le Havre!"

He could not believe his ears. What in the devil's name was Lady Beltham after doing at Le Havre? At a venture he questioned further:

"You know no other details? Be careful, the matter is serious."

"Why, no, sir! I'm telling you everything I know. I did ask the chauffeur if it was to Le Havre itself, to the town itself, he was going, and he told me straight: 'Yes, right into the town. I'm to stop at the Yacht Basin. My word! but it ain't no sort of a life traveling all night like this without a word of warning aforehand. I've been on my rank a week, but, if there's many jobs going such as this here, I shan't have much rest, I shan't.'"

"And you advised him which road?"

"Upper road."

"Good. Thank you." And Juve sprang back into his conveyance.

"Objective: Le Havre. Drive your fastest! Upper road!"

"I see," said the man. "Quick's the word, eh?"

"First-rate! Now I'm going to have a nap as we go along. Oh, of course there'll be a bit of a bonus if we reach the Yacht Basin before the others. And, of course again, you must wake me if the smallest thing occurs out of the common."

But, as a fact, Juve was not once roused throughout the long journey, not the smallest hindrance interrupting their progress. The police officer, worn out with fatigue, had hardly shut his eyes before he found himself overmastered by one of those deep sleeps that completely benumb all faculties of the mind. He had just time to reflect:

"A queer go this! I'm under orders to arrest Fandor, and it's Lady Beltham I'm going after. Hmm! A pretty welcome I shall have when I get back! And, then, it's forbidden to take service cars without an order signed by Monsieur Havard. Yes, I shall have a claim to the warmest sympathy if I fail to make some sensational discoveries."

But, as a fact, the police officer was destined to make just such a sensational discovery at the very instant of opening his eyes. Albeit he had slept soundly, in complete unconsciousness, all the time the car was in motion, Juve awoke entirely fit and alert as the vehicle, on slowing down, bumped over the stone setts of the Rue de Paris at Le Havre.

"There already!" he thought, and was just going to leave his seat when he overheard his chauffeur questioning a man in the street, a sailor:

"Hi! my man! The Yacht Basin, if you please."

"Straight before you, matey. D'you see that craft there? She's just going to put out. Is it the lady you're bringing?"

Juve was like to cry out with amazement. His car was being mistaken for "the lady's"—and what lady could that be if not Lady Beltham? So she was to embark on a pleasure yacht, it seemed? So, then, she was expected?

And at that instant the great detective gave fresh proof of his bold initiative. Chance no doubt had served him well, but now he was going to turn that chance to his own still greater advantage. Before his chauffeur found time to answer, Juve had his plan cut and dried.

"Hi! there, my man!" he accosted the sailor. "It is I, and not the lady. Pray, since when is it the right thing to talk of passengers in that fashion to strangers?"

He saw the man's face blanch, and went on in the same tone:

"D'you suppose you're obeying orders in chattering like that? D'you think *he'd* be pleased?"

Juve was speaking almost at random. This individual whose

displeasure he took for granted, did he indeed suspect who it might be? Dare he make a guess at his identity? Lady Beltham was expected. True, but might not the Englishwoman likely enough be joining a pleasure party on a cruise without *his* being there—*he*, the Ever-Elusive?

Meantime the man standing there, the target of these hard sayings had suddenly gone white as paper. Juve saw his advantage, and pursued relentlessly:

"So you've nothing to say, no excuse to make? You'd rather I informed *him* of the way you carry out his orders?"

"Oh, for pity's sake don't! He'd hang me soon as ever we were at sea!"

"Very good!" cut in Juve sharply. "Come along and have a glass."

"But my orders—"

"To wait for the lady, eh?"

"Yes, to see her aboard the *Lotus*."

"Well, we shall be back in time, if we look sharp. Besides, I have other orders to give you. See here! Get into the car."

"Get in?"

"Yes, with me. Now, in with you! Hmm! You're not over-smart at obeying orders, my fine fellow!"—and Juve gave a short laugh that by no means indicated the excitement he felt. What sort of new adventure was this now beginning? Barely arrived at Le Havre, already he felt a sinister presentiment of Fantômas' presence. Yet how could the Lord of Terror be there when but a few hours before he was still in Paris? If Lady Beltham had visited the underwater dwelling, did that mean she was by way of bidding him goodbye? Had Fantômas, leaving the strange abode, likewise set off by road for the Norman capital? Then was it to inform him of the explosion that had destroyed his extraordinary refuge that Lady Beltham had in *her* turn left Paris?

"Hmm! The last supposition is, at any rate, baseless," thought Juve. "If she had come on the spur of the moment, they would not be expecting her, as they seem to be."

However, it was no time to be puzzling out all these bewildering mysteries. The sailor was now seated beside him in the car, and Juve bent forward and spoke in an undertone to his driver:

"Straight ahead, and drive fast. Choose quiet streets. Take the Boulevard Maritime, if needs must—there's nobody there at this hour of the night."

Then, facing round on his companion the sailor, he laid a hand on his shoulder, and:

"Now," he said, "cards on the table!"

"What d'ya mean?" cried the fellow, with a start.

"What I say! Do you know who I am?"

"Why... a..."

"Yes, and here's my name: Juve—inspector at the Criminal Bureau."

"Juve! Juve!" stammered the sailor.

"Yes, Juve in person. And Juve bids you listen carefully to what he says."

"But I've done nothing. But—"

"Hush! Now listen, either you keep faith with your master, and I arrest you *instanter*— Oh, yes! you can see I know your record, eh?"

Juve was speaking purely at a venture, but there was not much chance of error. Anyone in Fantômas' service was pretty well sure to be a scoundrel.

"Or," he proceeded, "you don't stick to him, and help me in what I'm after. In that case I give you my word I'll let you bunk it at the first opportunity. Made up your mind?"

"But what d'you want me to do?" queried the mariner, his teeth chattering in absolute terror.

The police officer put on his mildest voice to reply:

"What do I want you to do? That's soon answered. I simply want you to help me get aboard the *Lotus* without anybody being the wiser."

10. A Vision of Beauty

"Sir, you astound me—simply astound."

"I know I do, and I am sorry for it. But what would you have? It's no fault of mine."

"Upon my word, sir, I really don't know what to say."

"Oh, come!"

"And at this moment I'm asking myself just what I ought to do."

"But, Mr. Purser, you have no choice"—and Fandor went off in a hearty peal of laughter. The purser of the *Paris* was speaking nothing but the truth when he frankly confessed himself bewildered, astounded. Half an hour before, as he was fixing up the final arrangement for the dance to be given on board, and now due to begin in a few minutes' time, he had been informed by the chief steward that an emigrant passenger insisted on seeing him.

"Tell him to go to the devil!" he had protested.

"I've done my best, sir, but…"

"I'm busy settling about the cotillion. Tell him I'll talk to him tomorrow."

But at that moment the door of the purser's cabin burst open, and Fandor appeared.

"Ever so sorry to disturb you, my dear sir," he began, with his own inimitable self-assurance. "But the matter is urgent. It is just because of the ball I must ask you to hear me."

Thereupon, taking advantage of the other's bewilderment, with a peremptory wave of the hand the journalist dismissed the chief steward, and went on:

"You know my name, perhaps? Jerome Fandor, reporter on the staff of *La Capitale*. At this present moment a warrant of arrest is out against me. Into the bargain, I boarded the *Paris* by fraud, without even a ticket to show!"

After that the two men got into talk. The arrangements for the dance were in a fair way to go askew, but the purser let them slide. Breathlessly he listened, divided between admiration and stupefaction, to what Fandor thought good to tell him of his adventures.

"You see," the young man concluded, "Helene, the young lady I want to get in touch with, has no doubt decided to appear at this function. She is bound to do so under penalty of attracting notice. Besides, not knowing I am on board, it is obvious she has no motive to induce her to keep hidden. In one word, I must attend the dance myself. I could not, therefore, make any longer delay in coming to you, sir, and making my position clear." And then, feeling the purser was more than half won over—for Fandor had an ingratiating way with him, and well knew how to gain over people, when needful, to his side—he continued:

"No, you have no choice, my dear sir! Either you've got to string me up here and now on the main yard—which would be highly regrettable—or clap me in irons—which would be quite illegal—*or* help me get hold of a dress suit. Now come, isn't the last alternative the best?"

Finally, never leaving the purser a chance to reply, Fandor wound up:

"Needless to add, of course, I am quite ready, if you wish, to pay you my passage by check. I hope you will trust me so far, won't you? Moreover, when we get to New York, if nothing turns up, you will always be at liberty to hand me over to the American authorities. In any case, I have no passport."

"Sir," replied the purser, "your case is unheard of. No matter. To avoid a scandal—"

"You agree to do what I ask you?"

"On condition you pledge your word to obey my orders."

"Good Lord! What orders?"

"To stay in the cabin I am going to assign you. If it should seem necessary to put you—"

"Under arrest? So be it. You have my word of honor, and I'm quite sure I shall not force you to take stern measures."

"So am I convinced, Monsieur Fandor, I shall not have to treat you harshly. But—well, you've had a stroke of luck in coming across one of your readers and admirers."

Fandor bowed and said no more. It was certainly a true piece of luck, but it must be admitted the journalist had counted on it. Is it not, indeed, one of the great satisfactions of the author and journalist to know how he possesses up and down the world a host of unknown friends? Fandor quite realized his own popularity. He was no less aware of the fact that if the official authorities, for the moment exhibiting an intentional blindness, still persisted in regarding him as a criminal, the public, more clear-sighted and more generous, looked upon him as a hero.

Was it, then, to be wondered at if the purser of the *Paris* had been won over as he listened to the young man's story? Bending over his desk, the officer was now engaged in scribbling sundry orders to his subordinates.

"You shall have stateroom No. 3, on the promenade deck. For the moment it is unoccupied. I don't enter you under your own name, eh?"

"Good Lord, no! Put—put 'Jean Marmont, merchant.'"

"I take you."

"And about the dress clothes?"

"True, you were bound to remember that. Well, we're about the same build. I've got a stock of shore-going things I use when the ship is in dock. I'll send you what you'll need."

"Indeed, sir, I have no words left to thank you, no way of showing my gratitude."

"Oh, but you have," returned the officer gravely, while a look of melancholy veiled his features. "You can do so easily. Arrest Fantômas. Help Juve to arrest him. My brother was first officer aboard the *Gigantic*. He lost his life in the catastrophe."

Without a word Fandor wrung the other's hand. Alas! how often had he met, like this, on his way through life strangers who besought him to avenge them on the ill-omened Torturer! And with what emotion he would press the hands offered him.

"Sir," stammered the journalist, his feelings touched, "my life is vowed to this work of justice."

He could see tears standing in the purser's eyes, and, bowing once more, left the cabin.

Twenty minutes later, in the stateroom that had been put at his disposal, Fandor was completing his preparations to attend the dance. Again his mind was agitated by ever-fresh anxiety—doubts and uncertainties that never ceased tormenting him. Had he not acted wrongly in boarding the ship? Was it really true that Helene would appear at the dance? They are veritable floating cities, these gigantic transatlantic liners, carrying thousands of passengers across the seas, and, in spite of storms and tempests, providing them with all the luxury and comfort of the finest hotels. Was it not quite possible Helene might see fit not to take part in the entertainment? He knew his fiancée never suffered from seasickness. Moreover, the weather was calm, and the great vessel rode smoothly over the waves. But were there not many other reasons that might confine Fantômas' daughter to her cabin?

"In truth," Fandor owned to himself, "I cannot tell why, but my mind is not at ease. I am afraid of I know not what."

He knotted his tie with a trembling hand. Into his trousers pocket he slipped his Browning, after carefully examining the chambers.

"Now I am ready," he assured himself. "In another quarter of an hour I shall make for the main saloon."

He smoked a cigarette as he counted the minutes, listening meantime to the distant echo of the dance tunes that reached him along the alleyway. It was the first dance given since the ship had sailed, and on this fine night, there was sure to be an exceptionally brilliant function. In fact, during the three days they had been at sea the passengers, according to their divers predilections, had struck up many friendships.

"Now for it!" Fandor suddenly reminded himself. "The time is come. Am I going to see her or no?"

He felt his heart thumping against his ribs with mingled excitement and hope. Yes, surely he was going to see Helene, to win a look from her to reward his daring and his untamable energy. He was confident that, knowing him to be near her, ready to share her dangers, to second her efforts with blind devotion, to do her will, Helene would be happy and reassured and strengthened.

Fandor left his stateroom, but so numerous were the passengers that nobody seemed surprised to see him. Nobody, indeed, had encountered him so far, those traveling first class being little in the habit of visiting the steerage.

"Going capitally!" the journalist thought. "I shall lose myself in the crowd and watch the guests as they arrive. I shall see her! Indeed I shall!"

The doors of the main saloon stood open. Chairs, tables, all the elegant furniture, had been removed, and in the vast free space a throng of dancers moved rhythmically to the strains of one of the ship's bands.

"Now for it!" the young man was telling himself when next moment, within a yard or two of him, he caught sight of a ship's officer evidently watching him suspiciously.

"Never mind," thought the intruder. "Let's give him a smile to reassure him." But hardly had his lips curved in an ingratiating grin when a gasp of surprise rose in his throat. He was hardly inside the saloon when a hush fell on the company. All were gathering round a piano at which a woman stood ready to sing. His eyes had not yet fallen on the performer when he heard her voice, and knew it instantly.

"It is Helene!" he cried, and would have fallen but for the support afforded by the nearest bulkhead. Yes, she was the singer, and she was singing divinely an Italian aria, of a melancholy, almost mournful, cast, but into which she breathed all the splendor of her soul and spirit.

The young man turned in her direction, but dared not for the moment look at her. It called for an effort, even when the audience broke into a salvo of enthusiastic plaudits, to fix his eyes on his fiancée and drink in the pure vision of beauty and charm that met his gaze. Wearing a plain, close-fitting frock of crêpe de Chine, at once modest, elegant, and graceful, Helene, the intrepid Helene, had the air of some innocent and timid schoolgirl. Who would ever have guessed in her the unhappy daughter of the dastardly criminal, the mere utterance of whose name would have blanched the cheeks of all that crowd pressing forward to congratulate her?

But presently it seemed as though his gaze possessed some magnetic power. Hardly had it fallen on the girl before she turned her great eyes upon him. And instantly her face paled—paled with mingled pleasure and pain, but with no touch of surprise. Fandor was quite near, almost at her side, ready to protect her. Why should she be surprised at that?

He drew back to allow her admirers to finish their felicitations, which he knew instinctively she never heard.

"She is coming out. She will pass by me, and I will follow."

For the moment Fandor saw nothing. He forgot the dance, and the steamship plowing the high seas, and the roar of the waves pouring past the open ports. More than all, he forgot that Helene was Fantômas' child, and how between her and himself stood threateningly a grim figure—the legendary figure of the Man in Black, the man without a face, whose features were ever hid beneath a hideous hood of black.

Making a supreme effort, he threw off the overmastering torpor. "I mean to speak to her," he cried, "now, at once."

But, looking again in her direction, he felt his heart stand still. Slowly Helene had walked to a door at the other end of the saloon. He saw her slip through it like a shadow and disappear.

"She avoids me?" he asked himself, and sprang forward. Mounting to the deck, he made a circuit, and at the top of the grand companion leading to the reserved cabins he caught a glimpse of a slender, white-clad form hurrying away.

"Oh, yes! I shall come up with her," he reassured himself, and plunged down the stairway. But his quarry had turned into an alleyway, at the far end of which he could see her walking fast—running almost. Then she stopped at a cabin door. At the distance Fandor could not make out the number. What matter? He would easily find it. Breaking into a run himself, the young man dashed down the long corridor.

But a steward barred his way. "Beg pardon, sir. Nobody allowed this way."

"Nobody allowed?"

"No, sir! They're going to practice closing the watertight doors."

"What nonsense!"

"There's always a practice, sir, as a matter of precaution, when there's a dance on. But you can get up on deck again and go round."

"Very good!" Fandor agreed, for he dared not insist further, bound as he was by all the circumstances to act with the utmost prudence.

Turning back and remounting the main companion, he found another stairway that brought him almost opposite Helene's cabin door.

"No doubt she has been waiting for me here these five minutes I lost by going round," he told himself, and rapped at the door—in vain. "The other door, then?" And he knocked again, with the like result.

"Can she be refusing me admission?" And again his heart seemed to stand still with amazement and distress. What to do? Force the door? No, he could not dream of such a thing. Wait? But how long must he remain on watch? Was it possible Helene would not open her door, refused to say so much as good day to him?

Then suddenly in the narrow corridor came the sound of a bolt being drawn. Did it mean Helene was coming out? Next, he saw a door come ajar, then open wide, and he stood dumb with stupefaction and horror, nailed to the spot. It was not Helene who came forward to greet him, bowing courteously. It was the Vicomte d'Oultremont!

"Monsieur Fandor," the young nobleman announced, "we have serious matters to discuss. Will you be good enough to come into my cabin?"

Fandor crossed the threshold like a man walking in his sleep. He could not tell what to think or what to believe. This Vicomte d'Oultremont, was he not Fantômas' lieutenant? How came he, then, to be on board the same ship as Helene? Was it with him the girl had taken flight?

Glaring wildly about him, the journalist scrutinized the little stateroom he had entered. It was practically empty. Besides the customary furniture, there was only a great trunk from which all the contents had been removed, while no one save the two young men were in the place.

"Monsieur Fandor," proceeded the other, "you will excuse my not asking you to sit down. Our interview must be brief. I am directed by the individual you know of—"

"By Helene?" struck in the journalist.

"To beg you to forget her presence on the ship. The direst results would follow any unreasonable persistence on your part. In fact, the individual I mean has besought me to ask you not to reveal your presence to anyone whatsoever, to efface yourself, even to make up and disguise yourself, so as to give yourself the look of a poor emigrant. Your life is at stake."

But Fandor's patience came to a sudden end. No, he would not endure that Helene should send him her orders by the mouth of this brigand, this outlaw. No, he would not allow himself to be hoodwinked by this scoundrelly fellow. Slowly and quietly he inserted a hand into his trousers pocket. Then, quicker than lightning, he pulled it out, leveling his Browning at the Vicomte.

"And I, sir," he cried, "I have another thing to tell you, and that is: I hold your life in my hands, and I shall shoot you down without a moment's hesitation unless you put me in the way of meeting Helene."

"Impossible!"

"Perhaps. But I will have it so."

"I give you my oath…"

"Useless… I do not believe you!"

"But surely—"

"Sir," said Fandor, "it is my turn to speak out, and speak peremptorily. I do not know who you really are, or what part you play, but I tell you this: if I have to search the ship from masthead to keelson, I mean to see Helene."

"No, sir!"

"But I say yes!"

"I will not allow it."

"An unwise speech that, Vicomte d'Oultremont! Now, as it is you who hide my fiancée from me, I have no scruples left."

"You are going to kill me?"

"You know very well I am no murderer. I am going to lock you up!"

"In this cabin? I shall shout for help."

"Wrong again! I am going to lock you up in this trunk, and you will not shout for help, for I am going to gag you. Come, do as I tell you. Lie down in that box."

The revolver in the journalist's hand possessed undeniable powers of persuasion. Without another word the Vicomte d'Oultremont stretched himself in the trunk.

"Capital!" Fandor chuckled. "I shall let you out if Helene bids me."

Rapidly he bound a gag over the young Vicomte's mouth, the latter offering no sort of resistance. Then he tied his hands, and shut the lid upon him, carrying off the key.

"And now I'm going to find Helene, and she must surely tell me who this man is and what authority he has over her."

The fact is, the young man was boiling with rage. Two minutes more and he opened the door and left the cabin, his purpose being to start the search for his fiancée there and then.

But he caught sight of his friend the purser hurrying past at a run.

"My dear sir," he called after him, "I should like—"

"Can't stop," returned the officer, without halting. "There's a yacht called the *Lotus* signaling for help on her wireless. She's in distress not twenty miles away. I'm doing what I can to see to her passengers presently. We shall be on the spot in half an hour."

But Fandor little knew what a suspicious craft this *Lotus* was, and the news meant nothing to him!

11. "It Is I!"

Five minutes afterwards, however, Fandor had to recognize that no time could well be less favorable for the prosecution of the search he proposed to make.

A man must have known those moments of agonizing suspense on board ship that prelude the rescue of a vessel in distress to realize fully the noble spirit of mutual help, the true brotherhood of feeling, that reigns among seamen. Directly an S.O.S. has been picked up, we may say without exaggeration that the everyday life and routine of the ship stop dead. From that moment all thoughts are devoted to those in peril, the men who are anxiously searching the horizon, watching impatiently for the coming of some vessel to the rescue. With one accord officers and crew—in this case passengers too—forget all customary preoccupations.

Very often it is unknown what the particular danger is that threatens the craft appealing for succor, but instantly all make ready to bring aid. Is it storm? The boats will be launched. Is it fire? At the risk of perishing themselves in the flames the rescuers will snatch from death those menaced by the encroaching conflagration. A leak? Serious damage to the hull? A hundred volunteers will be ready to risk their lives in the wreck that may founder at any moment and help to transship the crew. For is not every seafarer at the mercy of countless accidents? May not each in his turn have need of the succor he has generously afforded his neighbors a few hours before?

No sooner had Fandor left the cabin where he had just imprisoned the Vicomte d'Oultremont so effectually than he found himself bound to admit that the tale of his private troubles would meet with little sympathy. No man aboard the *Paris* had thoughts for anything save the yacht that had sent forth the most laconic, the most startling, of all messages—the S.O.S.

that provokes a shudder in all who hear it.

"I can do nothing without the purser's help," he reflected. "I have no authority to institute a search of the ship, and the purser will not, of course, listen to me at a time such as this! One can only wait with what patience one may. After the rescue, who can say if, under the excitement of the moment, Helene will not betray her presence?" But, as a fact, he hardly expected this. Since observing the way the girl had taken to flight on recognizing him, still more since he had encountered the Vicomte d'Oultremont, Fandor seemed to see a dreadful reason for the actions of Fantômas' daughter. Might it not be that, as lieutenant of the Lord of Terror, this Vicomte d'Oultremont was actually a sort of jailer on guard over Helene? In that case, finding it an impossibility to show herself, his fiancée must be waiting for her lover to come to her deliverance. Again, was it a moral or physical constraint this nobleman—or this self-styled nobleman—exercised over the lady?

"Oh, I'm going mad!" the young man exclaimed, debating in his mind all kinds of possibilities. "Who will give me the key to these mysteries?"

Then his thoughts turned to the strange commissions the Vicomte d'Oultremont professed to have been entrusted with for him. Did they not plainly show that in truth Helene was unable to express her true wishes?

"No, it was not Helene saw fit to send those messages to me; they were simply made up by d'Oultremont to forward his own purposes! Everything goes to prove it."

It may well be the young man was ready at this moment positively to curse the *Lotus* and her passengers. Was it not an atrocious act of cruelty to waste time that might be so precious in saving a craft of that sort?

"A pleasure yacht," he grumbled. "Ought there to be such things? Why should folks want to play games with the sea?" Yet at the very moment he was indulging these selfish thoughts he felt ashamed of his own attitude of mind. In truth, he loved the sea too well himself not to understand the glory and charm of this noble sport of yachting, unfortunately limited to the rare possessors of great fortunes.

"Come, come!" he chided himself. "I am going on like a ninny. Let's up on deck. Possibly I might be good for something. No man is entitled to stand aside and make no effort to be useful. And perhaps action will make me feel less discouraged."

Fandor climbed the companion and emerged on the upper deck. Not a passenger but was filled with excitement by the strange drama wherein they were soon to be actresses and actors. Meantime mattresses were being hurriedly brought on deck—sick and wounded might be among the rescued—while the ship's doctor was busy laying out the contents of a case of surgical instruments and medicines, and the stewards were brewing hot drinks and comforting beverages. And be sure never a telescope or pair of binoculars on board was left unused. For a boat of the speed of the *Paris* twenty miles was a trifle. Very soon the yacht would be in sight.

"We have had no squalls hereabouts," explained an officer. "I wager it must be fire."

"Unless the *Lotus* has been run down?"

"Perhaps. But these latitudes are far from crowded with shipping. A collision is very unlikely in these parts."

But suddenly all voices fell silent as the lookout in the crow's nest on the crosstrees bellowed through his speaking trumpet:

"A yacht on the beam!"

"Where? Where?" asked a thousand voices. But suspense was short-lived. Under forced draft, belching torrents of black smoke from her four funnels, the great liner was tearing through the water at such speed that in less than ten minutes the distressed craft was clearly visible.

A pretty vessel, the yacht *Lotus*. With her white hull, her two raking masts, she made a fine show of a vessel, both seaworthy and swift. Big and luxuriously appointed, it seemed evident she had been bound on a lengthy cruise when she was forced to send the message that had turned the *Paris* from her course. The knowing men whispered to one another:

"A French ship, flies the Yacht Club flag. In a bad way, too!" And soon all could verify this for themselves. With a formidable list to port, the *Lotus* lay motionless, ready to sink apparently at any moment. The lee nettings were almost awash, and the sea was lapping softly over her sloping decks.

"Not a doubt of it!" declared a voice, hoarse with excitement. "They are badly holed under the waterline. The pumps must have jammed. In ten minutes the poor hulk will be at the bottom." And no one thought of disputing the statement.

Fandor himself, for all his personal doubts and difficulties, felt his heart beat high with excitement. What a stroke of luck, indeed, for the *Paris* to have picked up the S.O.S. as she had. Judging by the position of the yacht, she could never have reached any other vessel with her message.

"Yes, and, her engines being flooded out," reflected the journalist, she could not even sound her siren to summon help. Ah! That's no doubt the reason she has never told us what exactly her damage is." Then the young man lost all count of the minutes that followed, so absorbed was he in the tragedy passing before his eyes.

By this time the *Paris* was checking her speed as she neared the yacht, maneuvering to get to windward of the unfortunate craft. Suddenly a sailor appeared on one of the masts, hand signaling with strings of flags.

"Anyone here can read the signals?" demanded the passengers of the *Paris,* and Fandor stepped forward. Loving all things connected with the sea as he did, he had long ago made himself familiar with the code. In a loud voice he translated:

"Keep your offing… bring her to two cable lengths away… Put down your quarter-ladder… we are launching the boats!"

Involuntarily the journalist put in a remark aside:

"Very odd they still don't tell what's wrong—and there's not a soul on deck—"

But, before he had time to finish, colors were broken at the tip of the yardarm—a flag the mere sight of which drew cries of frantic fear from every passenger. It was a flag the meaning of which was, alas! only too plain. Of black bunting, it bore for all device a grim symbol in white—a death's head.

"Pirates!" screamed a chorus of trembling voices. But the

cries were drowned in the sharp explosion of a volley from the *Lotus'* guns. Raked at point-blank range, the powerful steamship shuddered from stem to stern.

A hideous panic ensued. A disorderly mob, yelling with terror, the passengers, pushing and shoving, almost fighting their way, rushed for the companionways and dived belowdecks.

"Pirates! They are pirates!" came from a hundred terrified mouths.

For his part, Fandor had anchored himself to a rail to stem the torrent of fugitives. He was excited like the rest, but he felt no fear. Pirates? No, he could not believe it!" Are there pirates on the high seas in these days?"

Then, in a flash, he knew, and was indeed afraid. High on the yacht's mainmast a man had appeared, clinging precariously to a shroud and followed by a sailor carrying a hailing trumpet, a man whose form was clad in a close-fitting suit of black—a hellish figure at which Fandor had no need to look twice to recognize! No, there were no pirates nowadays sailing the seas. But there was Fantômas, the Lord of Terror, the Prince and King of Criminals!

And how admirably he had laid the trap into which the *Paris* had fallen! Could the great liner have refused to act on the wireless appeal received? Could she, once alongside the pirate yacht, no doubt powerfully armed—could she, the vast steamship with her rich freight of human life and precious cargo, offer any effective resistance?

But was it indeed a stroke of original genius on Fantômas' part? Nay, were not the Germans credited with having recourse to the like ruses during the blockade of the seas by von Tirpitz's submarines? All the scoundrel could actually claim was to have dared to fit out a pirate yacht, and in the open ocean to have adapted for his own vile ends the treacherous maneuver. Yet it was indeed a thing no robber had ever conceived the possibility of, no criminal had ever so much as dreamed of. What finer haul than a transatlantic liner? What wealth on board to be seized! What treasures in her holds to be stolen!

But Fandor had found little time to think of all this before the drama was carried further. Slowly at first, the *Lotus* came to a level keel. The comedy was ended, the *Paris* brought to a couple of cable lengths from her guns, the muzzles of which now showed undisguisedly from the gun ports, what need to go on pretending the yacht was in distress? And now the speaking trumpet was transmitting Fantômas' orders to the captain of the unfortunate ship:

"The whole staff of officers of the Paris will assemble, unarmed, on the bridge. Any officer found belowdecks will be shot on sight. Seamen and firemen will take stand on the forecastle, barring the hands needed to launch the ship's boats. These to be got overboard in good order with the least possible delay. Passengers will be put aboard the boats, one and all without exception. Any person found afterwards in the vessel will be incontinently hanged."

After all, was it not precisely the fashion in which the enemy submarines in the Great War forced the merchantmen they looked upon as lawful prize to haul down their flag? Fandor would hear no more. So well could he guess the rest of the tragedy he felt no wish to follow its further developments. They would embark the passengers in the lifeboats? Well, was not that equivalent to sending the poor creatures to their death after days of tossing helplessly on the waves, at the mercy of cold and storm and tempest? And the crew and officers—what was to become of them? Unfortunately, in an Atlantic liner there are never boats enough to save all the human beings aboard.

"Odious, abominable!" thought the journalist. "Perhaps the most atrocious, most murderous of all Fantômas' crimes…"

Then a thrill of acute horror brought to his lips the anguished cry: "Helene? But what of Helene?"

Now, at all costs, he *must* find her. Unaware of the catastrophe, in hiding or held prisoner, she might perish at the hands of the wretches Fantômas was sending on board to carry out his orders.

"If she declares she is his daughter, they will not believe her," he thought, with a shudder that shook his very soul. "And then," he added, "would they spare his daughter's life if they did know?"

Thereupon, heedless of consequences, without a thought of the bullets whistling past his head—for now the crew on the yacht were amusing themselves by firing on the steamer—Fandor turned on his heel and, leaving the deck, made for the cabin where he had left the Vicomte d'Oultremont locked in the trunk.

"I will blow his brains out if he refuses to tell me where Helene is. A life for a life! I have every right, surely?"

Jerome Fandor debated the point in all seriousness before deciding on an act of violence that, after all, revolted him. But could he yield to any scruple now? Was it not significant, the mere presence of Fantômas' lieutenant on board? Doubtless he was to play the part of traitor, see to the due execution of his master's orders. Nay, it would be he perhaps who would take command of the pirate crew that in a few minutes more would board the ship.

"Yes, I have every right!" Fandor told himself, and tore open the cabin door. A voice cried:

"I was expecting you!"

"Helene!" gasped Fandor, for, indeed, it was she and no other who stood before him.

"Yes, it is I," declared the girl in a broken voice. "What I dreaded has come to pass. Oh, Fandor, you cannot conceive the agony I suffer."

Tears stood in her eyes, tears that seemed to well from a torn and bleeding heart. In very truth she was suffering atrocious torments, Fantômas' unhappy daughter, at this terrible moment when, at once eyewitness and victim of her father's atrocious attack on the defenseless leviathan, with its precious burden of human life, she was torn between the sense of her filial duty to a parent and her instinctive longing to save the lives of the doomed liner's passengers and crew. For, in spite of all that had gone before, in spite of all she knew of his hideous past and the fearful record of his crimes and cruelties, the unhappy girl still loved, as well as feared, the Lord of Terror.

"Oh, Helene, Helene!" the young man went on in a shaking voice, "tell me how it comes you are on board this ill-fated ship. What motive prompted you to risk your life—your life I hold so precious—in an adventure that can lead to nothing but disaster—disaster and, it may be, death for yourself and for me who loves you?"

"I am here, Fandor," came the reply, in a firm and determined tone, "I am here to save, if I can, the passengers of the *Paris*."

"Give your orders, Helene, and I will obey them."

"Fandor, hide yourself in that box."

"In that trunk?"

"Yes! you will be released on board the *Lotus*. I shall say—"

"But, Helene, you do not know! I have locked the Vicomte d'Oultremont in that trunk."

Then the journalist thought he was losing his wits. A melancholy and fleeting smile had crossed the girl's face, and it was in a voice soft and low, yet not innocent of a touch of gentle mockery, that Helene answered him:

"The Vicomte d'Oultremont? So you never guessed? There never was a Vicomte d'Oultremont! *I* was the Vicomte d'Oultremont. I it was, made up to play that part. I it is who, in that guise, am my father's chief lieutenant. Did I not play the role, should I know my father's plans? Should I be able to rescue his victims from his hands?"

And again, for all her force of will, Helene failed to check the tears that brimmed over from her beautiful eyes.

*   *   *   *   *

But Helene was of far too energetic a nature to yield to such weakness for long. Next moment she was herself again, a very fire of determination burning in her eyes.

"Fandor," she began again, "I cannot tell what the coming hour has in store for us, but I would fain not die."

"Die?" broke in her lover. "Nay, I will save you."

"Who knows—and what matter either? But listen to what I say. Every second is precious."

"Speak, speak!" the young man exhorted her. "I would fain not die thinking that any doubt may linger in your mind. The Vicomte d'Oultremont, Fandor, and I are one and the same person but not a soul in all the world knows it."

"You have taken in Fantômas, then?"

"I inherit my cunning in disguise from himself. Someday perhaps I will tell you by what fantastic means I have succeeded in giving myself an appearance so utterly unlike the real that you yourself, like my father, were deceived by my skill. For the moment, what I want you to know is this—that with my father I am playing the part of a pitiful accomplice in his plans, and how this gives me the chance to save innocent lives from the peril that threatens them. Fandor, you do not doubt what I say?"

"I do not doubt you, Helene."

"And you do not think either that to succeed in this playacting I must have shamed myself?"

"You shame yourself!"

"Yes, by lying? By taking false oaths? By making odious promises?"

"I do not understand you now, but I do not doubt you in any way, whatever."

"Fandor, it was because I am the Vicomte d'Oultremont that the Vicomte refused to take the oath Fantômas demanded of his accomplices before deciding definitely on robbing this vessel."

"What! it was—"

"Yes, that was the villainy already being plotted. But hear me further. That day Fantômas learned how a part of his fabulous hoard had been stolen. He found the safe from which you had just emerged entirely empty. Alas! elsewhere he had other stores of gold. What cared he for the petty theft I had attempted in the hope of disarming him forever?"

The girl's voice, which had trembled a little, grew firm again as she proceeded:

"Since then, Fandor, I know that the gang of scoundrels who are Fantômas' associates regard me as a traitress. Yes! that day, Fandor, when you were struck down, I thought I too must die. I hardly know what lucky chance it was let me make my escape. I have given my pledge I will recover the lost treasures, and they have spared my life for a few weeks. But my days are numbered."

"Helene, Helene! Why interfere in these terrible adventures?"

"Is it not my duty?" And, checking her lover's appeal with an imperious gesture, Helene continued:

"Listen—only listen! We have but a few seconds to come to an understanding. Never let us waste them!"

Indeed, she looked so white, she seemed to be suffering such torment of soul, that Fandor, full of pity for the gallant creature, whom the accidents of life involved in such cruel predicaments, listened in respectful silence as his fiancée went on:

"Yes! My life is threatened. Meantime I have let them understand—without giving a promise—that perhaps the treasure will be restored. In that way I hope to divert on my own head the vengeance of these ruffians. I imagined that, thinking only of punishing me, they would refrain, at least for a while, from committing fresh crimes. You understand? I said to myself: 'They will search for the Vicomte d'Oultremont. Never once has Fantômas left unpunished an accomplice who has abandoned him.' I felt confident of holding them on my track and drawing them on to a false scent."

"You offered yourself a victim to their hatred? Yes, I do understand!" admitted the journalist, trembling with pity and admiration.

"No need for big words!" Helene interrupted. "One cannot but do what conscience declares one's duty. The time is ours. I found out—I will not tell you how—that the *Paris* was to be attacked. Then I set out."

"Again flying in the very face of danger, Helene!"

"It was to retain the hope of being of use. I do not know by what ruse you were able to board this steamer."

"I, too, only did my duty—just that."

"But I was horribly afraid when I saw you. Oh, Fandor, my father hates you and Juve. What vengeance might he not take on you if he knew you were here?"

"We shall find out in an hour or so," laughed Fandor. "I don't see how I can escape Fantômas, as he is going to search the ship and sink her, no doubt."

"No, no! Do not say so. I mean to save—save us—"

"Us? Only us?"

"How can you think that?"

"What! You suppose, then, you can save all the passengers? Impossible!"

"I do not believe anything is impossible to those whose will is strong and bold."

"Tell me your plan," said Fandor simply, once more stirred to admiration by his fiancée's energy, and it was with equal plainness the gallant young creature replied:

"Listen carefully, Fandor! I know how things are on the *Lotus*. In the meetings I attended as the Vicomte d'Oultremont I have heard speak of the arrangements on board the pirate. Well, she is fitted with wireless. A powerful installation is fixed in a deck cabin—the first on the port side."

"First on the port side!" repeated Fandor.

"Now I know," proceeded the girl, "I know the English squadron is not far away. You guess what I would be at?"

"You mean, once transshipped on board the *Lotus*, we are to call up the English squadron by wireless?"

"I mean to signal to them the pitiful lot of the passengers Fantômas no doubt intends to abandon in the boats. The English will rescue them. I want us—"

"Us, Helene?"

"Yes, you will come with me, I know. Why surely, Fantômas will let me transship the chest here—the chest in which Vicomte d'Oultremont will pretend he has locked the vanished treasure."

"Oh, admirable!" Fandor broke in, with newly awakened enthusiasm, for truly Helene's scheme struck him as marvelously ingenious. Of course, he told himself, the Vicomte d'Oultremont, bringing back the lost treasure, had every chance of getting aboard the *Lotus*, and that, hidden in the chest, he too would reach the yacht along with Fantômas' daughter. That done, might it not be possible to outwit the surveillance of the crew, slip into the wireless room, and dispatch the message that should bring the English fleet to the rescue?

The young man's heart bounded with a sense of triumph. Once the English squadron, so strong and well armed, had mustered round the *Lotus,* the pirate yacht would be bound to surrender, and Fantômas would be forced to haul down the ill-omened colors he had so proudly displayed.

But his exultation was short-lived. Another thought struck him. If Helene's plan succeeded, if it could be realized, was not that the end, almost for certain, of the wretched Lord of Terror? And, that being so, would it not be Helene who had knotted round her father's neck the rope that would end his career of infamy on the London gallows? Was Helene, then, forgetting this?

Suddenly the girl's hand fell lightly on his arm. "Now, Fandor," resumed the heroine, "I continue. I cannot deliver up my father to justice, and you know I cannot. Wicked as a father may be, one must remember his blood flows in my veins. I have therefore resolved—"

She broke off, breathless, made a violent effort to master a sudden fit of weakness, and went on:

"No sooner shall we have dispatched the message indicating the position of the boats in danger, and so saved the passengers of the *Paris,* whom the English will pick up, than we shall send out another message. In it we shall state where the *Lotus* is bound, where to intercept her, where to capture her—"

"And this message will be a lie? Our information will be worthless?"

"Entirely worthless!" And the two looked in each other's faces, trembling at thought of what they had said, at thought of what they dared not say.

Oh, the tragedy, the horror, of this conversation that passed between the pair of lovers, who felt between them as a grim barrier, separating them inexorably, all the crimes of another!

Softly Fandor asked the question:

"And we, Helene?"

"Ah!" sighed the girl, with a melancholy smile.

"Better say, 'And you,' for I know it is my fate that alone moves you."

"Well?"

"Well, our messages duly sent, our duty done, my father's crime repaired so far as I can repair it, we will be gone again. We will leave the *Lotus,* quit the accursed vessel. We can try to find a boat, to escape, to come up with the boats carrying the marooned passengers. We should be rescued along with them."

Looking straight in the other's face, she demanded:

"Do you agree to help me, Fandor? Alone I should doubtless have little chance of success…"

But Fandor was looking down, thinking deeply:

Of a certainty he was ready to give his life to save the shipwrecked passengers of the *Paris.* To board the *Lotus* and attempt the desperate ruse that his fiancée had devised in no wise alarmed him. But ought he to bind himself not to deliver up the brigand to the English fleet? Ought he to consent to the sending out of a bogus message?

But, just as though Helene had been able to divine the struggle going on in the soul of her companion, the girl went on to add:

"The thing once done, you will be free again to act as you will. If I ask you today to save my father, it is in view of this that you have the chance of saving hundreds of innocent lives."

"I agree," said Fandor softly. "You have a great soul, Helene. But for success—"

He had no time even to finish the doubting words that had sprung to his lips. At that same instant along the alleyway outside a wild rush of trampling feet met their ears… and screams and oaths…

"It is they!" cried Helene. "Quick, I say! Quick!" No need for her to speak more definitely. Fandor, too, had guessed the truth as soon as she. The tumult, the cries, the mad stampede of panic-stricken passengers, were proof enough that Fantômas' men were already aboard the ship. How much more time would they lose before starting their search? How long before the cabin door would be burst open?

"Quick!" reiterated Helene, pointing to the chest. Fandor demanded hoarsely: "How am I to get out again?"

"See, look, there is a secret mechanism. I had foreseen the possibility of using this chest as a hiding place. Here is the contrivance. You can open the lid, whenever you see fit, from the inside."

"Good! But you? The fellows will mistake you for a passenger."

"Make your mind easy! In five minutes the Vicomte d'Oultremont will stand before them." And now Fandor felt he had no right, and no time, to hesitate. He must perforce obey the behests of this astonishing, this undaunted child of the Lord of Terror, and he stepped into the open trunk.

"But, Helene," he made bold to say, "answer me one question first."

"What is it?" asked the other, her face paling suddenly with emotion.

"If we escaped, if Providence suffered us to come safe out of this fearful adventure—"

"Well?"

"Our happiness, Helene, in that case?"

The girl could not fail to understand. She knew what he would say. The beating of her heart repeated the echo of her thoughts. She was his promised bride. He loved her, and she loved him. If he questioned her thus, was it not because he was fain to know whether all hope was denied him? Was it not because he longed to hear a word of encouragement from her lips? Pitiful indeed was the look in her great eyes, but again Fantômas' unhappy child proved herself a true and brave woman.

"No!" she said, "happiness is not for us."

But next moment, a blush mantling her fair face, involuntarily almost she amended:

"No, not for us—yet!"

And with the word that still allowed the possibility of a smiling future, with a thud the ponderous lid of the chest fell back on the young man.

The lover's heart leapt up in joyous exultation. He was well aware the happiness of wedding Helene could not *yet* be near. Nay, he was convinced this happiness would never be his so long as Fantômas remained free and triumphant. But would he—Fantômas—always be victorious? If he, the Lord of Terror, displayed the reckless audacity of a fiend, did not Fandor and Juve show themselves no less prepared to go to any extremity of daring?

"I am going on board his yacht," thought the journalist. "I shall be within a few yards of him. Who knows but I may pick up a hint that will put him at my mercy?"

Then his reflections were cut short. For a moment Helene had left the cabin to pass into an adjacent dressing closet. Now she was coming back, she was there beside the chest, the locks of which seemed to all appearance intact. He could hear her footsteps. But how changed was her gait, now become imperious, sharp, decisive. No doubt the girl had resumed her disguise as the Vicomte d'Oultremont. He gathered she was opening the door. "If only Fantômas' men are taken in," he muttered doubtfully—and involuntarily he gripped the revolver he had concealed in the pocket of his evening coat. If Helene were in any danger, he would surely regain all his rights as a fighter...

But his thoughts and forebodings stopped dead, so enthralled was his whole attention by the scene unfolding near him. No sooner was the cabin door open than Helene shouted:

"Hi, there, you fellows! Two men to me—and quick's the word."

Instantly cries of surprise and alarm broke out:

"D'Oultremont! Is it you—you, d'Oultremont?"

"Why, am I so altered you must call out my name?"

"But how come you?"

"Oh, you'll know that later on! Two men—didn't I order two men?"

"Order? Hmm! Order?"

"Does that strike you as odd?"

"Why, yes. Is it for a traitor to the brotherhood to give

orders?"

Jerome Fandor in his trunk began to tremble, guessing a wrangle to threaten—nay, to be inevitable, seeing that Helene, in her guise as the Vicomte d'Oultremont, would be deemed a traitor to the cause and would find it hard to enforce her commands.

"Very well," the journalist made up his mind. "If it must be, I will show myself."

But he was forgetting that Fantômas' daughter was capable of the most perfect coolness and the most consummate daring.

In a voice quivering with indignation she replied:

"My good man, do what you think fit with me—seize me as a hostage, bind me hand and foot, if you so choose. All you will gain will be the knowledge of what the master thinks of your cleverness. Come, I asked for two men. I want rollers slipped under a chest in my cabin. Now, hurry, I say! And remember, you will have to answer for what you do with your lives."

Then Fandor heard a match struck. With an amazing assurance the girl had evidently lit a cigarette in token of her absolute self-confidence. But hardly had she spoken the word "chest" before the brigand she was talking to seemed to change his tune. He knew, of course, how the Vicomte d'Oultremont, accused of having stolen part of the master's treasure, had pledged himself to restore it. How fail to guess that this same treasure now lay in the chest referred to? In an altered voice he resumed:

"Come now, d'Oultremont, why dispute about it? Fantômas doesn't like one to make a personal question of matters that concern the whole company."

"Was it I who sought to quarrel with you?"

"I don't say anything of the sort. Nay, perhaps I was a trifle short-tempered. Anyway, they are at this moment transshipping the passengers into the boats. And there's a fine old gale blowing up. See here, I'm going straight off to have your chest carried aboard the *Lotus*. Then I shall get on with my job, searching the cabins to make sure there's nobody hidden in the ship. Just a ten minutes' job. I've only got this alleyway to look after. Then a good mine, and then *Paris* goes to the bottom. Will you wait for me? We'll leave the ship together."

"If you please."

"Agreed, then. In twenty minutes at latest you'll have it out with Fantômas."

At that moment, for all his intrepidity, Jerome Fandor felt a shudder run through his limbs. In twenty minutes he, too, would be on board the pirate yacht commanded by the portentous Lord of Terror.

12. Shooting the Moon

"Very badly managed! Shockingly badly—so badly I shall withdraw my custom from the damned firm. Don't know how to shift furniture, they don't. Oh Lord, my head! Good Lord, my ribs!"

Inside the chest wherein he had ensconced himself, with a courage that bordered closely on recklessness, Fandor was bewailing his lot—not without good reason, but yet in a merry mood, that was a bit surprising under the circumstances.

His situation was indeed a tragicomedy. Imprisoned as he was, knowing he was being transshipped on board the pirate craft commissioned by Fantômas with a criminal daring that would stick at no wickedness, he should surely have been shivering with distress and terror. On the contrary, faithful to his habits of gallant adventure, he was first and foremost turning the whole thing into a joke.

Head downwards one moment, tossed sideways the next, he was tasting the tender mercies of the callous ruffians Fantômas had no doubt recruited from the dregs of the out-of-works who prowl about the docks of seaport towns. Such gentry, we may be sure, showed precious little gentleness in handling the heavy package the "Vicomte d'Oultremont" had just entrusted to them. Growling and groaning, a bit drunk into the bargain, they hauled it over the carpets in the alleyways, banged it against every corner, and finally hoisted it from step to step up the grand companion.

"They're going to break my neck," thought Fandor, as he felt a bump of more than ordinary violence. "For the future I shall certainly have a suit of padded clothes made, and insist on their putting 'glass with care' on the package."

The journalist's gaiety was entirely unforced. Never a trace of show-off about it. He was one of those men who look danger straight in the face, weigh the cost, and conclude it has to be confronted. This done, they treat it with sublime contempt.

"One thing or the other," he summed up the situation; "either I shall come off all right—and in that case what need to worry?—or I shall not, and, in that case, may as well laugh as not during the last few minutes of my existence." A perfectly sound piece of reasoning, but that presupposed just one little thing to hold to it—to wit, Fandor's gallant personality.

As a fact, there was little to laugh at in the series of events now happening. After being hauled on deck, Fandor's trunk was deposited beside a creaking apparatus which the journalist, though he could see nothing, concluded was a steam-winch.

"And that," he argued, "means I'm going to be lowered into the hold at the end of a rope. I only hope the rope won't part!"

Purposely he forced himself not to think about Helene. Such profound anxiety tortured him whenever he called up the lovely form of Fantômas' daughter that, entirely unable as he was to protect her, he thought best in these agonizing moments to drive the memory of her from his mind altogether.

But the rope selected by the ruffians to effect the transship-ment from the liner's deck was evidently a stout one. Fandor suddenly felt himself swaying uncomfortably in space. Then he heard the engine creak louder than ever, and next moment had the extremely unpleasant sensation of falling down, down at a giddy rate.

"I've never been properly sorry," he thought, setting his teeth hard, "for horses they swing ashore in this fashion! Poor beasts! It's anything but a pleasant experience."

Luckily there was not far to go. A shrill whistle and a pretty sharp shock told the journalist he had now been dumped in the bottom of a boat rocking gently on the waves.

"No more to come?" a voice asked.

"That's all. Push off!" Followed by a loud order: "Pull away, lads!"

The chest was hermetically closed, and its thick, solid sides prevented the young man from seeing anything whatsoever. To make up, he found not the smallest difficulty in hearing all that was said beside him.

"You see the master, d'Oultremont?" asked a voice, evidently belonging to the pirate leader to whom Helene had appealed a little while before.

"Certainly I do. He is leveling his telescope at us."

"And you know why?"

"I suppose he wants to see who I am."

"Just so. Our orders forbade us to make a single prisoner. No doubt, seeing someone in the boat besides the crew, Fantômas is asking himself who it can be."

"Well, he's going to know soon."

"Don't it make you afraid to meet him?"

"Afraid? Why? Never trouble your head, my dear man, about what doesn't concern you."

Helene's tone was perfectly calm and composed. Yet how difficult and arduous a task it must have been for the girl thus to alter her voice so as to give it the semblance of a man's.

"Poor Helene!" Fandor groaned internally. But again he resolved to master his feelings of love and pity. Such powerful emotions have a way of undermining a man's energy. And he had such sore need of all his vigor and force of will at this crisis.

Meantime for some minutes the boat in which sat Helene, or, to be more exact, the Vicomte d'Oultremont, and which likewise carried Fandor's chest, forged ahead without other sound than that of the oars as they parted the waves.

Then came a hail, at which the young man's face paled with fury where he lay in his prison.

"Boat ahoy! Who is it dares to come aboard the *Lotus*? Who is it you are bringing with you?"

"A self-invited guest, Fantômas!"

"My orders cannot be gainsaid! I will have nobody on board the yacht! Pitch your passenger into the sea!"

Fandor clenched his fists in rage. No need for the brigand's lieutenant, in command of the boat's crew, to have pronounced Fantômas' name for Fandor to know who it was had given the cruel order. Who but the Arch-Criminal could have shown himself so atrociously inhuman? Who save the Lord of Terror could have had the heart thus callously to order the stranger his officer had thought well to bring to be thrown overboard? Fantômas' orders must never be disputed. Never would he suffer any one of his directions to be infringed.

But now Helene had turned to face the scoundrel who was her father.

"Throw me overboard—me, Fantômas?" she protested calmly. "Is not the Vicomte d'Oultremont more than your other officers?"

"The Vicomte d'Oultremont!"

Involuntarily Fantômas had suffered a note of surprise to sound in his voice. There was no doubt the presence of this lieutenant of his struck him with amazement. Could he really believe him a traitor? Did he in very truth suspect him of having stolen the vanished treasure? But, if that were so, why had he not already brought the dread weight of his implacable anger to bear upon his faithless comrade?

Fandor had no time to ponder the question. Playing her part with splendid boldness and absolute coolness, Helene had resumed:

"Why, yes, it is I, Fantômas—come to clear myself of the accusations you level against me."

"What next?"

"Don't you see the chest I am bringing you?"

"Which you are bringing me, d'Oultremont?"

"Why, certainly!"

"Bringing because you are obliged!"

"Not at all. I was expecting your attack."

"You lie!"

"If I am lying, why should I have made myself known to your men?"

"It was they who recognized you."

"Ask them if that is true. Master, it was I who asked to be brought to you."

"Not to be cast away in the boats?"

"If I had felt myself guilty, tell me, was it less terrible to appear before you than to be left in one of those boats, which may yet find safety? Have you ceased to be the one men fear worse than all else?" And the pretended Vicomte d'Oultremont broke into a mocking laugh.

Where he lay concealed, Fandor at that moment was like to give a cry of sheer admiration. How each one of Helene's replies to her father had nonplussed him. How he adored—admired is no word to express all he felt—the brave girl who rose so gallantly above the fear and timidities of her sex, playing with such consummate art this daring comedy!

Meantime Fantômas for a moment found no answer to make. Never, surely, had he been defied like this before! Yet was it this only that made his voice tremble of a sudden?

"Good and well!" he ordered at last. "Let the boat pull in. The question will soon be settled!" A threat this, or was it the admission of a doubt?

But again Fandor had no time given him to form an opinion. Hardly had Fantômas issued the order for the boat to draw to before a sharp bump told the journalist it had ranged alongside under the yacht's quarter, while immediately after a character-istic swaying to and fro assured the young man that crew and passenger were disembarking.

"Oh, ho!" He heard the voice of the pretended Vicomte d'Oultremont raised in a jeering laugh. "So Fantômas comes to the gangway to welcome me, eh?"

"To lead you to my cabin. I always hate prolonging matters forever."

"Very natural, master. But you will let me see first to the hoisting of the chest on board?"

"My men will take care of that."

"And they will take care to check the contents, no doubt. No, I mean to look after it myself."

"What now, d'Oultremont! Do you presume to give orders in my presence?"

"Why not, Fantômas? If I offend you, you have only to kill me. The thing is perfectly simple. So long as you let me live, it means you approve of me."

"Or that I wish to hear your story, the better to make mock

of you?"

"Well, then, I shall afford you that pleasure. You ought to thank me."

Surely never had Fantômas heard himself addressed in suchwise by a mere accomplice. Indeed the trembling of his voice—a circumstance Fandor did not fail to notice—was token enough of his agitation. He now went on:

"Agreed! The situation is so extraordinary I will do as you ask, just out of curiosity... Have that chest on deck at once!" And again Fandor was to appreciate the doubtful delights of a rough-and-ready transshipment.

What passed after that between Fantômas and the *soi-disant* Vicomte d'Oultremont he could scarcely guess. In his cramped hiding place he was being so shaken up, so violently bumped about, that he felt bruised and beaten, and had to think first and foremost of the best way to wedge himself against the sides of his prison to avoid attracting overmuch attention on the part of the sailors by pitching about inside. But again the torture was of no very long duration. With a quick heave, like men who are tired out after a heavy job and give a sigh of relief to be rid of it at last, the hands who had transshipped the chest now pitched it heavily on the deck, where it rested aslant, partly leaning against the bulwarks. At that moment, as ill-luck would have it, Fandor found himself standing on his head again.

"Charming!" he growled. "Anyhow, it will teach me a lesson. Evidently 'Glass with care' is not enough. Next time I shall put 'This side up' as well. Meanwhile I've got to turn." And slowly and painfully, supple as an acrobat, twice over convinced he could never succeed, and all the time dreading an apoplectic stroke, the young man at last managed to assume a more natural position.

"Ah, but that's a relief," he sighed. "But what is Fantômas saying now?"

Once more he listened. Hearing less distinctly, for the speakers seemed to be somewhat farther away, but, still clear enough for him not to miss, the journalist overheard a further conversation:

"So, Vicomte d'Oultremont, you are satisfied now, I take it?" mocked Fantômas in his hard voice. "The chest is on board and safe now."

"No doubt."

"So, then, you are ready to come to my cabin with me, and explain your behavior?"

"No!"

"No? You still refuse?"

"You *must* understand why, Fantômas."

"Understand? Nay, I have not a notion what you mean. Indeed I begin to think you are playing or—"

"You are quite wrong there."

"Wrong? *I* am wrong? What next?"

"Never get in a passion, but listen! You shall decide—"

"I have decided."

"You are mistaken. You have *not* decided. You do not know what it is I want to tell you."

The girl's voice was no less serious now than Fantômas', and it was in impressive tones she resumed:

"One day, before all the comrades, you accused me of betrayal. You would have it I had stolen the treasure you had buried, and which was to have been shared between all."

"It was the truth!"

"It was false, Fantômas. I took no heed of the treasure till after it was discovered by the police."

"Lies! lies!"

"I can prove the contrary. However, that is not the question. You accused me before all. Have I or have I not a right to be judged by all and before all? You charged me with treachery; I wish to clear myself of that accusation before the assembled comrades."

"That is your last word?"

"My last word, Fantômas."

"But you should surely see that if I choose to question you in private—"

"I see nothing of the sort! I claim a public trial after an insult that was public."

"As you please, then!" came the reply in a high-pitched, imperious voice, in which sounded the far-off echo of an implacable hatred. He proceeded:

"But, seeing you prate of justice, Vicomte d'Oultremont, we will copy in all respects the ways of judges. You lie under my suspicion. I am going to commit you to prison pending your trial."

"As you please."

"What need for you to authorize me to do what I see fit? Moreover, your fault having been public, as you say, and your trial having to be in public, as you demand, it is likewise in public I am going to have you undergo this confinement."

"In public? Explain, Fantômas!"

"I am going, Vicomte d'Oultremont, to have you bound to the mainmast. In an hour's time, when the *Paris* is at the bottom of the sea, we will judge your case. You understand?"

"Yes! This time I understand."

"And you agree?"

At that moment the prisoner in the trunk felt his heart stand still. A wild notion had burst upon his mind. In all the replies Fantômas made to the pretended Vicomte d'Oultremont was not a touch of forbearance apparent that was very far from being the brigand's usual way of speaking? In suffering one of his accomplices to express an opinion in his presence, surely the Lord of Terror was exhibiting an extraordinary clemency?

Fandor reflected: "No, it cannot be possible. I am deceiving myself."

But nevertheless his conviction grew stronger. He could not deny its force, do what he would. To act in this way, to endure that anyone should almost defy him, surely Fantômas had divined his daughter under the guise of the Vicomte d'Oultremont…

"Yes, he has recognized her," thought Fandor. "That is why he desires to speak to her alone—and it is this odious interview Helene insists on avoiding, even at the cost of her life."

But, if the journalist had guessed right, was not the unhappy girl's fate more terrible than ever?

High-spirited and courageous as she was, Helene would never consent to avow her birth to her father. Never would she buy his forgiveness at such a price. But Fantômas—was not Fantômas capable, even against his own daughter, of exacting the direst vengeance when she braved him to his face?

"Oh, it would be appalling—appalling beyond all conceivable bounds of horror, that he should kill her after recognizing the truth. She, despite all the scorn she felt for him, has ever refused to imperil his life, to make our task easier for us, for Juve and myself!"

Then the young man felt an icy chill through his limbs, paralyzing the very faculty of thought. Fantômas' imperious voice—that pitiless voice that had again grown hard and callous—had issued the order:

"Lash that fellow to the mainmast. And, mark me! the ropes must be stout, and two men keep guard over the prisoner. He is dangerous. He is to die at sundown!"

*   *   *   *   *

A prisoner as he was, condemned to inactivity, yet hearing every word exchanged between the villainous father and the heroic daughter, Fandor was enduring a veritable martyrdom.

"Has he recognized her or has he not?" he kept asking himself. "Can he really have the heart to threaten her with death, knowing it is his own daughter who stands before him? Or has he conceived a doubt, and, in view of Helene's defiant attitude, persuaded himself that he is mistaken?"

Next moment he left this question that could never lead to any practical decision unanswered, as he reflected further:

"I must, in any case, argue as though Fantômas had not recognized Helene; I have no call to trouble my head about such problems. One thing, and one thing only, is of account—the plans we have agreed upon." And, by a heroic effort, no less an act of courage than was Helene's calm defiance, he recovered his gaiety.

"I'm in a cashbox," he grinned. "Suppose I use the opportunity to do as cashiers do, and make up my accounts"—and he proceeded with mock gravity:

"Item No. 1—to escape from jail by using the keys in Helene's possession… Give it up, inasmuch as neither she nor I *are* in jail. Item No. 2—to slip into the wireless room… Again, give it up, for it doesn't strike me the Vicomte d'Oultremont is likely very soon to be in a position to move freely about the decks of the *Lotus*. Item No. 3—to save the unlucky passengers of the *Paris*… No good again. Hmm, seems to me things aren't shaping over-well."

Then, pulling a rueful face in spite of himself, the journalist proceeded, still obstinately maintaining the humorous vein:

"Ergo, balance sheet: general bankruptcy of all our hopes! I can't help thinking the game's going to end badly."

The young man fell silent for a moment, then resumed in a reflective tone:

"Unless, that is, I shoot the moon—cut and run, in other words. But maybe that's a trifle risky, eh?"

Still, with a man like Fandor it was hardly possible to hang back in face of a contingent risk. On the contrary, the mere thought of danger seemed to stimulate and stir him to action.

"That's the game," he chuckled. "Let's cut our stick. All poor devils do it, especially if they're the sort that belong to Fantômas' lot."

With a shrug, Fandor dived into his pocket, and produced a superb knife that was a veritable toolbox in itself.

"Now, trusty knife, do me the favor of working noiselessly!" he besought. "The least sound might easily betray me"—and opening a blade, he pressed the point against the wood of the chest and started to bore a hole.

"To come out of my lair," thought Fandor, "is all very well. Browning in hand, I can shoot down a few scoundrels—fellows who will be much better in hell than cumbering our poor earth. But that's not enough. Before deciding to leave my chest, I must first see to it there's nothing I can do to rescue my fiancée. For, once I show myself, it's pretty well all up with both of us."

He cherished no illusions as to any chances of safety the hole he was cutting might afford him, but, nevertheless, went on with his task in feverish haste. True, he could think of no way to make the girl's escape a possibility, but so often before, when all hope was denied him, had the journalist found an escape out of such scrapes that he never despaired, but was always ready to attempt the apparently impossible. Unfortunately the timber of which the chest was made was of a hard, stubborn fiber, far from easy for Fandor's knife to make an impression on. Moreover, as the steel bit in the wood gave repeated cracks, compelling the operator to exclaim:

"Why, surely the fellows keeping guard over Helene *must* hear!"

But he soon reassured himself:

"Bah! they'll only think it's rats or mice. Ships are always infested with rats."

Comforted by this reflection, and, in any case, so firmly resolved to go on with his job that no risk whatever would have made him desist, Fandor continued his operations. Alas! very soon after a fresh difficulty arose. Trampling heavily along the deck, a man had marched up to have a look at the chest. Fandor guessed he had been heard, but it was even worse than that. Someone, probably one of the men guarding Helene, had calmly sat himself down on Fandor's chest.

"Confound it!" groaned the journalist, as he realized what the fellow was doing. "Devil take the fellow, coming to interrupt me like this!"

But, undaunted as ever, he went on working his blade just the same, and at last the desired result was gained. The wood split, leaving an aperture to which Fandor immediately glued his eye.

The sight thus revealed filled the young man with indescribable fury. No, it was impossible Fantômas could have recognized his daughter under the guise of the Vicomte d'Oultremont. Otherwise how could he, infamous as he was, have treated the girl in this atrocious way? If he had entertained doubts—it was conceivable he had—as to the identity of his former lieutenant, Fantômas had evidently overcome them. How else account for this abominable outrage? Lashed firmly to the mainmast, Helene could not make the slightest movement. The rope binding her was wound tightly round her lower limbs and body, while her arms were tied behind her back.

"Wretched girl!" sighed Fandor. "She will not say a word. She absolutely refuses to tell who she is."

Then an agonizing thought struck him: To save her life, to regain the good graces of her father and his gang of desperadoes, she had but to speak one word. Let her but reveal that he, Fandor, was there, let her betray him to these men who hated him—their lifelong enemy—and she would be fêted, flattered, made much of by one and all.

"Her ransom!" thought Fandor. "Yes, I might be her ransom!"

But well he knew that Helene would never, never agree to such a thing. Besides which, was it not quite likely the girl would never even think of such a possibility of betrayal?

"Yet I cannot," he reflected, "very well be my own betrayer. That would not have the same result at all. We must find some other way."

But was it possible to find "some other way"? A prisoner as he was, the journalist could only suffer events without the power, whatever happened, to direct them. Fists clenched and face pale with rage, the young man forced himself to look elsewhere to discover, on such part of the *Lotus* deck as he could see, something that might suggest one of those brilliant notions that so often came to him and enabled him to perform veritable miracles. But alas! he saw nothing helpful. On the foredeck some hands were busy dragging off the tarpaulins from the hatchways, giving access to the hold.

"Why, of course," concluded the journalist, "they are getting ready to stow away the booty from the *Paris*." And he to shuddered again to think of this tragedy, so easily played out on the lonely ocean—the great liner answering the call of the wireless that announced a yacht in distress, and so falling into the trap set by the pirate vessel. How many would escape alive of the hundreds of passengers who had been forced to embark in the ship's boats? By abandoning them to the mercy of the elements,

Fantômas was inevitably dooming them to certain death—a terrible death—that of shipwrecked mariners tortured by hunger and thirst, till at last a merciful wave overwhelms them and puts an end to their sufferings.

"Yes, it was a massacre he organized," thought Fandor, "and now a gale is blowing up and the sea is rising. The boats will very soon be swamped." Then he broke off abruptly. The man seated on the chest had just got up. Through his peephole the journalist could only see his legs, but that sufficed to show him that their possessor was making for a heavy-looking package left lying on the deck by the yacht's bulwarks. On reaching his objective, he bestowed a kick on the packet that burst it half open. It was clear he had been asking himself what was inside. Having discovered this, he turned about on his heels and walked away.

But Fandor, no less than the other, had been able to check the contents, and therefore, drawing his revolver from his pocket, he gripped the butt with a look of triumph.

"Death no doubt?" he muttered. "Yes, but a painless death—a death of one's own choosing." And once more, in another three minutes, he was attacking the wooden walls of his prison. Widening the hole already pierced, he made it big enough to put the muzzle of his weapon through.

But if Fandor at that moment was anxiously making preparations obviously implying the speedy use of his Browning, there stood not far from him another individual who, with equal care, was inspecting the magazine of a heavy pistol.

"A first-rate weapon!" the said personage observed. "A good thing I appropriated it. True, it's a bit clumsy to carry in one's pocket, but, as I have no idea of surviving—" And a slight shudder shook the speaker's limbs.

"Half a dozen shots," he went on. "Far more than I want, for the very good reason that most likely I shall find no occasion, or rather no time, to fire them all. So let's try to settle the most judicious order. It's a case where nothing must be left to chance."

The man appeared to be struggling hard to master an access

of feverish excitement as he pursued these reflections. Presently he resumed:

"Honor, where honor is due, of course—my first cartridge will be for him. I have no scruples whatever now. To take the scoundrel alive would have been best, but, there, impossibility knows no law, and to rid the earth of this monster will already be something gained. As for my second shot—hmm! This Vicomte d'Oultremont might claim it—a fellow who dares betray Fantômas well deserves some attention. The third—upon my soul!—the third—"

Who was this personage thus mentally deliberating on the right distribution of his cartridges? Juve it was, and no other!—a Juve very far indeed from suspecting he stood within barely a yard or two of his best friend, Fandor, very far from so much as dreaming that the latter had been a passenger on the *Paris.* For many hours now that gallant police officer had been living a life of the most terrific happenings. Reaching Le Havre a few minutes before Lady Beltham, he had endeavored to intimidate one of the crew of the *Lotus,* and by dint of threats induce the man to take him on board the yacht without anybody suspecting.

But Juve had quickly abandoned this plan of action, the fact being that the seaman in question seemed to be so arrant a scoundrel that the astute officer had concluded:

"As for you, my lad, you'll go back on me the first chance, and, if the opportunity doesn't occur, you'll take good care to make one without the smallest compunction."

So, changing his tactics and not caring to take the risk of casual gossip rousing suspicion as to his own personal intentions, Juve had simply handed over the fellow to the care of his chauffeur, himself an agent of the Criminal Bureau and excellently well-fitted to keep an eye on him.

"Keep him with you till I come back," were the orders. "Put up at some hotel and play cards together. If need be, wait a fortnight. If by that time I have given no sign of life, let the chap go, but shadow him. Possibly he will lead you to me."

Then, with a light heart, ready to risk the impossible, resolved at all costs to solve what he was already designating in his own mind as "the mysteries of the *Lotus*," the police officer had returned to prowl about the neighborhood of the yacht basin, watching that vessel unobtrusively from a distance. For a detective of his caliber, trained in all the tricks of the trade, it was an easy enough job, and he had not failed to see Lady Beltham as she crossed the light gangway that still offered a means of communication from the quay to the yacht before she sailed.

"So," he had told himself, "Fantômas is on board."

Then he had marked how the preparations for putting to sea were speeded up, and concluded that this was the only passenger they had been expecting before casting off. A quarter of an hour later, however, he had altered his opinion. Contrary to his expectation, Lady Beltham had left the yacht again, only finally walking away after being escorted as far as the quay by a man whom she appeared to be eagerly beseeching for something, and who, while refusing the boon she asked, yet listened to her with a courtesy there was no mistaking.

"Fantômas! It is Fantômas!" thought Juve, and he shuddered. He had been on the point of hurling himself at the brigand's throat, but had nevertheless restrained himself. That was no way to arrest the Prince of Daring. Far from it, that was the way to risk certain failure, to attack without first taking all possible precautions.

"Patience!" the police officer urged himself. "We must have patience."

And he had given proof of infinite patience. In ambush on the wharf, convinced the yacht would not sail before daylight, the tide not suiting till then, he had watched for the propitious moment to spring on board. None but Juve would have succeeded here. Unobtrusively indeed, but still ever watchful, sentinels stood on guard. But the detective was not the man to be hindered by such a trifle. Calling in at a slop-shop nearby, he disguised himself as a sailor. Then, jumping into a dinghy with the hardihood of an experienced mariner, he clambered onto the yacht's deck under pretense of having a job to do—a rope's end to belay and carry to the dockside.

The hands of ships in harbor are constantly in the habit of climbing aboard vessels lying alongside their own, as their work requires. Nobody taking any notice of him, he had seized the opportunity to take hiding.

Nor had he hesitated very long in choosing a place of concealment. He well knew that the simplest is the best. With an agility that proved his limbs were still supple as a boy's, he had hoisted himself into the hollow mouth of a windsail—one of those ventilators or wide tubes to be seen mounted on the deck of every ship for the purpose of supplying the cabins with air—and crouched down inside.

There he had spent a wearisome and dreadful time. As a precaution, before going on board the yacht, he had provided himself with three big tins of preserved food and a quart of water, but had had no other nourishment for five long days.

Little Juve cared for that. It was something very different that kept his blood at boiling point. Right before him, under his very eyes, Fantômas, wearing his hateful and notorious costume, face hidden by a black hood, had more than once appeared. To feel him so near, to hold him at his mercy under the muzzle of a heavy service revolver he had boldly snatched up one night from the deck—and not to fire: what a hideous nightmare for the man in hiding!

Nevertheless Juve realized he had no right, save in some desperate emergency, to shoot down the villain at sight. As a police officer it was the scoundrel's capture he was bound in duty to effect.

But now circumstances had changed his point of view. Helpless to interfere, as incapable as Fandor of modifying the course of events, he had been witness of the attack on the *Paris*.

Surely the monster's cup of iniquity was full? Ought he not, at all costs, to put an end to the foul villain who had dared such a crime as this?

"My first shot for him!" Juve had declared—and he cocked his pistol.

At that instant, however, a mighty clamor broke out on

board the yacht.

*　*　*　*　*

At those critical moments when unlooked-for events lead a man of sense completely to change or modify his ordinary line of conduct—and the act of shooting down Fantômas was for Juve something of the sort—it needs a mere trifle, an incident apparently insignificant, to cause renewed hesitation in face of the final decision to be arrived at. Whereas, on hearing Fantômas' words a few moments earlier, he had found it impossible to refrain from the longing to kill him, now, gathering that something new was on foot, he experienced the same perplexity as at first.

Not by any means that he felt any undue scruples at the notion of doing justice on this monster, unworthy of any sort of pity. But his mind was too active, his intelligence too great, for him not to know that Fantômas' death here on this vessel would not produce at all the same effect as would his execution on the scaffold in virtue of the sentence of a court of justice. To kill Fantômas with a revolver shot, as one kills a noxious wild beast, was merely to deliver the world of him. But to give him up to justice was to punish him, to manifest in the eyes of all men that the mastery belongs always, sooner or later, to the law.

Besides, when the police officer should announce the scoundrel's death—supposing by any unlikely possibility he had not himself been killed on the spot—was there any certainty he would be believed? Nay, was it certain even that some lieutenant of the Lord of Terror might not take it upon him to continue the same hideous exploits, assuming his dead chief's personality? No man had ever seen Fantômas' true features. How, unless the monstrous villain were publicly unmasked, hinder some stout-hearted subordinate from taking his place?

Deliberately, but only at the cost of a vigorous effort to curb his rage, Juve uncocked and laid down his weapon.

"Not yet!" he muttered. "Best wait. I am neither judge nor executioner. Presently, yes, if he means really to murder this Vicomte d'Oultremont, it will be time to intervene. Brigands possess no right to execute justice on one another; but at this present moment I should not be justified in firing." And he shuddered once more as he listened. The noise he had heard, and which had checked his murderous impulse, Juve was quick enough to identify. It simply meant that the ruffians Fantômas had sent to board the *Paris* were returning to the *Lotus*. Now they had reached the accommodation ladder, and were swarming on deck with yells of triumph, demonstrations with which the liquors in the liner's storerooms had surely had something to do.

One fellow, the first on board, dashed up to Fantômas.

"So, master, here we are!" he vociferated, "and the trick's done."

"Really and truly?" questioned the chief.

"Really and truly indeed. Not a doubt of that! In three minutes you'll hear an explosion—and the *Paris* will be at the bottom of the sea."

Behind the man other hands of the pirate ship crowded up one after the other.

"A first-class mine!" reported one. "We're going to see some fireworks worth looking at."

Another of a more practical turn, bellowed: "And the swag we've brought along! Gold ingots that lay deep down in the hold. A little more and we'd never have spotted them! They were a shipment to the Bank of New York."

Yet Fantômas never moved. Impassive, indifferent almost, he seemed hardly to hear what his men were telling him, to pay no attention to their clamors.

But now appeared at the ladder-head a young man whose very bearing sufficed to mark his superior rank among this pirate crew. He too wore a haughty, scornful air. Fantômas advanced a step to meet him.

"Well?" he questioned.

"Everything quite successful, sir!" replied the officer.

"The liner?"

"Will founder in three seconds."

"The cargo of specie?"

"The ingots you told me your inquiries had satisfied you were on board I discovered myself, sir. They are locked up in the chests you see there in front of you."

"And the passengers?"

"All put aboard the ship's boats."

"The officers?"

"Tied up prisoners on board their ship. Not a soul will survive."

"Are you sure?"

"Yes, perfectly sure! Each boat was well holed before my eyes. They will all founder one after the other."

"So then we can forget this business? It is finished and done with." Yet even as he spoke the words Fantômas seemed to find some difficulty in checking all signs of satisfaction.

At the very hour an ignoble crime was being carried out at his orders—a crime that was to cost the lives of hundreds of innocent victims—he knew no compunction, no hesitation, no feeling of pity. But, had he known that close beside him were three enemies, shuddering with rage and horror as they listened to his words, he too must have trembled with apprehension. Helene, unhappy child of the wretched villain, was hardly choking back the tears that welled to her eyes. Fandor was swearing under his breath. Again and again he had, like Juve, been on the point of leveling his revolver and making an end of a monster no longer fit to be counted among the race of mankind he disgraced with his crimes. For Juve, he had put back his weapon in his pocket, fearful of even yet yielding to the temptation to shoot. Fantômas was at his mercy, but he was resolved to kill him only when there was no other course to pursue.

Suddenly Fantômas waved a hand for silence. "Hear me!" he commanded. And in the cold, calm voice that, with its deep reverberations, filled men's minds with a haunting sense of terror, he spoke:

"The booty taken on this vessel belongs to all—all of you have the right to a share of it. I propose, however, that we do not share it out immediately." And, as murmurs of dissatisfaction were already breaking out, he continued:

"Wait, I say! You know neither the plans I have formed nor the reasons that lead me to make them. In one short word, the English squadron is in these waters. In one word, it is possible—one must think of every possibility—that a radiogram may have given them the alert and that at this moment they are steering for us. Do you want to be hanged right away, my lads?"

Fresh murmurs answered the chief's appeal, but now they had ceased to be protests of displeasure, and had become cries of fear.

"If you don't want to be hanged," Fantômas resumed, "we must take measures of precaution. We have on board—you know that—an airplane all ready to take the air. Six of you will haul her from her hangar, while the rest are thinking things out. Are we agreed on that?"

A voice from the crowd made itself heard in trembling accents:

"We must obey you, Fantômas, for you are stronger than all of us. But, if you mean to leave us in order to put away the treasure in a safe place, we—we cannot trust you."

"Silence!" thundered Fantômas, who had shuddered from head to foot at the insolent speech. More scornful than ever was the voice in which he continued:

"I propose that we load the treasure on the plane, and that the pilot take six of you with him on his first trip."

"His first trip?" repeated the crew in questioning tones.

"Why, certainly. The plane will come back of course, and, six by six, you will all leave the yacht. No need to hide the facts. The *Lotus* must disappear and founder like the *Paris*. You must every one quit the vessel. Our plane is for that and nothing else. The English coast is not far off. In a few journeys back and forth the pilot can land you all there."

"But the treasure?"

"You will guard it till I come."

"You will be leaving too, but when, Fantômas?"

"I cannot tell you, and I do not choose to be questioned. But I am quite ready to inform you of my intentions—I shall be the last to leave."

"The last? And if the squadron between now and then…?"

"I fear nothing—not even a squadron!" And the laugh with which Fantômas accompanied the boast had an ill-omened ring in it.

Neither Juve nor Fandor nor Helene had lost a word of these strange announcements.

"Odd!" thought Fandor in his trunk. "What the devil does it all mean? Fantômas is to let them carry off the treasure? But the trusty comrades of his gang will never be such fools as to wait for him. The first six landed by the plane will share the hoard amongst themselves, and the pilot will not come back at all."

As for Juve, he was frowning in perplexity. No more than Fandor could he deem sincere the announcements made by the Lord of Terror. This generosity, this trustfulness he was displaying was not in character. For sure his scheme concealed some sinister design. Yes, but what?

As for Helene, her eyes were cast down in very shame. Each word her father spoke but added to her horror, for did not each reveal the depths of degradation to which he had fallen?

Then suddenly the pretended Vicomte d'Oultremont gave a start.

"This plan once adopted," Fantômas was announcing peremptorily, "it remains for us, before putting it in execution, to carry out a work of justice. You have all seen the Vicomte d'Oultremont, once my lieutenant and our one-time comrade, bound to the mast yonder? You have guessed his crime? What punishment do you choose for him?"

But Fantômas had not done speaking before Helene raised her head proudly.

"To talk of my crime is very well," she protested, "but the word is too vague. Of what am I accused?"

"Of robbing us—me and your comrades!" retorted Fantômas curtly. "You have stolen the treasure I had buried. A mere chance has brought you on board the *Lotus*—and for the chest there…"

Fantômas had no need to complete his sentence. Till that

moment, perhaps, Helene had counted on one of those turns of fortune that come sometimes to the help of unfortunates crushed under the blows of unjust fate. But now she realized her last chance was gone. Nothing had happened—nothing could happen—to avert the catastrophe.

In vain she had striven to gain a few seconds' respite, hoping to untie her bonds and, with Fandor, seek hiding somewhere on the yacht. Now the hour for such wild hopes was past. To go on temporizing, to prolong the effort to keep up an ineffectual comedy? No, the unhappy girl knew no time was left for such useless attempts. At the first word she should utter, would not the pirates fly to open the chest, and discover Fandor? Was she—she herself—to help them find her lover, to betray him into their hands? In ringing tones she declared:

"Be it so! I confess. Do with me what you will! If I have seen good to rob you, it was because I hoped to stay the execution of crimes that fill me with horror. Yes, what I did was to try and rescue your victims from your hands."

But by this time cries of hatred and yells of fury filled the air, when an incident occurred that, for certain, neither Fantômas nor his crew had foreseen. First the dull thud of an explosion, followed instantly by a dense smoke—a black, impenetrable cloud that wrapped the *Lotus* in absolute darkness as of night, so thick the ship's crew could not so much as see one another's faces. At the same moment almost, a man's voice rang out joyfully:

"Courage, Helene! Quick, quick! We are going to escape."

Then came a deafening noise, the rattle of an engine that is starting to turn and is speeded up in jerk after jerk of the accelerator. Be sure it was not without a motive, not without foresight for future needs, that Fandor, a few moments earlier, when he saw one of the pirates kick open a packet lying on the deck, had smothered a shout of delight. The truth is that in the eyes of the alert young journalist the smallest facts had a meaning of their own—that for his inventive mind no discovery was without its value.

Indeed, Fandor had observed that the packet in question

contained rockets, ship's rockets, such as all vessels going to sea are bound by law to carry, and which are used for making signals of distress. At first the journalist had looked at these fireworks without much interest. Then he had given a sudden start. If these rockets had been thus deposited on deck, this was undoubtedly because Fantômas had thought he might need them to let the *Paris* know she was steering in the right direction in answer to his wireless calls. But since then the weather had changed and the sea risen. A wave had swept the deck and wetted the rockets.

"So now," it had occurred to the young man, "these rockets would never go off. They would only smolder and give off clouds of sour, black smoke."

Sour, black smoke! A light had broken in on his mind as he repeated the words. Under shelter of a smokescreen could he not make a dash to Helene's side, tear her from the hands of her enemies, and drag her to some corner of the yacht where it would, at any rate, be possible to sell his life dearly? In the first instance he had paid little heed to the idea, but little by little a wild hope had sprung up, growing greater from second to second, in spite of his terrible position bringing a light of joyful expectation into his eyes. Was not Fantômas speaking of an airplane, ordering the machine to be got ready on the yacht's deck? Hardly listening to the directions the brigand was still giving, the young man had watched from his hiding place the execution of the master's commands.

"Excellent! A first-rate machine!" Fandor muttered to himself. "Oh, a fine chance this!"

And next instant, when Helene's fate was trembling in the balance, with supreme daring, he played the terrible game he had just resolved on. Drawing his Browning and passing the muzzle through the hole he had some minutes before bored in the wood, the journalist took aim at the packet of rockets and pulled the trigger.

"The first ball to secure our retreat!" he told himself. "The second for Fantômas!"

Little *he* heeded the scruples that paralyzed Juve's action.

Against an enemy of this sort, a monster of crime, who signal-ized each day by a fresh villainy, the journalist's conscience was untroubled by any reluctance to be the first to fire.

But once again destiny was to frustrate Fandor's plans. His shot had fired the rockets, and explosion after explosion followed, throwing off so dense a smoke that the journalist, himself drowned in the inky vapor his act had let loose, could not now dream of using his weapon for a second shot. Nay, he was hardly conscious by now of Fantômas' existence, every thought concentrated on Helene. Before firing, he had careful-ly taken his bearings, and could have made a beeline to her blindfolded.

"To the rescue!" he cried, in the fierce excitement of a peril-ous hope. A second or two sufficed to set in motion the secret mechanism the pretended Vicomte d'Oultremont had told him of on board the *Paris,* and he was out of his prison and on the point of dashing forward.

But he was forced to pause. His limbs, numbed and stiffened by long inaction, trembled under him, and he could barely stand. Next moment, however, with a supreme effort of will, the young man had mastered this weakness and reached the mast where the girl he must save stood helpless.

"Quick, quick!" he panted. "Courage, Helene, courage!"

His knife was in his hand, and he set to work to cut away the lashings that bound the *soi-disant* accomplice of the Lord of Terror. To the impatient young man it seemed hours before she was free, and vaguely, meantime, as in a dream, he had felt as though, at the moment he had called Helene's name, a stifled exclamation had met his ears.

But, stopping for nothing, Fandor bore off his fiancée in his arms, muttering as he ran: "The plane! The plane! We are going to escape in her."

Before long, however, he halted in bewilderment, doubtful which way to take. Just before the explosion the air had been so still—the same thing happens before great tempests such as sailors in the Indian Ocean call typhoons—that the smoke still hung about as thick as ever. And in the black darkness he could hear a pandemonium of oaths and shouts and orders:

"Keep your heads! It's only the rockets."

"Don't move! Stay where you are, my lads!"

"The prisoner! Look after the prisoner!"

Little cared Fandor for these clamors. It was the airplane he was bent on finding. Suddenly, when all but despaired of coming upon it, he felt himself stumbling against one of the wings.

"Quick, Helene!" he besought. "Get in! Are you right?"

But she stood bewildered, stammering:

"I cannot! I am still tied!" And so it was. In his haste to set her free, for all the smoke cloud, at once a friend and an enemy, he had not succeeded in cutting all the bonds that held her.

"No matter," cried her lover, "I can settle you in the cockpit by myself without your help." And he found strength to do the feat. Holding the girl at arm's length, he lifted her bodily into the machine, scrambling in himself after her.

"The joystick?" he panted, breathless but sublime in his force of will. "The electric contact?"

He was fumbling, still in darkness, at the controls, trying to discover which was which, asking himself the while if he had not counted overconfidently on his experience as a pilot. Now and again at an airdrome he had flown a machine for the novelty of the thing and out of keenness to master the whole secret, and had actually given proof of a hardihood and handiness that amazed his instructors, delighted at the promise he showed.

But now, what a novice he felt, what a bungler! It was only by juggling with the levers under his hands that he managed presently to get the spark plug working and the carburetor flushing the cylinders with petrol vapor. Then, with a cry of joy, he saw the pistons moving, and next moment the engine was in full swing. It seemed like a hundred years since the moment he had let fly at the rockets; barely two minutes had actually elapsed!

"Quicker! quicker!" cried the young man, as he sped up the motor to its highest power, at the same time setting his elevating rudders—and waiting.

At last she took the air. Under traction of the propeller, turning at top speed, the machine tore itself loose from the ropes that held it down as a precaution against the rolling of the ship, and went soaring heavenward like a gigantic bird.

Almost vertically rose the plane under Fandor's reckless guidance, at an angle a more experienced airman would never have dared to take.

"Saved!" laughed the daring pilot—while behind him he heard a voice growl out:

"A pretty trick! Only I am here! Ho, ho! A bullet through the head will soon teach the fellow to play at flying."

13. A Fatal Mistake

None but Juve could have planned and attempted and carried through what he had just successfully done. Courage, however great, has its limits, but the gallant police officer's had none. Having long ago vowed to sacrifice his life, what had he to fear? To die was nothing to him; to win the day was the one thing needful.

When he heard Fantômas propose to his accomplices to carry away with them the gold ingots, the booty from the *Paris,* he had been struck with amazement.

"There is something else underneath!" the detective had told himself. "Fantômas cannot be so trusting as all that."

Now, this very same "something else" that he suspected to underlie the villain's behavior he concluded he was now witnessing when suddenly a black cloud of smoke spread over the deck of the *Lotus.*

"Oh God!" thought Juve. "Just what I expected! Fantômas is going to take advantage of the smokescreen he has contrived to make off." And he was more than ever confirmed in his suspicion when the smoke grew heavier still, and he heard the unmistakable hum the screw of an airplane makes.

"Oh, ho! So he is making a bolt of it, leaving his comrades in the lurch"—and the police officer ended his sentence with a laugh in which could be read the echo of a threat. Be sure he felt not the smallest pity for the pirates thus cheated of the guerdon of their crimes, but he was sore and angry to think how their master was yet again—for so it seemed—only too likely to score the victory. Was it not, indeed, certain that, if Fantômas, was leaving the ship, he was doing this after taking due precautions to ensure her destruction? He was duping his accomplices! No doubt of that! But equally undoubted that he was doing so only after making sure they would perish. The brigand was not one to leave behind him aggrieved comrades who might prove dangerous, while a few murders the more would never deter him. All this Juve had realized in a flash, and he hesitated no more. Crawling out of his ventilator at the risk of being seen if the wind should clear away the smoke, he leapt on deck.

"Oh! So we are for running away?" he growled between his teeth. With hands outstretched, at random he dashed forward, making for the airplane, guided by the roar of the screw revolving at top speed. Another instant and he felt the furious wind of the propeller, and knew the machine was that moment lifting to take flight.

"Too late!" he groaned. But, taking a wild leap, be felt his hands touch something that was plunging forward with incredible force, and laid hold of it and hung dangling. In fact, he had caught on to the fuselage of an airplane, which was mounting in the air at a giddy pace.

"All the better!" he cried. Then, in a voice of menace, he hissed out the words:

"A pretty trick! But I am here. Oh, ho! A bullet through the head will teach him to play at flying!"

No trace of hesitation was left to impair Juve's purpose. It was Fandor piloting the plane, Fandor saving Helene's life by snatching her into the air, *but* he, the police officer, was convinced it was Fantômas taking to flight. Unaware of the journalist's presence on board the *Lotus,* equally unaware that the Vicomte d'Oultremont was in reality Helene, could he have had the smallest suspicion of the true state of things? The mistake was tragic, but in a way inevitable.

It was no less fated that nothing should occur to remedy it. Still pinioned, unable to move a limb, Fantômas' daughter, who had rolled to the bottom of the hull, was struggling furiously to break her bonds. Fandor, for his part, intent on his steering, and far from confident of his own skill, never once thought of turning his head. Hence it came that, when the machine rose presently above the smoke cloud, and was flying in clear air, neither Fandor nor Helene saw or knew anything of Juve.

For the latter, he could only see Fandor's back—or, to be more precise, he did *not* see it, he, too, having other things to think about than the pilot's face. Having gripped the fuselage of the machine at random, Juve had lighted on anything but a good point of attack. Directly he could see plainly he found that, as ill luck would have it, he was clinging to the extreme tip of the hull, within a few inches of the rudder. From there it seemed an impossibility to creep to the body proper of the machine, the spot where the places reserved for passengers are usually found.

What to do under these conditions? To begin with, Juve came to the conclusion it was best not to look down. Thrown out of balance by his weight—as could not fail to be the case— the tail had dropped, and the machine was mounting higher and higher, leaving a terrifying depth of empty air below the unhappy police officer, a depth that was growing greater every second, and which the tossing billows far below rendered yet more appalling.

"Surely I am not getting giddy?" thought Juve. "That would never do." But he was wrong to doubt his own powers. Summoning all his strength, he hoisted himself by his arms up to the fuselage, rested his chest on it, then, heaving a leg over, he soon found himself mounted astride of the airy mount fortune had given him to ride.

Thereupon he laughed again. Looking towards the pilot— Fandor—he thought:

"I've got him! He is at my mercy!" And he felt for his revolver. But the heavy pistol was not in his pocket. Had it fallen out when he was hanging on to the hull? Had it jerked away when he was gripping the airplane as it took the air? He never troubled to inquire.

"I have my fingers left," was all he said, and, without further hesitation, he made up his mind to a desperate enterprise and started crawling along the fuselage, regardless of the abyss that yawned below. Fantômas was in the pilot's seat. Well, he would attack him there, armed though he would certainly be.

"I will half strangle him," the police officer decided, "and in another second I shall have snatched away his weapon. My word! I suppose the machine, left to itself, will make a fine dive at that moment… But Fantômas will bring her level again. It is an instinctive act with every pilot to right his machine that has got out of control." And again, a marvel of boldness, a miracle of willpower, Juve calmly calculated:

"If we don't kill each other while I am disarming him, I'll undertake to reduce him to helplessness. To clap the revolver to his head, and so force him to steer for England, is not impossible. Otherwise, if he *will* resist, I shall only have to shoot him."

How conclusively these last words proved the true nature of the man! To fire and kill Fantômas, supposing he would not yield, meant certain death for Juve, but he never so much as thought of that.

"Now for it!" he repeated, and began his perilous advance. Any noise he made was drowned in the roar of the wind, against which the machine was fighting, and Juve was actually in a fair way to carry through his dreadful scheme when two explosions crashed out, one a second after the other, while simultaneously a fierce gust of wind set the machine rocking so violently as to threaten disaster.

"Ah, yes!" exclaimed Juve, with a shudder of horror, "the *Paris* and the *Lotus!* Two more crimes to the villain's black record!" And, leaning overboard, he had the courage to examine the abyss below him. Of the two vessels, the great liner and the yacht Fantômas had fitted out as a pirate ship, naught was left but fragments of wreckage tossing on the stormy waves.

"All gone!" gasped the police officer, and strove to make out the small boats in which the passengers had been embarked. But not one could be seen. All, one after the other, must have foundered, swamped by the weight of water that had poured in through the holes Fantômas' lieutenant had shamelessly boasted of having had made by his orders.

"Horrible! Horrible!" he groaned, and, forgetful of his own danger, he felt half stupefied by the horror of these crimes of which he was an eyewitness, without the possibility, for all his superhuman energy, of hindering their perpetration. But quickly this torpor was succeeded by fierce anger that gave him new strength and a yet more passionate determination to have done with this monstrous criminal of genius, who terrorized the whole world under the increasing threat of his abominable daring.

"Fantômas, you shall pay for your villainies!" he declared solemnly, as he cast another, a last look of anguish, at the rolling waste of waters that showed never a sign of life to the farthest horizon.

"We are the sole survivors, we aboard this airplane!" he faltered. "But no matter, duty must be done!"

A fresh idea had occurred to him. He had thought to arrest Fantômas, force him by dint of threats to make for England and land there, where the police would capture him, a beaten man. He had been wrong. Horror-stricken by the atrocity of the crime he had just witnessed, Juve forgot his part as a police officer, his mission, his duty. He thought, and rightly, how Fantômas had again and again escaped, had invariably found means to evade pursuit. Was he to risk a repetition of such failures?

"No, no!" he swore. "His cup of iniquity is full. To let him live on is to run the danger of his committing fresh enormities. I will kill him! Yes, I will kill him."

He began to creep on again. The desire of murder was in his heart. To destroy Fantômas, was this not, after all, to abolish a curse, a scourge, that threatened every living being? Was it not the deed of a hero, that should save millions of men's lives?

And it was so easy to do. To creep, creep along the hull, to reach the cockpit where the villain sat, to grip him and paralyze his action for a few seconds. No more was needed now to annihilate Fantômas!

"Why hesitate?" thought Juve. "It is humanity at large I shall benefit. I should have every chance of success on my side. A few short seconds will suffice, once the pilot is incapacitated. Once out of control, this machine will crash. Yes, I will attack him from behind."

Here, perhaps, was the hardest point for Juve to settle. Loyal-hearted as he was, the mere thought of mastering his enemy by an attack in the rear was horribly painful to him. But was it not his duty, after all? Had he the right, out of mere bravado, to expose himself to the blows of a ferocious beast men must slaughter to save the victims it threatens with destruction?

"To work! My mind is made up," declared the police officer. "In a few minutes I shall be dead. Poor Fandor! Poor lad!"

Now, as every time he was face to face with death, it was the thought of his beloved comrade that stood first in his mind. He believed him so far away—this friend whom a merciless fate seemed bent on having him murder.

Juve resumed his cautious advance. Then suddenly he stopped, with a start of astonishment. He had caught sight of the Vicomte d'Oultremont in the hull, where he still lay bound. No wonder the poor man was amazed—albeit he never suspected, never for one second suspected the truth. When Fantômas and Fandor had both been deceived by the girl's admirably conceived disguise, was the detective likely, in these few, frenzied seconds, to have the smallest inkling? It was really Helene he saw, yet his first thought was:

"All the better! I shall rid the world of this scoundrel, too. So, forward!"—and he slipped down into the hull. Fighting the giddiness that was gaining on him, he took another step forward—and his face lit up with pleasure. He had caught sight of a revolver lying on the bottom boards within reach of his hand. Natural enough that a plane belonging to Fantômas should be armed, but this in no wise diminished Juve's delight at the sight.

"A second will do it now!" he cried. "I think I am only doing my duty!" And, stooping, he picked up the revolver, pulled off the safety catch, and leveled it at the pilot.

Another second would have done it. Let him press the trigger and fire, and the hideous deed would be accomplished. He would have killed Fandor, killed his dearest comrade, the man he loved as a father loves his son!

But Helene, lying there in the hull, had realized with a spasm of horror the fearful, fatal mistake. Unable to get free of her bonds, incapable of stirring from where she lay to stay the murderer's arm, she broke into wild screams.

Not for one instant had she hesitated to recognize Juve, not one second had she remained in ignorance of his intention, and she yelled in desperate tones:

"Juve, Juve! It is Fandor! Fandor!"

But the noise of the engine drowned her woman's voice—that noise and the tearing wind together.

We know how pilots and mechanics on board these machines are compelled to communicate by means of a telephone. Yet they sit close together, and, thanks to their airmen's helmets, have not the whistling of the wind to deafen their ears.

Helene was quick to realize the dreadful truth. Juve did not hear her! He could not possibly hear her! The girl made a desperate effort to burst her bonds. To see Juve, the noble-hearted Juve, the man whose devotion and heroism she so admired, assassinate her lover Fandor! The dreadful thought was so replete with horror the unhappy girl felt her very heart stand still.

"It must *not* be! He must *not* fire!" she gasped, and lo! her whole being rising in revolt, the tender girl found an almost supernatural strength at her command. One of the cords that held her gave way somewhat, granting her a little more freedom of movement.

Now she was on her feet, repeating her wild cry: "Juve! Juve!"

But he never heard her, and she could not get to him. She was in the portion of the hull reserved for passengers, whereas Juve had now reached the seat behind the pilot intended for a mechanic. High screens, fitted with miscellaneous gear and accessories, separated them.

If only Juve had turned his head! If only he had seen how, tearing off a mask—made of what strange material?—that concealed her face, Helene had revealed her true features as a woman. But, utterly absolved in his deadly purpose, the police officer had his eyes riveted on the back of the pilot's head, taking sure aim, thinking only of the death he was about to deal—the death he was resolved to inflict in punishment of the Monster's crimes.

In a flash the girl realized the grim purpose of the police officer, on whose determined features a sterner, fiercer expression had settled. Sick with horror, she saw him finger the trigger, steady his aim, make ready to fire.

Then, her purpose outrunning in swiftness the consummation she dreaded, Helene took her decision. She had not thought of it before. She had not calculated, foreseen, resolved, on what she would do. It was her woman's wit, her loving heart, her unsullied soul, that prompted the deed instinctively, without the concurrence of the conscious mind.

Juve was firing—had fired… Well, the ball must not strike Fandor! It must miss its mark! And, above all else, Fandor must tum round and see Juve, and Juve see him.

In a lightning flash she accomplished the dreadful deed of heroic self-devotion she had resolved on—hurling herself headlong into space. It was to save her lover's life! She leaned far over the side, let go, and plunged into the depths. At the same instant the shot rang out, and at that same instant, relieved of the girl's weight and losing balance under the hands of the inexperienced pilot, the airplane seemed to rear on end, and took a wild leap upwards. Juve would have fallen had not the mere instinct of self-preservation made him cling on for dear life.

But now Fandor, startled by the revolver shot, turned round to look, instinctively cutting off contact and stopping his engine.

Then came two cries—cries that expressed all the terror and joy and horror the human heart can feel:

"Fandor! Fandor!"

"Juve! You, Juve!"

Then from the abyss, rising from the giddy depths, like the last groan of the dying, came the faint farewell of the girl who had sacrificed her life for others.

"Helene! Helene!" groaned Fandor, who had abandoned all control of the machine.

Dark clouds, heavy with storm, were surging up on the horizon, ominous and threatening. A squall struck the machine from below and tossed it up like a straw, half overturning it.

But neither Juve nor Fandor heeded the impending crash. Leaning far over, fascinated, the two men were gazing at a woman's body whirling in empty space, in a moment to plunge headlong into the foaming waters.

14. An Atrocious Revenge

A tragic moment, a moment of horror and sickening suspense, that came near robbing Fandor of his wits.

Then, with one voice, police officer and journalist broke into a wild cry: "There! look there!"

Amid the sullen waves swelling higher and higher under the furious gusts, a dark mass showed up like a gigantic spindle two hundred feet long. They saw it cleave the billows, forge ahead, swing round.

"A submarine!" declared Juve, and, "Saved! Helene is saved!" yelled Fandor in response. Instinctively he turned about again and gripped the joystick, bringing the plane to a level keel, checking the downward dive, restarting the engine, hardly conscious, it may be, of what he did, yet doing it all with the admirable adroitness of a trained and intrepid pilot.

"Saved!" reiterated the young man. He had seen, and Juve had seen, a boat put off from the submarine and toss on the crest of the waves. He had seen her crew lean over the side and drag Helene's body from the water.

Yes, beyond a doubt, by a miraculous chance her life was to be saved. Certainly a drop from such a height might involve serious consequences. Plunging from such an elevation the girl might well have been killed or badly injured on striking the surface. But for once destiny had taken pity on the heroine whose perilous leap had prevented the most hideous of calamities. At the very moment her body touched the surface a huge wave had caught it sideways, borne her on its crest, and broken the fall. She had struck out and was alive.

"Saved! Saved!" again and again came the same delirious cry of joy from the lover.

All the while Juve, at the young man's side, no less frantic with delight than his companion, had not an inkling how

Fandôr and Helene had come to be in the airplane, but, never doubting the evidence of his eyes, he was vociferating with equal fervor:

"Saved! Saved! Helene is saved, and she has saved your life!"

Next moment he bawled:

"Down! steer down! It is the English squadron!"—and he had no doubt he was speaking truth. Had he not gathered from what Fantômas had said that the English were near at hand? Was he not now convinced that this submarine formed part of the British Fleet?

"Down, I say, Fandor. Steer down!"

But the journalist was now fighting the whirlwind. None who has seen how gales spring up in a moment in mid-ocean can doubt the fury and sudden onslaught of these hurricanes. A minute before it was broad daylight; now it had grown pitch dark. A few seconds earlier the wind was strong, but steady; now it was coming in squalls of incalculable violence. Stays groaned and controls bent. So light, the tempest made a plaything of it, tossed about by every blast, the airplane was fighting for its life.

"Down, down, I say!" Juve kept shouting. "They will pick us up."

But at that moment, cutting short his exclamations, something whistled through the air close past their heads—something that burst and flew to pieces with a deafening crash.

"How now," began Fandor. "One would think…"

But he broke off suddenly, as the other had done, never finishing his sentence.

Again came a dull roar, then the whistling of a projectile, then again the crash of an explosive.

"They are firing—firing with anti-aircraft guns—firing on us!" faltered Juve. While Fandor gasped:

"It is not the squadron! It is not a friendly submarine! It is Fantômas! Fantômas!"

The truth had dawned upon him in a flash. If Fantômas had bidden them load the chest of gold ingots on the airplane, if he had assured his accomplices he would be the last to leave the deck of the *Lotus,* it meant simply that he was lying—lying atrociously. Long ago, doubtless, the Monster had planned out this last of his treacherous villainies. Without the crew of the yacht ever suspecting it, the vessel was escorted by a submarine manned by men genuinely devoted to the Lord of Terror's service.

Here was the scoundrel's scheme: he was to have the hoard, the sole possession of which he coveted for himself, loaded upon the airplane. The machine would sail away. Yes, but he would bring it down with a well-aimed shot, and the chest would plunge to the bottom of the sea, whence his submarine would easily fish it up again. Then, taking refuge himself on board the submarine, he would have every facility to send the *Lotus* to the bottom and his accomplices with her, and could make sure of being the sole surviving witness of the loss of the transatlantic liner.

"Oh, the double-dyed villain!" raged Fandor. "And he is for shooting us down? Well, we shall escape him in the end."

About Helene he was now easy in his mind. If she had been rescued alive by her father, she had no doubt revealed her identity to him. For what motive could she have had to conceal her true name and relationship, now that none, alas! was left for her to try to save?

"Fantômas loves his daughter," thought the journalist. "Possibly he will threaten her, perhaps try to punish her for her seeming acts of treachery. But he could never condemn to death—"

He had no time to continue his reflections. Suddenly the fury of the elements was redoubled. Such dense clouds accumulated overhead that black night seemed to have fallen—a night of horrid darkness shot through by the zigzagging fires of forked lightning.

"We must rise higher," declared Fandor. Beside him he could see Juve clinging to the fuselage to save himself from being hurled from his perch by the frantic bounds the machine was taking as squall after squall struck it. For himself, as he gripped the controls with bleeding fingers, he was afraid of being bodily pitched from his seat in the cockpit.

"We must rise higher," reiterated the young man—and he tilted the elevating rudder and speeded up the screw, already going at racing speed.

At a higher level, in the wide heavens above the storm clouds rolling in dark confused masses and driven hither and thither by the furious wind, the blue sky was clear and calm.

But now, after its upward leap, the plane seemed to be stopping, the engine working less effectively, the tractive power of the screw apparently diminished. Powerless against the wind, the machine began to drift backward.

"Should I turn tail and run before the storm?" Fandor asked himself, thinking to regain control by a bold stroke.

But alas! he could lay no claim to the superb expertness of trained pilots who sport with the fury of the elements. He felt the gale was his master, that the wind was playing with him, doing what it would with his machine.

How long could he continue the struggle? Casting a look at the compass: "Yes, England lies yonder," he muttered. Two hours more on the line indicated by the magnetic needle, and he would be safe. But could he hold out so long?

"Courage, Fandor," Juve breathed in his ear. "We shall crash perhaps, but we shall have done our best."

Then, once again, the two men uttered a simultaneous cry of terror and surprise. Right before their eyes, almost touching the nose of their machine, coming from the surface of the sea and reflected in a great square of light on the dark background of the clouds, the dazzling beam of a searchlight had flashed out.

"That finishes it," wailed Fandor. "They want to see us clearly to get a surer aim. We are the mark they are shooting at." There seemed no doubt of the fact; evidently the searchlight was mounted on Fantômas' submarine.

But Juve was not so sure. With a shrug:

"Come, come," he protested. "We are too high up for them to hit us. Besides, the submarine pitches and rolls in this heavy sea far too violently to allow any certainty of aim. Fantômas is not going to open fire again."

And Juve was right. To cover an airplane is difficult enough on terra firma. From the deck of a submarine—a wonderful modern invention, but one that in the nature of things gives an unstable foothold—this was practically an impossibility.

"Then why the searchlight?" demanded the journalist.

"I cannot say. Wait—ah, look there!"

On the background of the clouds right ahead of the plane that was still buffeted by the winds as if the tempest were resolved to dismember and break and tear the wings of the frail machine, lettering had suddenly appeared.

Truly Fantômas kept well abreast of the very latest inventions in all parts of the world. In thus throwing gigantic letters on the clouds as on a screen was he not copying the New York tradesmen who every night above their amazing city thus advertise their wares in this fantastic fashion?

Breathlessly the two men read the first message—a stroke of irony:

"*Fantômas congratulates his enemies on their gallantry and ingenuity.*"

Then the lettering changed and a new sentence followed the first:

"*He warns them, however, their victory is only temporary.*"

Then suddenly, in enormous characters, a threat showed up:

"*Fantômas has decided that the hour of his vengeance is at hand.*"

"Good God!" gasped Fandor. "What vengeance?" But the searchlight was still at work, its beam again reflected on the stormy heavens.

"*Helene, my daughter, is in my hands! Helene will expiate her wrongs against me by killing you both with her own hands.*"

"A lie!" vociferated Juve.

"Foolishness!" shouted Fandor. "Fantômas has not caught us yet, nor will Helene ever consent—"

He said no more, unhappy man. For, just as if he had guessed the thoughts his threats would suggest to the gallant pair, Fantômas replied to their doubts, their incredulity, by this sinister phrase:

"*Fantômas informs you that Helene will only know afterwards the crime she has perpetrated.*"

Then, a moment more and this daring boast:

"*In an hour from now you will be in my hands.*"

"In an hour, eh?" sneered Juve, who for the first time in his life was pale with foreboding. "What nonsense! You can hold out, Fandor?"

"Yes, Juve, yes! But—"

"But what?"

"The engine—"

"Well, what of it? You drive splendidly!"

"Look, Juve, look there!"

Once more on the dark, gloomy background of the lurid clouds letters flashed out, clearly spaced, plainly legible:

"*In an hour you will be in my hands for your machine does not carry petrol enough for an hour's flight, and the engine is already running slow.*"

"If he speaks the truth—" groaned Fandor.

"We must find out," said his companion. And again Juve risked an unparalleled feat of daring. While the journalist sat still in the pilot's seat, from which he dared not stir, the unfortunate police officer, the man who dreaded giddiness, dragged his unwilling limbs halfway along the fuselage, reached the petrol tank, and checked the gauge.

"Well?" faltered Fandor when the other had rejoined him.

"It is too true," said Juve; "our petrol is nearly exhausted. But…"

"But, Juve…"

"I have thought of something."

"What do you mean? Speak out!"

To make themselves heard they had to bawl in each other's ears.

"Wait a moment," shouted Juve. "Let me look"—and, leaning over, he scrutinized the waves, now white with foam and running mountains high.

"Yes," the detective resumed, "the submarine is following us.

It is there, steaming on the surface—waiting for us to crash."

"Well?"

"The engine of this machine weighs how much, Fandor?"

"I don't know—a big weight. Why ask?"

"Because, my boy, we might plump it right on top of that cursed diving boat. Death for death. *Our* end would, at any rate, serve a good purpose. What think you? We should destroy our motor, but we should kill Fantômas and his accomplices."

A flame of fire blazed in the detective's eyes, but next moment the light was extinguished.

"And Helene, Juve?" Fandor had interjected. "You forget Helene. She is on board that submarine. Can we kill her?"

"You are right," asserted Juve sadly. "So be it! To kill is cowardly, anyway. Best wait and drive ahead! Who knows? Who knows?"

But the hurricane was waxing fierce, the wind redoubling in violence. And they were alone and helpless, doomed inevitably to speedy disaster, hanging precariously between the heavens where the tempest howled, waiting in ambush to wreck their frail craft, and the waters tossing in fury below, where prowled, following them, watching for them to drop, Fantômas and his submarine.

"Best wait," Juve had declared, "and drive ahead." Alas! was not their fate already fixed immutably? Was not Fantômas' vengeance complete, even now?

THE END